# THE HOURS IN BETWEEN

## A Novel

## OLIVIA BARRY

Copyright © 2022 by Olivia Barry



To bring author to your life event use the Contact Form at www.olivia-barry.com

Interior design by Alexandra Amor

Book cover design by Hannah Lindner

Edited by Camilla Borgogni

Printed in the Unites States of America

Library of Congress Cataloging-in-Publication Data (is available)

Names: Barry, Olivia, author

Title: The Hours In Between: a novel/Olivia Barry

Identifiers: ISBN 979-8-9863882-1-2 (paperback), ISBN 979-8-9863882-0-5 (e-book)

Subjects: FICTION/Contemporary Women. FICTION/Romance

Paperback: ISBN:979-8-9863882-1-2

E-book: ISBN 979-8-9863882-0-5

*For Camilla and Cosimo*

**Diary** [ˈdī(ə)rē ] — noun: *a book in which one keeps a daily record of events and experiences, and* **occasionally a secret**

A book lying by itself on a desk in the living room, at first sight, might look like nothing special. That, however, isn't the case with the red notebook, velvety and thick, now resting on the otherwise empty antique desk.

A breeze enters the peaceful room, moving the thin, eggshell white curtains a few inches to the left, enough so that if you sat in the desk chair in front of the notebook, you would catch a glimpse of the blooming garden.

# DAY 1

## NOVEMBER 27 | NEW YORK CITY

*This can't happen to me. Not to me. No. Not me,* I thought as the revolving glass door of yet another newly built skyscraper swirled around again and again before spitting me out into the blinding sunlight.

The world around me suddenly felt distant. People passed me as if they were characters in a movie, and I was the audience. My breathing became shallow, and I had to steady myself as a tall man in an expensive-looking suit brushed against my arm, mouthing, "Sorry," before rushing along with the crowd and leaving me wondering if I ever could have been his lover.

What a silly thought, especially at a moment like this, when my world was caving in. Then again, that random thought made me realize two things: One, it was time to move. And two, I was not done. Not yet.

That's when I took the first step of the last one hundred and forty days of my life.

# DAY 2

## NOVEMBER 28 | NEW YORK CITY

Since yesterday afternoon, after a few moments of lucidity, my life turned into nothing more than a blur. I can't remember how I made it home or what happened after that. Hazy images of me meandering along Fifth Avenue, past St. Patrick's Cathedral, Saks and the Empire State building still muddle my mind. There were stores, restaurants and cheerful people everywhere. Many people. But as hard as I try, I can't recall a single detail.

For most of my life, details were so important to me. Keeping things in a particular order and being overly efficient kept me on track—especially when I suffered from anxiety and the ground would slip away underneath my otherwise down-to-earth self. My thoughts would race and go to unrealistic places as I lived through months, and ultimately years, of sporadic panic attacks.

Today I feel unusually calm. Dr. Sternenberg's face—piercing blue eyes behind a pair of round glasses and a prominent, symmetrical nose—keeps reappearing in my mind. I imagine his face will most likely haunt me forever. A polished guy, stern in a professional way, in his mid-fifties and head of the oncology department at Mount Sinai.

Less than twenty-four hours ago, he informed me that I have twenty weeks to live, maybe less. One hundred and forty days. Of course, he wasn't too sure about the number and didn't want to commit to an exact timeframe.

There have been moments in my life when six months would have sounded like an eternity. But while sitting in one of those deep brown leather chairs—the ones that make everyone look insignificant—six months suddenly seemed like no time at all. It's final. I have twenty weeks left to live. Maybe.

He compacted my rare form of fast-spreading acute leukemia into a cascade of complicated words while, for my taste, pronouncing my first name far too slowly and—considering he's a stranger—in a far too familiar way.

"Liz, I'm sorry. There's not a lot we can do to change the outcome." How often had he said those words before?

Anyway, I knew the devastating news before he said anything. I could see every fact displayed on his face. I could see it in his eyes.

That was yesterday.

# DAY 3

## NOVEMBER 29 | NEW YORK CITY

This morning, I made a point of not getting up at my usual time. I was sick of all the meaningless, self-imposed rules governing my life. Instead, I laid there until the sun's rays caressed my face, and then I did something I hadn't done in years: I spent the day in bed.

I cuddled up with *this* old notebook I've occasionally been using as a diary. Not that I've ever been good at journaling—my diary more so resembles a work of fiction than a journal. It doesn't help that for the last twenty years I've wanted to write a novel but didn't have the courage to do it. I've been waiting for my life to change; I've been waiting for my life to become perfect.

Foolishly, I always thought that someday there would be a better moment. But as it turned out, November 27th was the day my life changed in a way I could have never imagined. That day for me, time became a different dimension.

Lying in bed, thoughts about my past and my minimal future—about my kids and the people and things I love—raced through my mind. Once in a while I reached out to the other half of my bed, letting my fingers slide across the crisp, cold linen. There was nothing but emptiness. The way I felt for the last fifteen years.

There's a lot of news on how sadness and loneliness can become a deadly combination. Am I looking for some half-witted reason to explain what was happening to me, the reason for my cancer?

CANCER! The word alone makes me shiver. Cancer will be my biggest challenge, while Pete will always be my biggest disappointment. He's supposed to come home from a business trip tonight. Business trip? He must think I'm a fool. And home—what home?

**Home** [ hōm ] — noun: *the place where one lives permanently, especially as a member of a family*

Home. A word I once was so fond of now sounds so foreign. Years ago, this house—with its warm brick walls, fireplace and oversized windows—was filled with laughter and joy, playdates, dinner parties, Christmas trees, and Easter egg hunts. It's difficult to remember those long-gone days, the many moments that then felt indestructible, now crumbled, and lost forever.

After staring at the ceiling for a long time, I picked up my pen again and doodled. Lots of circles and clouds. I tried to make sense of my thoughts and feelings until I dissolved into self-pity. The 'why me' pity kind of thing. Or was it more the realization of how many moments of my life I've wasted? I can't tell.

Why me? Why do I have to die? Why do I have to die before turning fifty-five? There was nothing but merciless silence as the red ink, mixed with my tears, ran across the page while my questions stayed unanswered.

What am I supposed to do now? Let it all happen? That seems a tad overwhelming. The truth is, I am going to die before my kids get married. I am going to die before I can do the many things I always wanted to do but never did.

~

Between thoughts of dying and counting my many regrets, I must have fallen asleep because a buzzing sound woke me up. As I opened my eyes, I saw a fly crawling at a leisurely pace along the silver frame of one of my favorite paintings: an empty bench in a flower garden. I've often daydreamed about a time when, far into my eighties or even my nineties, I would sit on a wooden bench like that one, looking back on a life well-lived.

But this time, I stopped. *That won't happen. There will be no older version of myself. That's a fact.* As I continued to study the painting—the bright-colored flowers, the weathered bench that would forever remain empty—I couldn't help but wonder: How I could possibly die now?

~

Finally, I checked my phone. Thirty-two messages! One was from Pete, forewarning me that he might not make it home tonight. The second was from the hospital, with more information about groups I could join, helpful pain management centers and my next appointment. Then three funny and sweet messages from my kids, Julia, Matt and Isabella. Matt was just checking in, and so was Julia.

And then Isabella's, "Mom... mom... call me back. Love you!" Followed by a smacking sound, resembling a kiss. I miss my kids and I want to see them. I need to see them.

The other twenty-seven messages were from yesterday. And they were all from my two best friends, Erica and Freja.

"Where are you? Everybody is here," Erica had whispered into the phone. Oh fuck, I missed our most important meeting of the year. Erica and Freja aren't just my best friends, we also co-own and run a gallery together in Chelsea. Every year for the past twelve years, we've hosted a charity event to raise money to provide underprivileged kids with free art programs.

The next message was from Freja. "Where the fuck are you? You better have a good excuse for this." Freja is the type everyone wants as a best friend. At least I do. She's assertive and always says what's on her mind. I listened to all the messages. Erica, who is sensitive by nature, freaked out after her fifth message and threatened to call the police if I didn't call her back. Freja threatened to kill me, which made me laugh.

I wasn't ready to reveal my news to anyone yet. (Not sure if I'll ever be ready.) I needed time to think and decide what to do next. So instead of calling, I texted Erica to let her know I was fine. I lied. Obviously. I am not fine. I'm a total wreck.

Time passed as I stared out of the window and the quiet street in front of my beloved nineteenth-century brownstone turned into a busy zone—honking, yelling, clattering. During all the noise of the evening rush hour, along with my racing thoughts, I reminded myself over and over: *I am still in control.*

In the distance, a male voice shouted, "Fucking bitch..." The remaining part of the sentence swallowed by traffic and the rattling of the familiar, comforting glass bottles in Pietro's kitchen—a cozy, garlic-smelling Italian trattoria only a few houses over. I love Pietro's! I love this city. And despite my many past failures and too-frequent wrong decisions, I still love this life.

Thoughts popped in and out of my mind. Like, *Maybe the diagnosis is nothing but one giant mistake. I have no pain. I'm just a little tired, but I feel good. The doctors must be wrong. People are misdiagnosed all the time.*

This sucks! All of it does. I have to accept the truth. But I don't want to. Right now, I want my analytical mind to shut up. I take a deep breath, thinking *I've never been a desperate kind of woman, and I certainly don't intend on becoming one now.*

**Desperate** [ˈdesp(ə)rət ] — adjective: *feeling, showing, or involving a hopeless sense that a situation is so bad as to be impossible to deal with*

My pen flies across the page as I'm writing this, and I declare in big, bold letters: **I don't want to tell anybody I'm sick. Not yet. This is my battle, and I am not ready to share my news with anybody. Mainly, I don't want the people I love to worry about something irreversible, nor do I want people to treat me differently. These six months belong to me until I am ready to let go.**

And there it is again, this annoying, nagging inner voice of mine saying, *Liz, live on your terms.* If only I knew what my terms were.

For now, I will write. I will think. I will walk. And maybe, just maybe, I will be strong.

After all, I will have one hundred and forty days. Of course, that's only if I'm lucky. Lucky to die. How ironic.

# DAY 4
## NOVEMBER 30 | NEW YORK CITY

Pete never came home last night, as expected. A mixture of anger and fear made me wallow in despair until the early morning.

When I got up it was still pitch-black outside and deathly quiet for such a vibrant city. Earlier, I heard a couple of garbage trucks passing by, rumbling loudly along the otherwise deserted street until silence embraced me once again.

That's when I thought about all the books I've read on how to live mindfully.

**Mindfulness** [ ˈmīn(d)f(ə)lnəs ] — noun: *a mental state achieved by focusing one's awareness on the present moment*

They conveyed how to stop thinking about the future and the past and instead, how to live in the moment. At the time it sounded too taxing, and I immediately dismissed the very thought of it. Now it's clear that it might be the only way for me to continue living with some joy. Not only do I need to live in the now, but I also *want* to live in the now. I want to experience every moment of my life, and considering that I have no real future, it shouldn't be too hard.

A few days ago in Dr. Sternenberg's office, it took thirty seconds to irreversibly demolish my entire already-scattered-and-so-incredibly-fucked-up existence. Just like that, my life became a ticking time bomb and simultaneously, a luxury. There was no place to hide any longer, the truth screamed at me—loud and clear. *Life is happening right now.*

After my third cup of coffee, I gathered all my strength and called my kids, ignoring the insanely early hour on the West Coast. I needed to hear their voices. Phone calls that, only a few days ago, would have been so easy and joyful were now emotionally challenging. With each of my kids, my conversations were usually as different as they are. We talked about finals, work, friends, books, and a new TV show I 'absolutely' have to watch. In their eyes, I'm not 'up to date' on the happenings of the world. We didn't talk about cancer. That conversation will come soon enough. The thought of leaving my kids behind was excruciating, and as I hung up the phone, I lost it. I broke down howling like an animal in pain. Was that a sign of acceptance?

As I'm writing this, I feel dumb. All this time, I've pretended not to know what Pete has been doing and where he's been spending his nights. 'Pretended.' Of course I know. As long as I can remember, I've had this inner voice guiding me: *stop fooling yourself and face the truth, Liz.* I have no doubt he's with one of his many young lovers. Oh Pete, how pathetic. It makes me sad to think that the funny, passionate, considerate man I once loved so much has been emotionally absent for a long time.

Charming Pete, tall and handsome with salt-and-pepper hair and greenish-gray eyes.

I wonder if any of these women will ever see the real Pete: the man who can be cold and critical, the man with a short fuse, the man who can strip away all your confidence because you can't live up to his standards. Or will they just be blinded by the man who can talk for hours about almost any subject? The man with infectious laughter, the man who makes you feel loved. The good man.

I rid myself of these thoughts by taking a series of deep breaths, and then I slipped into my oldest and most comfortable pair of sweatpants—the ones Pete hates—and its matching sweater, another favorite item of mine. I bought it at the Portobello flea market during a trip to London, long before I got married. Back then, I was studying journalism and had so many dreams. I have to find my dream list! I used to make lists of everything. When did I stop writing them? When did I stop dreaming and living the life I wanted to live?

Many years ago, there were moments when I would hold my head high with so much confidence and I would tell everybody that one day I would be a famous journalist, like Diane Sawyer or Barbara Walters, and I would write and travel the world. Not just travel the world, I was going to change it.

Despite adoring my kids and loving being a mother, every time I gave birth the image of success that had been implanted in my head for so long had to surrender to my new circumstances. That's when I began dreaming a new and bigger dream. I wanted to be a novelist.

But my dreams were no more than illusions. I was barely able to cope with the reality of my busy daily life and my slowly failing marriage.

Without me noticing, one by one, all my dreams died and I gradually created a new life for myself. A life that fit Pete's life. I found new friends and meaning as a mother and as a co-owner at the gallery. I learned to love the new version of myself. But Pete, despite me trying so hard to please him, didn't like the 'new me' any better. In fact, he loved me less.

"*Now.* Liz, it's all about now." I repeated to myself as I grabbed my sneakers and ran for the door. I decided to stop feeling sorry for myself and go for a long walk. A very long walk. A walk through the city I love.

# DAY 5
## DECEMBER 1 | NEW YORK CITY

All bundled up in a long, navy blue winter coat, I stood in front of the house I've lived in for the past eighteen years. The air was brisk. It was the type of cold that hits New York every winter.

A cloud of breath formed as I slowly exhaled, and I felt a burning sensation in my lungs. That's how I began my second—or was it already my third—walk? When I walk my mind quiets, my breathing steadies, and my thoughts become crystal clear.

Today wasn't any different as I strolled east toward Union Square. New York City is the most seductive and ever-changing city. The many colors of displayed fruits and vegetables, and the smell of freshly baked baguettes from the nearby farmer's market distracted me from what lies ahead. The aroma of bread and homemade jam made me think of Paris.

After all, before New York there was Paris. Cobble-stoned streets, Le Marais, outdoor cafés, baroque buildings, and of course, French men. French men with their natural arrogance and their irresistibly passionate way of communicating with women. A French man can undress a woman with his eyes like no other man. And I can't forget the countless picturesque bridges I often crossed during my nighttime walks, always wondering if I would ever share those moments with someone special. I will not. Now I know.

I was the one who chose to give up Paris for Pete. My two Ps!

Then one day, New York became my Paris. It took some time, but in the end I fell in love with its diversity: the people, the art, the contrasting neighborhoods, and the non-stop bustle.

In a flash, morning turned into the afternoon, in a semi-dream about Paris and the life I could have had. For about two-and-a-half miles, I walked uptown along Broadway until I reached Central Park. I took in every sound, every movement. The way the light fell on the pond, all the shades of green, gold and umber. *This is a beautiful world.*

Hours later, I sat in the already—too—familiar waiting room with piles of used magazines, glass tables and brown chairs. I must have been put on a list of urgent cases because the minute I made myself semi-comfortable, I heard my name. A middle-aged nurse ushered me toward Dr. Sternenberg's office, into yet another brown chair facing the man himself.

"Would you like to wait for your husband? Or maybe a friend?" I shook my head in all four directions, thinking, *I am not ready to share my news.* He paused for a second, trying to interpret my gesture.

Then he cut to the chase. "Liz, you still have options. We have drugs that can prolong your life." My mind was racing and I couldn't speak. To be honest, I'm not sure I heard or understood everything he said.

He continued to explain lengthy treatment plans. "Naturally, you would have to stay in the hospital for about six weeks."

Although all the information clouded my brain, for one brief second I emerged from the fog and had a moment of sudden clarity; I was fully aware that he was talking about a considerable fraction of my remaining life. This wasn't a great offer. Honestly, it was a terrible offer.

My mind drifted off. I was thinking about my next steps while Dr. Sternenberg continued to rattle on about medications, side-effects, tubes and percentages.

"With some luck, you might live for another year." Did he just say luck?

**Luck** [ lǝk ] — noun: *success or failure apparently brought by chance rather than through one's own actions*

At one point Dr. Sternenberg leaned in and in his low-key voice said, "There is one more possibility we should discuss. It's a new clinical trial."

After I pressed him for more information, he finally admitted that if I would say 'yes' to the trial, I would have a five percent chance of doubling or tripling my life expectancy. Five percent! The possibility of spending most of my remaining time in the hospital, or potentially never leaving it, wasn't a price I was willing to pay.

That's when I decided I was going to forget all about clinical trials, and I was just going to take the necessary drugs and painkillers to stay comfortable as long as possible. I had a choice to make, so I made it.

That very moment I realized: I have full control over my life, and in the same way, I have total power over my death.

**Death** [ deTH ] — noun: *the end of the life of a living thing*

Finally I managed to speak, despite the foggy bubble engulfing me and the world around me turning into one muffled sound.

Although he had already told me, I had to ask again. "How much longer do I have?"

"Without the trial four, maybe five months."

I suppressed a sob, pretending to be calm. I'm a master at pretending to be okay when I'm not, but these numbers made me dizzy.

Not much later, I walked through a sea of people down posh Madison Avenue and sipped some green tea. A scotch would have been better, but I can't remember the last time I had a drink during the day.

Despite my desire to forget every second of what had just happened, my thoughts drifted back to Dr. Sternenberg and I wondered: Do we always need a plan in life? Doesn't a plan mean we're chasing something? And isn't that the opposite of living more mindfully?

His words replayed in my mind. "Liz, I understand how hard this is for you."

I thought, *No, you don't. You have no idea how I feel.*

The only 'lucky' part about my situation is that I

received a fair warning, and with that information came the luxury to do the things that are important to me. That's why I chose to hold my head up high and live the last days of my life with as little regret as possible.

# DAY 6

## DECEMBER 2 | NEW YORK CITY

Pete finally came home last night, then he surprised me by getting up shortly before six. He never gets up early.

Not much later, we sat in silence at the kitchen counter, sipping coffee and reading newspaper articles, predominately sad stories blown up into tragedies. Sitting together like this wasn't really a choice but rather a habit.

**Habit** [ habət ] — noun: *a settled or regular tendency or practice, especially one that is hard to give up*

The sound of the dripping faucet cut through the heavy air surrounding us, and at some point I put the paper down to watch Pete as he read. My heart broke one last time as images of a young Pete ruffling up my hair while kissing me floated through my mind.

Not being able to take it any longer, I finally broke the silence. "Will you be home tonight?" He lowered the paper and studied me for so long that I concluded he was comparing me to one of his lovers, and I was on the losing end. That's when I looked away.

"Yes. Why?" he asked.

"No reason. I'm going to see Erica and Freja for dinner."

"I'll be late anyway." And then he continued to read as if nothing had ever happened between us. And as if I was not about to die. (To be fair, he didn't know that part yet.)

For one moment I wondered if I should tell him about being sick. It would be the "correct thing" to do. But would it change anything? And for the first time it isn't about Pete. It's about me.

With every step, my city enfolded me, and I became intensely conscious of all my senses. I focused on the world that surrounds me, to examine every detail and not let it pass me by any longer.

It was cold and I wrapped my scarf closer around my neck. A pedestrian elbowed me from behind. Cabs honked and their headlights illuminated the night sky. I'm not sure what triggered it, but my heart started pounding and my mind began racing. I also wasn't sure how much or how little I wanted to reveal to Erica and Freja, or if I wanted to say anything at all. I couldn't breathe. I panicked. Tears flooded my eyes. I clearly wasn't ready to accept my fate. But would I ever be?

Dr. Sternenberg had advised me: "Liz, you should consider seeing a psychologist to help you cope. You will go through a lot of emotions, which will be difficult to handle." I was beginning to get the idea.

**Panic** [ 'panik ] — noun: *sudden uncontrollable fear or anxiety, often causing wildly unthinking behavior*

I looked up at the dark sky—something I vowed to do often in the days to come—I was looking up to heaven. Maybe I would pray. Maybe.

Once my shallow breathing returned to normal, I pulled myself together and made my way through the cheery Soho crowds towards the restaurant.

I was late. And I am never late. Balthazar, a bustling, romantic French brasserie, was as lively as always. I spotted Freja immediately. Standing tall at 6 feet with broad shoulders and short brown hair, she definitely doesn't blend in.

On top of it, she screamed in my direction, "Liz, over here!"

Smiling, I pushed myself through the people to a booth table in the back. Erica, half the size of Freja, was sitting in the corner. I leaned down to hug her for a little longer than usual.

I peeled myself out of my hat, coat, gloves and scarf, and squeezed in between my friends. A waiter with the walk and physique of a dancer approached. Freja scanned every inch of him before announcing, "Not bad at all." She's so no-nonsense that even he had to smile. Then she ordered half the menu while my stomach turned, and I wondered if I should tell them the truth or find some excuse to leave town and deal with my share of the gallery later.

Delicious food followed delicious drinks. Erica was in the middle of a story about an annoying neighbor while I leaned back observing my friends, when Freja suddenly said, "What's wrong, Liz?"

I jumped. "What do you mean?"

"I mean, what is it you aren't telling us?"

Erica dropped her food and stared at me. Her eyes widened and she looked scared. That's when I made up my mind.

"I love you both," I said, knowing that this was going to be much harder than I'd imagined.

"This can't be good," Freja said, putting down her fork.

I took a deep breath and reached for both their hands. "I'm leaving." I guess this was also the very moment I decided what I would do next.

"You're what?" Freja shouted. She's always so loud.

"I don't understand," Erica said.

In the end, I blurted it out. "I'm dying. I have leukemia." I did it. I actually said it out loud. It was over. Done!

Erica and Freja stared at me for what felt like a very long time. And under different circumstances, it could have been funny.

Finally, Freja buried me in her arms, and then Erica joined her.

After that, the evening took a turn. At first, they denied it, almost in the same way I did for the past few days. They looked for a reason why it couldn't be true, and for ways in which they could save me. Our little get together became "sad," precisely what I didn't want. So, I swore them to secrecy.

I need to tell my kids when the time is right. And now is not the right time.

# DAY 7
## DECEMBER 3 | NEW YORK CITY

Despite lying awake for most of the night, I woke up before Pete. Anxiety was inching through my body while my thoughts raced from one subject to another. Some of them serious, others not so much. It went something like this: *What kind of funeral do I want? Where should I be buried? Will I miss Pete? Should I be buried? I'm scared. Will Pete ever miss me? I need to clean the fridge. Pete will never remember to pick up the dry cleaning. Will I suffer a lot? My kids, I adore my kids. Will they be okay without me?*

As I watched Pete snuffling next to me, I thought about all the years we had spent together and the question that would remain forever. Why couldn't we make it work? I reached out for Pete one last time but stopped in mid-air; I couldn't.

I was lying next to a man who had made me cry too often. A man who no longer respected me and who couldn't—or didn't want to—see the real me.

After all these years, I finally grasped that the man I had once loved so much had never taken the time to notice that something had changed, that I had metamorphosed.

But if all that were true, I wondered: Why had I never dared to change my life? For too many years, I had postponed everything. There had been the fear of the unknown. The fear of failing. The fear of not fulfilling, to the best of my abilities, the limitless responsibilities of life.

**Fear** [ ˈfir ] — noun: *an unpleasant emotion caused by the belief that someone or something is dangerous, likely to cause pain or a threat*

Now was the time to make yet another choice: I could die with regret, or I could finally live.

I chose to live and to give up fear. I was determined to live these last months, days, hours, minutes, and seconds fearlessly. At least, I would try.

In my mind I created a bubble that descended on me and soothed me into a state of quietude, a painless world. I visualized it as a pink, unbreakable bubble, like the 'Bazooka' bubblegum I used to blow up as a child until it popped straight onto my face. I see myself in that pink cocoon, protected.

This morning I waited. I waited for Pete to get up. I waited for him to pack for his next trip. Another trip? I waited for him to hug me one last time, but it never came. Instead, I watched him close the entrance door. I watched him leave. He never turned around, so he never saw me crying. He didn't know that I concocted a plan during the night and that we would never see each other again.

The door clicked shut and I stood there, sobbing. Did my bubble already burst?

I texted my kids to let them know I was okay and that I would be in touch soon. Seconds later, my phone buzzed and a text from Isabella appeared. "Weird, Mom… What's going on?" I didn't answer but sent back a heart emoji. Next, I grabbed a suitcase from the coat closet and threw all my comfy clothes in it, turned off my cell phone and tossed it between my clothes in the suitcase. Then I took my jewelry and watches and placed them in my closet behind the dresses I will never wear again.

And finally, I wrote a note:

*Pete,*
*Please don't try to contact me or alarm the kids. I'm all right, and they know that I will be in touch soon. Although life didn't turn out the way we once dreamed, I don't want you to forget that I loved you the day we got married in that tiny church across from the Chinese deli, and I loved you for all the years that followed.*
*Be well.*
*Liz*
*P.S. I plan to spend Christmas with the kids (if they want). Please agree to this and don't question anything.*

I placed my keys on top of the note, while images of Pete and me floated around my mind: staying up all night and counting stars, running through the rain, painting the walls of our tiny apartment in bright yellow, feeding each other dumplings out of paper containers and Pete holding each of our babies. They disappeared as quickly as they came. One by one, I let them go.

The day Pete and I moved into our home, all I had with me was one suitcase. Now, I'm leaving him the same way.

For many years, Pete had been the best man for me. He made me feel secure and for a while he had been a man of his word. At the beginning, we were blinded by a fun life with only a few responsibilities, and we had dreamed up a future that later turned out to be nothing more than an illusion.

Life gradually evolved into a succession of tasks and duties: kids, the house, Pete's increasingly demanding work. Pete struggled, and eventually he gave up—first on the kids, then on me—and continued to live his life the way it had been before we got married.

But I'm not a victim here. I'm more of a participant. After all, I never tried to stop him.

The door slammed shut behind me, and I walked down the stairs thinking, *Why didn't I enjoy every moment as if it were my last?*

# DAY 8

## DECEMBER 4 | NEW YORK CITY

After spending a sleepless night in a small but fancy hotel in Chelsea, with its rose walls and fluffy white towels, I was on my way. However, my newly found freedom and the fact that I'm not used to making impulsive decisions made me feel discombobulated.

On my way to the airport, I started spiraling. Suddenly the thought of flying made my heart palpitate and I panicked. I loved flying, the sensation of soaring through infinite space. But flights end too quickly, like so many other things in life—and as I now know, life itself.

I was almost at JFK when I changed my mind. I needed time to think about what I was going to do next. For years there had been this little dream of mine: to travel cross-country on a train. With my death so imminent, this turned out to be the perfect opportunity.

The cab driver, Singh Rajed (that's what it said on his license medallion), by now irritated by my indecision, gave me that New York look. Seriously reconsidering my sanity (and I can't blame him), he made a sharp U-turn and drove through Queens back towards Manhattan.

Elated, I knew I made the right choice when the spectacular New York skyline once again came into view. This would be the last time I would see the city I had loved all these years. I tried to absorb all the colors, shapes and breathtaking reflections of sunlight on the glass windows of the skyscrapers. Then I closed my eyes and created a picture of it in my mind, an image I can recall at any given time. That was when I figured out how to say goodbye. Goodbye to people, places and things.

**Goodbye** [ go͝od'bī ] — noun: *a parting*

The incense the cab driver was burning (is this even allowed?) gradually lulled me into a state of peace. An hour later, a much calmer Singh—I doubled his fare— dropped me off at the Grand Central Station.

Train stations aren't supposed to be that grandiose! In my experience, train stations are filthy and either too cold or too hot. But those descriptions don't apply here. With its gigantic clocks, ornate mezzanine, old staircases, enticing food courts, long underground corridors, and its masterfully painted ceiling of angels and stars, Grand Central is mesmerizing.

I've always been attracted to the allure of train stations and the stories they carry. I often wonder: Where are all these people going, and why?

Train stations remind me of beginnings and endings, departures and arrivals.

As I stood underneath the opal-faced Main Concourse Information Booth Clock, knowing that in less than six months all of this won't exist for me anymore. I'll depart to an unknown place I can't even picture yet.

I whispered, "Liz, don't cry," and swallowed my tears.

It was almost funny that everybody was in such a rush except for me. And I was the one with no time left.

Behind the ticket counter sat a heavyset woman with meticulously braided hair. There was sadness in her brown eyes.

"Where to?" she asked.

"Los Angeles," I said.

A weird moment of silence followed while she looked through a timetable. In the end, she broke into a half-smile.

"You're in luck, girl. There's one leaving in two hours. But not from here. You have to go to Penn Station." Of course! How silly of me. I should have known better.

There was a pause, and I thought she was about to say something else, but what followed was only a look of desire, as if she wanted to come with me. I forced my attention back to her, thinking that maybe one day she could change her life and follow her dreams. I only hope if she does, it's not her last journey.

"Thank you," I murmured. And then I ran.

At Penn Station I bought my ticket (two tickets, I have to change trains in Chicago), and that's when anxiety hit me. It always comes out of the blue. Trying to breathe through it, I clung to my ticket and held on to my suitcase as I made my way through the crowd, feeling vulnerable. People transformed into nothing but moving figures, and I urged myself to take one step at a time. *Just one more step. Just one more step, Liz, just one more.*

# DAY 9
## DECEMBER 5 | ON THE TRAIN

The steady, monotonous beat of the train woke me up and my first thought was that more than one of my remaining weeks had already passed. Less than nineteen weeks left, and that's if I'm lucky. Less than five months. I have to stop counting.

I opened the shades and as sunlight flooded my train cabin, my mood lifted. I'm leaving one life behind to begin a brief new one. Am I insane? What am I thinking? What will happen when I'm too sick to take care of myself? Honestly, right now, I don't give a fuck.

I unlatched and opened the window and screamed as loud as I could. "I want to live!" It felt so good. Then I did it again. And again.

Later, curled up on my quite comfortable berth, I watched the world fly by. Stretched out in front of me was a fertile plain of cornfields—endless green and yellow bathed in the sun, swaying in the wind. After some time, the fields disappeared and stretches of ever-greens, standing tall, replaced them. So beautiful.

There are a few ways one can travel on a train. In my case, there were two options: the rustic and straightforward way economy or the more luxurious first-class version. I opted for the latter. Paying a bit more—actually, a lot more—secured me one of the single occupant compartments. The things money can buy! Plush pillows, blankets and vanilla-scented soaps. I should have felt a little guilty; after all, I used Pete's money. But instead, I silently thanked him, knowing that he would be more than fine.

**Guilt** [ gilt ] — noun: *a feeling of having done wrong or failed in an obligation*

I closed my eyes and tried to let him go—with every mile, Pete became less present.

Being in a single occupant compartment granted me the freedom to spend time alone. I've always disliked small talk with strangers, but I especially dreaded it now when I needed to be by myself.

This train ride is my way of taking the first step toward departure from this world. I want to leave this place with a sense of tranquility, hoping that wherever I go something better is waiting for me. Maybe I will see my parents again, and my older sister. I miss them.

The train sped along, and as I drifted from thoughts to sleep and back to thoughts, I lost track of time and space. I had no idea where I was. Now and then I wiggled my toes, just to make sure that I was still part of this earth.

This is a one-way journey, and it feels unsettling to realize that I will never return.

# DAY 10

## DECEMBER 6 | SOMEWHERE IN KANSAS

After changing trains, I didn't feel too good. This was the first time since the day I saw Dr. Sternenberg that I felt pain. My body ached, and occasional sharp pains ran through my legs and arms, followed by inevitable waves of uncontrollable panic.

Since my diagnosis, there have been moments when I wanted to believe (I read that's quite normal) that some miracle might happen. That is a foolish thought!

I made myself comfortable on my foldable sofa bed, cuddled up under a soft blanket I wisely carried along-- the last reminder of my previous life. Waves of dizziness and nausea crept up on me—an indication, perhaps a warning, of what will come.

Dr. Sternenberg mentioned the acute pain won't set in for another three months. "Acute pain," I had repeated to him, before I added, "I don't need to hear anything else. Not now."

Evidently, he had dealt with patients like me before. "As you wish, Liz." I hated the way he said my name.

After leaving the doctor's office that day, the meaning of the word "time" changed for me.

**Time** [ tīm ] — noun: *the indefinite continued progress of existence and events in the past, present, and future*

Suddenly, time became a gift, and now I'm painfully aware that I'm running out of it. But I'm still alive and lucky to see the world unwinding right in front of me.

That's exactly what I did today as I sat on my bed while the reddish colors of the early sunrise turned into a bright yellow, until the sun disappeared behind a series of oddly shaped, first-white-then-grey clouds. Finally, it rained.

Rain always has a cleansing effect on me. Today wasn't any different. It washed away my gloominess. In the end, today is all I can ask for. There is nothing else but the present. There is only *now*.

I took my medicine: seven pills and Chinese herbs such as Panax Ginseng, Curcuma, and Oldenlandia. Then I laid out all the books I brought with me, and I slowly began to feel better.

Reading has always been a way for me to find my serenity. I used to read a lot. As a kid and later as a teenager, I would spend countless hours in bed reading, escaping into different worlds with my heroines and heroes, taking part in their journeys.

Before leaving New York, I narrowed my reading list down to a few books. Books I wanted to read again. My hours are numbered and reading seems like a waste of time. Why would I even consider reading books when every minute is so precious?

There's a paradox. Knowing that I will die soon makes me want to continue to live my life as ordinarily as possible. Then again, here I am amid an adventure of traveling and changing my life (for one last time).

Now and then, I catch myself looking for comfort in the familiar. Maybe that comfort is nothing more than some false reassurance that everything will eventually turn out to be one big mistake, and life will continue as usual, even for me. But right now, I need familiar. And reading is familiar.

Reading not only calms me, but also carries me to different worlds. I can travel from Thailand to the 18th century, from ballrooms to the streets of Calcutta; I can experience love and tragedy; I can swim in lakes and ride camels through deserts.

Ultimately, I'll have to let go of everything that I love the most. Soon, but not right now.


MY READING LIST
1. Last Lovers by William Wharton
2. A Perfect Stranger by Danielle Steel
3. Outlander by Diana Gabaldon
4. The English Patient by Michael Ondaatje
5. Out of Africa by Isak Dinesen
6. Jane Eyre by Charlotte Bronte
7. All the Light We Cannot See by Anthony Doerr
8. Gone with the Wind by Margaret Mitchell
9. The Bluest Eye by Toni Morrison
10. Pride and Prejudice by Jane Austen

*Julia, this list is especially for you. You will understand and ultimately find your comfort in reading the books I once loved so much. By the way, Elizabeth Bennet in Pride and Prejudice reminds me of you. I love you, Mommy*

Jane Austen, the most courageous and untouchable writer of her time. I've read all her books many times before, but Pride and Prejudice will always be my favorite. In the end, isn't it all about love? Isn't it love we're living for?

As I'm writing my final story, I'm thinking of all the love in my life—all my love stories. I can't help dreaming about the one I'll never have.

# DAY 11
## DECEMBER 7 | ARIZONA

The morning air was balmy as I stood by the open window of my compartment. I felt the wind blowing on my face and moving through my hair.

Sprawled out in front of me was Arizona, with its dry land, red rocks and scrub bushes. Old roads wound through the desolate landscape, and I envisioned how people must have traveled through here centuries ago. Carriages drawn by oxen, mules and sweaty horses generating clouds of dust. Cowboys and shootouts.

To my surprise, I felt great today. But as I became cognizant of yesterday that momentary feeling of lightness could disappear in seconds. Not wanting to focus on my health, I shifted my thoughts to the now, which wasn't that difficult because I was starving. My empty stomach ultimately forced me to emerge from my cocoon in search of some food.

Up until this point, I hadn't been privy to the actual length of the train. At first, I walked in the wrong direction—fitting, since I've been walking in the wrong direction for twenty years. Walking the wrong way turned my initial intention of getting something to eat into a rather long and undesirable experience as I swayed with the rhythm of the train, occasionally losing my balance.

At last I made it, and the dining car was packed. It was like a picture of the past: old-fashioned red curtains, booths with wooden seats. Cramped. Smelly. Loud.

Standing in the middle of all the commotion, I took in the noisy happiness of travelling people, the anticipatory excitement foreshadowing their journey. A server, dressed in a ridiculously ill-fitting black suit, pushed me into the only free seat, next to a pretty, dark-haired woman. She must've been in her thirties—her features were delicate and her deep, sad brown eyes fixed themselves on me. She studied me a bit until finally deciding to say something; her voice was so soft that I had to lean closer.

"Hi, I'm Mary."

I wasn't sure if I wanted to make a new friend or have this conversation.

**Friend** [frend] — noun: *a person whom one knows and with whom one has a bond of mutual affection*

Over the years, friends have come and gone. Only a few good ones have remained to live with me through my journey as I've lived through theirs.

Considering my circumstances, making new friends appeared contradictory. I hesitated, but some inner force—I can't explain what—drew me towards her.

"I'm Elizabeth. Liz."

She continued to stare at me and for a moment I felt that I should be the one to initiate a conversation. But Mary, despite her shyness, jumped ahead of me.

"I'm scared," she said.

"Scared?"

"This is my first time on a train. Everything is so new."

I tried to hide my surprise, but it was most likely plastered all over my face.

She continued, "I've never left my town before." Then she corrected herself. "That's not true. Sometimes, I take the bus to Tulla. It's a bigger town next to ours."

"How much bigger?" I asked, suddenly feeling curious.

"Not sure, but it has a Walmart and a small movie theater."

I nodded, while images of Manhattan floated through my mind: people rushing along 5$^{th}$ Avenue, cabs honking, the smell of burnt chestnuts, mothers holding their kids tightly, tourists—loaded with shopping bags— winding through the crowds.

"What's your town like?" I asked.

"My town?" She looked at me, astounded. Maybe she wasn't used to people asking about her life.

"How many people live there?"

"Less than 2,000," she said.

The same two thousand people, day in and day out. Everybody probably knows everything about everybody. It must be unsettling to be exposed like that and have a limited amount of privacy. Then it dawned on me that this might not be the reason why she's traveling, and I wasn't sure why I cared to continue the conversation, but I did anyway.

"So, where are you going?" I asked, not at all expecting what I heard next.

She blushed and took a deep breath. "I'm on my way to meet a man. I met him a year ago." She glanced at her wedding band. "I know it's not right… you know, my husband drinks. He drinks too much, you know, he… he gets angry." She swallowed hard, once again looking straight into my eyes. I could only imagine.

And then I thought, *A man*! This unassuming woman is having an affair. Something I occasionally contemplated but never dared to pursue. Not even in my loneliest moments. And there were many.

I wanted to say something but couldn't find the right words in time. Instead, I reached for her hand. Over the years, I've understood that there's something very profound about touching another person. The slightest comforting touch can often mean far more than words.

There was a long pause before I asked, "Do you have kids?"

"Four." I waited for her to continue. "They're with my mom until next week. I'll get them when I get back. My mom knows about…. the man."

"I have three kids," I said.

"How old are they?"

"My youngest, Isabella, is 20. Julia's 25. And Matt is 28."

"That's nice." The pause that followed was so long that I thought this might be the end of our conversation.

"My husband left for a mining job and won't be back for a month. I have to leave him. I know I have to."

"I understand," I said. And I did.

"I love him very much."

"Who?" I asked, slightly confused.

"Mark. My…" She struggled to find the right words. "Not my husband."

When she said his name, I felt the power of love emanating from her, and it hit me hard.

Mary! This gentle woman. Her sudden unexpected

presence, her story, and her passion for life will stay with me for the rest of mine. She trusted me with her deepest secret, a stranger. She, who had never traveled more than twenty miles outside of her self-imposed boundaries, had found the courage to do what I had failed to do for twenty years.

**Courage** [ ˈkərij ] — noun: *the ability to do something that frightens one*

# DAY 12

## DECEMBER 8 | SOMEWHERE

Today was the fourth day of my train ride and it was—well, I'm not sure how I can describe it, uneventful. One could call it uneventful. Still, it was a peaceful day with no aches and pains. A day that instantly made me wish I could have a thousand more. I closed my eyes and thought about all the things I could do if I had that many more days.

Those 'imagined' days, in the form of tiny circles, filled my head, shouting out all the things I'll never get to experience. I had to remind myself to forget about the past and to stop thinking about the future. No more pondering on how to achieve more in life, it's such a bad habit! Here it is. This is it!

Today, I'm pain-free and astonished by how little discomfort I'm experiencing. Dr. Sternenberg must have given me magic pills. Or am I living in a state of illusion?

**Illusion** [ i'lo͞oZHən ] — noun: *a thing that is or is likely to be wrongly perceived or interpreted by the senses*

I know I have my moments of denial; it's easier that way. On the other hand, I'm amazed at how I find peace, even if only for brief moments, with the condition I'm finding myself in right now.

Nowadays, internet sites offer explanations for everything with the click of a button. And I'm sure that somewhere there's a formula for how a person should behave in a situation like this. But I haven't searched for it, and I never will. Back in New York, I tried to research the form of leukemia I have. All I did was type one question, and Google came up with over 5,000 results—a bit too much to sort through considering the little time I have left.

All I know is that this is my life and these are my choices, and the farther I travel west, the more I'm preparing myself to live life—every day—fully and fiercely until the end.

Knowing this, I relaxed and felt ready to hibernate in my cozy compartment. I read *Last Lovers* until I drifted off into a dream.

*Last Lovers* is a story about Jack, a successful middle-aged executive living in Paris. Dreaming of becoming an artist, he spends his days painting in a Parisian park. Jack—now Jacques—soon becomes friends with Mirabelle, a 71-year-old blind woman. And gradually, their friendship turns to romance.

In my dream, a deep, soft voice told me that everything is going to be fine. *Fine* is a word my mother often used when I was a little girl. She promised me that everything would be fine, but it never was.

Later, after I woke up, I prayed—something I hadn't done in years.

In some form or another, I have always believed in a higher power. Although I have to admit that until today, I had ignored that belief most of the time. Over and over, I observed people reaching out to God in times of trouble, only to forget about him when life turned out the way they wanted. Evidently, I'm one of those people. After all these years, I finally had a conversation with my God (or shall we say the Universe).

This was real: my prayer, the swishing sound of the moving train, me sitting on my daybed looking out the window.

As I'm writing this, my fingers clasped tightly around my fountain pen—a gift from my father. Growing up, I believed that each of us has our own God. Mine is a wise man sitting on top of a mountain. He understands that I don't want to leave this earth, the people I love, the beauty that surrounds me, the many challenges ahead.

Earlier, he asked me, "Why do you want to stay, Liz?"

It took me by surprise when I heard my own voice. "There are so many things I have to do. I want to spend time with my kids. Go to dinners. Take long walks. I want to write a novel. I want to be a grandmother. I want to live in a house with a blooming garden. And I want to be in love again. I want to be loved."

# DAY 13
## DECEMBER 9 | ALMOST THERE

T he on and off conversation between my wise man and me turned out to be much longer than I had expected—through the night—and nobody was winning. A little faith had slipped back into my life, but that doesn't mean I'll change who I am. The conversation turned out to be exhausting and somewhere between feeling furious and terrified, I fell asleep.

When I woke up hours later, I was well into my last day of this marvelous train ride, just six hours away from reaching Los Angeles. *This is it!* I thought. *The last chapter of my life is about to begin.*

(Final) **destination** [destəˈnāSH(ə)n] —noun: *the (final) place to which someone or something is going or being sent*

I threw my clothes into my suitcase and took a long, hot shower before slipping into my favorite dress. I love how it flows around my body with every movement I make—perfect for the sunny California weather. After a glance in the mirror, I approved of my look. But I also noticed that I'd lost some weight.

With nothing else to do, I went to find Mary. Once again, it proved to be a rather tricky task. The train was speeding along, and I was bouncing around, touching walls as I made my way towards the observation car.

I found Mary sitting all alone in a corner. Her eyes were swollen from crying and my heart instantly broke for her. I knew she needed to be comforted, so I sat with her as she told me more about her life; she's a waitress and on her off days she does housekeeping for the elderly. Even days into her journey, she was still in awe of her surroundings. Imagining that she had no money to spare, I invited her for brunch.

I was not trying to make a difference in her life, but I prattled along anyway: "The steps you're taking now will determine your future. You are doing the right thing for your kids and yourself. There's nothing selfish about wanting to be treated well and wanting to find happiness."

All of a sudden, I heard myself and became cognizant that I had said too much. That's when I stopped, creating an awkward pause.

"Liz, love is happiness," she said. Four words—one of them being my name—and it became apparent to me that all this time she had understood what life is all about, much better than I do.

Love. There it is again, that word: *love*. Life is about love.


**Love** [ lʌv ] — noun: *an intense feeling of deep affection*


The train stopped in Prescott; I hugged Mary, and she left me staring at a tiny piece of paper in the palm of my hand. On it she had scribbled her lover's phone number, the only way I could reach her. The paper weighed a lot as I closed my hand and crumpled it into a ball; I knew I would never see her again. We had met at a crossroad. It was her first journey, and for me, it was my last.

# DAY 14

## DECEMBER 10 | LOS ANGELES AND SANTA MONICA

Surreal Los Angeles: the land of palm trees and convertibles, where everything sparkles, glitters and shines. Everybody appears to be gorgeous, healthy and wealthy. But I've quickly understood that all of it is nothing more than a perception born from movies, ads and magazines.

On my previous visits to Los Angeles, I was always rushing—settling kids into dorms or apartments—with no time left to wander and explore. This time it was different, and reality hit me sooner than expected as I strolled along the almost-empty, stretched-out Santa Monica beach.

In a travel magazine, I once read that this beach is about three and a half miles long. The Westside (that's what Angelenos call it) was more beautiful than I remembered. The Pacific Ocean spread out in front of me with its majestic roar—a perfect picture of both tranquility and movement. Plus, I felt the sand rubbing between my toes. I love the beach! The air! The ocean!

**Perfect** [ ˈpərfikt ] — adjective: *having all the desirable elements, qualities, or characteristics*

I can recall times in my past when I wanted to be perfect, and to be viewed as perfect. Ultimately, I understood that there's no such thing as an ideal place or person.

For most of my life, I was an optimist. But as things gradually got worse at home and my confidence shattered, I began to believe less and less in myself.

More often than not, I struggled to comprehend how my life had changed in ways I could have never anticipated. For years, my heart leapt with joy every time I saw Pete, then one day I realized he didn't love me anymore.

**But I am strong. So damn strong!**

*Stop it, Liz!!! That's such bullshit!* I'm neither bold nor strong. People always perceive me as such, and I hate it. Right now, I feel like screaming. I want to be weak. I want to break down. And I want someone to tell me I'm going to be fine.

Don't we all need a soulmate: a husband, a wife, a friend, a parent we can count on when it matters? That someone we can love and trust, someone who accepts us unconditionally.

On my way back to my rental car, I climbed up a bunch of stairs. In my mind I was ready to dash up, but in reality I had to stop several times to catch my breath.

The wooden stairs lead from the beach to a pathway

along the ocean. From there the view was stunning: to my left was Santa Monica Pier, with its lit up old-fashioned carousel and rollercoasters; to my right was the Malibu coastline.

But Los Angeles, the place where dreams come true, isn't the *perfect* place.

And later as I drove through the heavy LA traffic, I concluded that I came to this city for only one reason: I wanted to be close to my kids. Kids can't be your soulmates, but they can feed your soul.

My kids are the three people who define my version of love. And California turned out to be the place they call home. Julia went to Berkeley, Matt to Stanford, and as I am writing this, Isabella is in her second year at UCLA. They all opted to go to college, follow their dreams, and build their lives on the West Coast. From a very young age, they had a powerful connection with each other, and I want to believe that's why they ended up in the same city.

I miss my kids, and by now I'm sure they're wondering where I am and why I'm not reachable.

As much as I want to see and hug them, I also need more time before I find the strength and courage to talk to them. I need time to decide what to tell them, and what *not* to tell them.

I turned off my rental car and stepped into the wintery California light. It took some time before I snapped out of my reflective mode and drew my attention to a cloud that looked like a heart floating through the sky. I visualized a ladder from where I stood going straight up to heaven—a ladder just for me.

# DAY 15
## DECEMBER 11 | BEVERLY HILLS

The palm trees swayed lightly in the morning breeze. The cool wind and rose-colored walls of the Beverly Hills Hotel should have made me happy, but they didn't. Instead, I felt lonely and apprehensive.

Not that long ago, I loved staying in beautiful hotels. Each time there was the wonderful sense of novelty and excitement that came with a luxurious hotel in a foreign place. But not this time.

Uneasiness stayed close to me today. I felt panic run through my body, and worse, through my mind. Whatever I did, nothing seemed to feel right. Just one of those days.

**Panic** [ ˈpanik ] — noun: *sudden uncontrollable fear or anxiety*

All I see while writing this are happy couples strolling past me. To be honest, it stirs up a lot of emotion in me.

Not that I don't cheer for them to be in love. I do. But I don't want to see it. Not right now. Their joy makes me aware of all I've lost. Tears are welling up in my eyes, and now I can't see what I'm writing. Everything is blurry and all I want to do is cry. Cry until it's all over.

# DAY 16

## DECEMBER 12 | BEVERLY HILLS

L ast night, while I was lying awake in bed, the panicky feeling left and "Worry" with a capital "W" crept upon me instead. Where will I stay? How long can I avoid a hospital? All these years, it never crossed my mind that I could die too young. Why hadn't I ever thought about it? After all, I know people who died young and, of course, I've read about so many others. But I've never thought about my own mortality.

I have so many questions, but none of the answers. What will happen to my kids? I'm certain they will miss me, but do they still need me? All three are fearless and independent. But what about Isabella, who just turned 20? My love for them is as deep today as it was the first time I held them in my arms. In those moments, the amount of joy and contentment I felt seemed almost unimaginable.

**Unimaginable** [ ˌənəˈmaj(ə)nəb(ə)l ] — adjective: *diffi-cult or impossible to imagine or comprehend*

While waiting for the real estate agent to call me back, I was sitting by the pool in one of the hotel's fancy lounge chairs—they were pink, just like everything else around here—when I noticed a boy no older than four standing right in front of me. He was amused that I hadn't seen him until then. He giggled and I reached out to touch his tiny hand. Laughing, he retracted it and ran back into his mother's arms. That's when I decided for the hundredth time that despite my anxiousness and occasional nausea, I would pretend, for as long as I can, to be healthy. I will ignore the deadly sickness inching through my body. *Yes, that's exactly what I am going to do.*

# DAY 17
## DECEMBER 13 | MALIBU

This morning, at an inconceivably early hour (it must have been no later than 5:30 AM), and after a light breakfast (bread with honey and jams) and a cup of green tea, I drove to Malibu. As I cruised along Sunset Boulevard, cranking up my music, I forgot about time. I felt happy. And as I had vowed to myself yesterday, I ignored being sick.

It's no lie that the Malibu coastline is one of the most beautiful coastal stretches in the world. The colorful houses form a half-moon surrounded by miles of sand.

I stopped at the Malibu Commons, which is an outdoor mall for the rich. It was still early and there wasn't one other person there as I sat for some time in silence on the porch of Malibu Kitchen—a pot-pourri of a deli—listening to chirping birds and waiting for it to open.

An hour later, I moved to one of the outdoor tables and indulged in a cup of coffee. The nutty aroma reminded me of the life I once had and memories from the past surfaced.

My emotions are all over the place today, one minute I'm giggling like a young girl and the next I'm crying. All the excellent physicians and none of them can save me. They give me more than enough useless advice, however—drink three cups of green tea every day, cut out coffee, don't eat fried food. That's ridiculous. It's not like I'll live any longer if I drink green tea for the next few months, nor will I die any sooner if I drink coffee. I love coffee, so I'm going to drink it anyway.

After—unapologetically—finishing my coffee, I wandered down to the beach and spent a couple of hours strolling around. The air was brisk and salty, and the fine sand wedged its way between my toes while the roaring waves drowned out my thoughts.

A couple miles in, I put on my sweater to fight the emerging chill and I sat on a towel I had brought with me to watch the waves rolling in and out in a rhythmic pattern.

Seagulls circled high above, and I looked up at the endless blue sky. Heaven. *It's so difficult to leave this earth.*

Moments that shaped my life flashed in front of my eyes as tears kept coming: Matt when I taught him how to tie his shoes. Me and Isabella happily twirling around in front of the Museum d'Orsay in Paris. The first time I saw Pete sitting on a bench in the park. He smiled at me, and I tried to avoid his eyes, until suddenly he was sitting next to me.

"How long are we going to play this game?"

"What game?" I pretended not to know what he was talking about. Our eyes met, and that was that.

# PETE

When I met Liz, she was sitting on a bench in Central Park, reading a book in French. Her hair was shorter and darker than it is now. I still remember her dress; it was vintage, with red and yellow flowers. That very dress made me notice her.

I had just failed the 'ARE' (Architectural Registration Exam), and I was in no rush to go anywhere. That's when I saw her, just sitting there, lost in her book. She didn't look at me, not even when I strolled up and down the path. I wasn't sure how to approach her. I was shy then. It was only when she looked up and in my direction that I gathered all my courage and walked over to her.

"Nice dress," I said. She ignored me at first. Later she teased me about that moment. Mostly for sitting down next to her without asking, so close we almost touched.

"What are you reading?" I asked.

"Les Livres de la Cité des Dames. It's French."

I laughed. "I know."

She looked straight at me, or straight through me. "You speak French?"

"No."

"Then I'll never be able to marry you." She said.

"Why not?"

"Because I only love things that are French, and soon I'm going to live in Paris."

"When?"

"Soon."

Six months later, we were married, and she never went to live in Paris. Liz became a wife and a mother. And in time she became a cook, a nurse, a decorator—all for her family—and a co-owner of a gallery. And I became a selfish jerk.

It didn't surprise me to see Liz's note. I knew it would happen one day. Secretly, I hoped for it. I wish I could say that I wanted to save our marriage, but I didn't. There was nothing left to save. I wanted to end it, but I didn't have the guts to do it. Still, I was surprised to see that she left everything behind: her jewelry, most of her clothes, her favorite worn-out Ferragamo's. That part unsettled me. I could feel that something wasn't right.

Despite everything, I still care a lot. If that makes any sense.

# DAY 18
## DECEMBER 14 | BEVERLY HILLS

Two weeks have passed, and I can't help but remember that I only have eighteen weeks left. Maybe less. Maybe there's a slight chance I can survive this?

Too many thoughts were crossing my busy mind when Susan Marble, the owner of a small real estate company, knocked at my door and stepped into my life. Despite being in her early sixties, she's stunning. And with her arrival—she stormed into my hotel room as if we had been friends forever—my life took an unexpected turn.

"Don't look at me. I had no time to do my hair, let alone go to the salon," she explained, immediately followed by laughter.

Sitting on pink chairs in the Cabana Cafe for lunch, Susan let me know that she's been a real estate agent for over twenty years, she's happily single, has a brother who lives somewhere in the Canadian woods, she loves dogs but doesn't have the time to actually own one, and that the real estate market in Los Angeles is impossible.

Susan reached for a French fry and dipped it into a porcelain jar filled with mayonnaise. "I could eat them all day. So, what are you looking for? And don't leave out any details."

Three hours later I could see that Susan's movie-star looks effortlessly matched her personality. Her vivid blue eyes were persistently fixed on me, and the most captivating thing was that she completely understood my want and need for a charming home. I couldn't shake the feeling that she knew more about me than she should.

After dessert (ice cream, berries, and whipped cream), we drove in silence along the winding Coldwater Canyon Road. No longer was there any sign that California had experienced a seven-year-long drought. Instead, a fresh breeze whipped through the car window, and I was entranced by the distinct scents of the flowers along the road. That morning my many thoughts, one by one, floated away while Susan maneuvered the car skillfully around sharp curves and up a narrow and pebbled dirt path, deep into the hills. Along the way, we passed two enormous houses with massive iron gates, temple-like pillars and marble fountains spitting water into the air.

Susan must have read my mind. "Far too pompous."

Not long after, we stopped, and there it was: the perfect house.

Compared to the others, it was small at two thousand square feet, but compared to New York apartments, it was huge. This house was the exact opposite of every mansion we passed earlier: the grass was too high and the flowers were a wilted mess. But the five palm trees— planted to form a heart with their huge leaves swaying to the rhythm of the wind, were what attracted me the most.

"Why don't you go ahead," she said. "The first impression of a new home is always the most important one."

Susan handed me a key dangling from a gold chain. One tiny key.

She continued, "I understand you want to rent, but if you change your mind and decide to buy this house… She paused. I'm certain you'll spend many months…," then correcting herself, "years here."

"My kids might," I said, regretting my words immediately. She didn't seem to notice the quiver in my voice. Why would I buy a home now? What a ridiculous thought!

Honestly, all I wanted was a home as soon as possible, and this had serious potential.

Conscious of every step, I approached the house. The pebbles below my soles made a crunching sound, and the sunlight illuminated the white and weathered wooden entrance door. I couldn't believe it. This house, with its chipped, rose painted exterior and white shutters, was the house I had envisioned for myself so often before. I turned around and what I saw took my breath away. In front of me, spread out in the distance, were canyon hills in sandy earth colors. They were studded with palm trees and colorful flowers. The light reflected on the earth, and for a second, it looked like the ocean. It must have been my imagination.

Water has always had a way of calming me, and the ocean's vastness has always soothed my fears. At first, I wanted to live close to the ocean, but something deeper and more profound drew me to the hills.

I had prepared to explore a bunch of neighborhoods,

never thinking I would find my house on the first day. My home. The Universe must be on my side.

Susan had to make some phone calls, which gave me time to take it all in. The house's many exquisite exterior details put me in a state of tranquility. There was something so strange but also comforting as I sat on the front steps of the very house I dreamt up, and despite I haven't been inside yet, I already was in love with it.

Straight away I knew, I wanted this house to be mine, even if it would only be for a short time. Besides, before I left, Freja had offered me a generous sum for my third of the gallery, which I accepted without thinking twice. Freja loves the gallery, and Erica doesn't want to invest any more money. That had been easy.

Curious to explore the interior and bracing myself for disappointment, I turned the key. The door sprang open, and I entered the house of my dreams.

Everything in the house seemed untouched. It was like walking through someone else's life: there were many photos of an older woman with shoulder-length gray hair and a soft smile, there was fresh wood in the fireplace, books piled up, rugs covering most of the old and chipped wooden floor, and paintings hanging all over the walls.

Many questions permeated my mind: *Who is the woman in the pictures? What is her story? What is the story of this house?*

I meandered around for some time, and there was no doubt in my mind that I would do anything to rent this little piece of heaven.

Knowing that the house was not only for rent, but also for sale, my inner voice kept whispering, *Buy it! If you can, Liz, buy the house!* —I'm going mad.

That evening, Susan and I drove back through the

hills in silence. This time, I was the one to break it, my voice cracking from excitement. "I might want to buy it." I said.

If she was surprised at all, she didn't show it. She just said, "Think about it."

One way or another, this will be the last place I call home. This will be the house I die in.

# DAY 19

## DECEMBER 15 | BEVERLY HILLS

Susan insisted it would be okay for me to rent the house and move in immediately.

Ever since I found out I was dying; everything has gone so smoothly that I can't help but wonder when things will fall apart.

Susan and I drove to the bank to transfer money, and I signed a rental contract with the option to buy, and just like that, I became a 'sort-of-owner' of a beautiful home in the hills. The universe, without a doubt, helped me out here.

I couldn't wait to move in! I packed my suitcase, loaded it into my rental car and drove up Coldwater. I had to stop twice along the not-yet-familiar narrow dirt path leading to my new home to make sure I was driving to the right place. My GPS went crazy before I lost the signal. My heart was beating out of my chest, and I felt —healthy.

Dim moonlight threw shadows everywhere and a mysterious feeling came over me, one I couldn't shake.

That night, I moved into my new home with nothing more than a suitcase and a handbag.

# DAY 20

## DECEMBER 16 | BEVERLY HILLS

This morning my place—I have to repeat this out loud so I can believe it—*my home*—was bathed in sunlight. It was uncanny how happy I felt, despite also feeling nauseous and dizzy. My body was rebelling against my mind.

I was in turmoil. And I want to see my kids more than anything, but I also need time to think. I'm struggling with the fact that I have to tell them I'm going to die. I must prepare myself for the journey that lies ahead of me—a trip I'm not ready to take.

I wish I would have taken more time for the little things in life. Instead, I rushed from place to place, from opportunity to opportunity, from one unfulfilled dream to the next. Too often I tried to please everybody, and in the process I forgot about myself. Regrets. So many regrets.

Later that day, my mind kicked into autopilot—something I rarely experienced before getting sick. I felt numb and empty. (My emotions are all over the place.) And the only way I could force myself out of the weird feeling was to pretend to feel better. So that's what I did.

Once I opened all the windows and an airy California breeze floated through my house, my worries, one-by-one, faded.

Holding a cup of green tea (yes, tea!) that smelled like a mix of exotic, rare Chinese flowers and lemongrass, I wandered through ***my new home,*** searching for what could become my favorite spot in the house. I'm sure I'll need one in the days to come, a place where I can sit and take in as many delightful moments as possible.

Like everything else in the past few days, my special place manifested itself while I was sitting in my backyard. Surrounded by a wild mix of oleanders, daisies, and colorful lilies, sipping tea and reading bits and pieces of my favorite book, *Pride and Prejudice*, I knew I had found my spot. The tweeting birds and the sweet, sensual smell of jasmine eventually lulled me into a daydream, in which I wished for a gardener to turn this piece of heaven into paradise.

**Heaven** ['hevən ] — noun: a place, state, or experience of supreme bliss

# DAY 21

## DECEMBER 17 | BEVERLY HILLS

Earlier today, I strolled from room to room of my new house studying every detail. It's not a big house, but it's filled with surprises. With every object I touched, my imagination ran wild, and I thought about all the stories that passed through its walls.

I can't help but be curious about the woman who lived here before me. Why was this house sold with all her belongings? Wandering around, I felt I was invading her space, and that I was just a guest in my own home.

She's gone, but her furniture, her pictures, her clothes, even her dishes are all neatly placed in spaces (I assume) she chose carefully. She must have put everything in its place for a reason, the way I would.

At this stage in my life, I don't expect to find a new purpose. But suddenly I have a goal. I want to figure out if there is a reason why I ended up in this entrancing home on the hill?

The voice of my father came to me. "Lizzie, what are you waiting for? Get going and find the answer." So bizarre! I haven't heard his voice in years.

In the afternoon, I sat in my favorite chair on the terrace. I was happy and scared and happy and sad as a tear rolled down my cheek. And damn, I need a better journal. This one is already falling apart like me.

# DAY 22

## DECEMBER 18 | BEVERLY HILLS
## AND UCLA

Snuggled up on the sofa with a tightly woven blanket that smelled of fading soap and a touch of history, I must have drifted into sleep before long.

The chiming of meditation bells in the garden had woken me up.

It took me much longer than usual to get ready, which had less to do with my lack of sleep and more to do with my slowly declining energy level.

Before leaving New York and during my cross-country travels, I made a pact with myself to take good care of my body and my soul until the day I die. And I intend to keep that promise.

Then I did another thing I've been avoiding lately. I looked in the mirror.

**Mirror** [ ˈmirər ] — noun: *a reflective surface, that reflects a clear image*

Despite everything that's going on in my body, I can

honestly say that my hair and skin still look pretty good. I had lost five pounds, but seeing the healthy reflection looking back at me gave me a surge of confidence.

It's been far too long since I've seen my kids. I ache for them, but the thought of having to tell them I'm dying makes me sick to my stomach. And I know the longer I wait, the harder it will be.

One by one, my kids left for college, and despite their frequent visits, I've felt a part of me missing ever since. Letting go is never easy. To be honest, I suspect that they have been my emotional buoy, keeping me afloat when everything else was pulling me down.

Today, images from my childhood emerged out of nowhere—my father, whom I admired and loved, would chase me until we were both out of breath, then he would lift me up onto shoulders and say, "Hey Lizzie, how does the world look from up there?"

He always made sure that I was looking at the bigger picture. With that in mind, I drove down the hill to UCLA. I wanted to surprise Isabella and I couldn't bottle up my joy at the prospect of seeing her soon.

I used to count the months, weeks, days, hours and minutes until certain events. Life was a lot about antici-pation. Now everything is about "now."

I whispered to myself, "Take it all in, Liz. This is all yours now. Listen to the sounds. See the colors." Not only do I see, feel, hear, and taste everything with so much more intensity, but I also have the urge to take it all with me to wherever I will go.

There were only two days left before winter break. I knew Isabella's schedule, but of course, there was always the possibility that it might change. Not sure how the day would unfold, I strolled around the half-empty campus until I found her building. The Southern California sun, even in December, made me hot and dizzy and I felt relieved when I noticed a small stonewall underneath a tree to sit down.

Once I made it to safety, I recalled a conversation I had with Isabella not too long ago.

"Mom," over-pronouncing the 'o' sound, "I would love to come home for Christmas, but I can't."

"It's Christmas, and I haven't seen you in a long time," I replied, trying to hide my disappointment.

"I'll be home for Easter. Besides, this will give you a chance to do something fun with Dad." I wanted to scream. Instead, I said nothing.

She continued, "I can't say 'no' to Lake Tahoe. Everybody is going. I mean everybody."

"I don't think everybody is," I said.

"Not *everybody*, but almost everybody," she emphasized, as if I didn't get what she was saying. I understood where she was coming from, but deep down, I tried to hold on to the little girl she once was.

"It's important," she said.

"Okay," I had said, feeling a touch of disappointment.

While I sat there, thinking, I had a nagging feeling that Isabella wouldn't be as thrilled to see me as I would like her to be. After all, I might ruin her important plans, but I am determined to spend Christmas with my kids. It's important to me, and one day, this will be important for them too.

I waited for an hour and was about to leave and drive to her apartment when I saw her striding down the path—tall, lean, beautiful. Her dark brown hair wound up in a ballerina bun. Classy Isabella. Sensitive Isabella. I watched her pass me. I could have reached for her, called out to her, but I didn't.

She looked so happy. What could I possibly say to her? I'm dying! Just like that. Tell her that her mother, the person she trusts the most, is going to leave her behind? Me revealing the truth now wouldn't change anything. It would just take away her lightness of living, take away the joy of our time together during my few weeks left. It would put a dark cloud above all of us. I would become "a patient" and I would hate it. That was not my plan. For now, I needed a good reason for being in California, for moving here.

I want to spend quality time with each of my kids. I envision us going for long walks and sitting around the dinner table engaged in conversations. I want to prepare them for later. I want to prepare them for a life without me.

What is the silver lining here? I will die. That's a fact. But I still have time to make an impact on people, however small. With some luck, I'll leave them with a little wisdom and a gigantic amount of love.

Seeing Isabella and letting her walk away from me broke my heart. But I had to.

Lost in my thoughts, I strolled back to my car. And while driving back up into the hills, I saw a grandmother pushing a stroller on a narrow sidewalk, *thinking I will never be able to do that.* I cried, my tears a mixture of denial and acceptance.

# DAY 23

## DECEMBER 19 | BEVERLY HILLS AND SANTA MONICA

Christmas was approaching fast. *Only five days until Christmas Eve*, I reminded myself as I jumped out of bed. It was going to be a good day. I could feel it.

Over the last few weeks, I've developed a ritual that helps me to overcome occasional nausea. It's funny how fast we can adapt as humans, even in the most unwelcome circumstances. Now, my mornings consist of a cup of green tea infused with fresh ginger and garlic. It sounds gross, but it isn't too bad if I drink it while eating a homemade oatmeal cookie.

After throwing on my most treasured sweats, I sat in the garden, in my favorite bamboo outdoor chair, looking at the world around me: palm trees, jasmine flowers, hummingbirds—despite everything, I felt grateful. Grateful for this moment.

A little later, I drove to Santa Monica to go on my daily beach walk. My walks are my therapy. They might not heal my body, but for sure, they're healing my soul.

And then a thought crossed my mind. *Can these walks cure me?* After all, they make me feel so good, and miracles do happen from time to time. But that thought was immediately followed by, *Shut up, Liz. Don't kid yourself. You can't be cured.* It's true. I know I will die.

This morning the beach was peaceful, and the ocean breeze carried waves of cold air towards me. *Why did I rush through life? Why did I fail to live in the moment?*

I was angry. Angry with myself. And angry with Pete for taking away part of my life and for not cherishing me. And I was mad at God (it's definitely easier for me to believe when I'm angry) for choosing me to join him earlier than planned. That's why I kicked a stone into the ocean, and of course, hurt my big toe.

*For Julia: Sweetheart, do you remember your mom frantically running around while you were laughing because I was doing the silliest things, like throwing the wash in the toilet instead of the hamper? The truth is, I did it on purpose just to hear you laugh.*

It's astonishing how quickly my mind can switch from hopeful to depressed. In seconds I can go from joyous to downhearted, and my body follows. One minute I'm full of energy and the next I'm totally lethargic, feeling slow and tired. It scares me. And I hate being scared. I hate being afraid of dying. But I will say, I'm getting a lot better at turning negative thoughts into positive ones.

~

Later I strolled along Third Street where Artists of all kinds—some talented, some not—populate the long commercial stretch between Broadway and Wilshire Boulevard.

My next stop was a gift and cards store, filled with frivolous pleasures. It took me a long time to choose three cards for my kids and countless Christmas treats.

*Isabella, Julia, and Matt: Today I went to buy tons of Christmas treats and cards for you. Choosing the cards was so paramount because I need to put in writing how much I love you.*

*I want to believe that I'll be able to watch over all of you from heaven. That way, I can see you celebrating Christmases, knowing that you'll remember our last one together.*

After I left the store, I made a mental note to write a list of all the people I need to call. For now though, I have to concentrate on how special I want my last Christmas to be.

# DAY 24

## DECEMBER 20 | WEST HOLLYWOOD

I long to see my kids. It's time. Christmas is fast approaching, and I need the three most important people in my life to know how important it is for us to be together right now: as an entity, as a family. Us without Pete.

The thought of never seeing Pete again still bothers me. How could it not? We spent a lifetime together. That's not something I can just wipe out.

Usually by now, we would have all talked and figured out holiday plans, but life has a way of falling apart in an instant, despite taking forever to build it up. It's like building a sandcastle and having one wave destroying it in a second.

The kids have known for years that the home we all used to share is now occupied by two strangers living separate lives. At some point, we all became masters at pretending. I did. Pete did. And they did as well.

Shaking off my negative energy, and wanting to enjoy every second of my life, I grabbed my car keys and hurried out of the house, only to stumble over a huge gift basket with a glittering pink bow sitting in front of my door. I carried it into the house, admiring it from every angle, and I decided I'd keep it as a surprise for later.

Before I could change my mind, I left the house and drove down the hill, relishing in the fact that I was getting familiar with LA traffic and streets (which is quite an accomplishment). I cruised along side streets and took in this alluring city with its canyons, beaches, glittering glamor, street art, and that-makes-no-sense architecture. LA has a mysterious, almost sinister, quality that's both attractive and unsettling.

Through many twists and turns, and with the help of the GPS, I somehow found my way to West Hollywood and Huntley Drive.

Once there, I parked in front of a small and inviting Spanish-style house with white stucco and terracotta roof tiles. My son Matt lives here with his partner Sebastian, whom I hadn't met yet. I was excited and apprehensive.

Before I got sick, seeing my kids would have been the first thing on my list, but now, I had to gather all my courage before strolling through the courtyard and ringing the doorbell. I waited, but there was just silence. Honestly, I expected they might be at work. Luckily, I came prepared. I slipped an envelope containing part of my Christmas plan under the door.

Last night, while I sat on my terrace looking out over my savaged but entrancing garden, I wrote a *Christmas Plan*.

Making a plan came with mixed feelings and insecurities. To be honest, I was terrified.

What if Matt isn't in town? Then my plan will fail. *Then... and then... and if... if...* I detest "if" thinking. It has so often limited me and caused me not to pursue my life. That tiny word "if" has kept me from doing so many things I dreamt of doing. Isn't life all about "now?" This moment. I'm gradually learning to pull myself out of the "if" and into the "now." And that's how I suddenly had the feeling that my plan would work.

In my note, I explained briefly that I came to California for some alone time. I didn't want to lie, and that was somewhat close to the truth. I asked Matt to come to my new home for a special Christmas meal and not to call me before. I didn't want any questions. I asked him to bring Sebastian and his sisters (plus their boyfriends if they wanted). Julia has been in a relationship for almost two years, but I wasn't sure if Isabella was still dating her boyfriend. Then I instructed Matt to bring one food item that reminds him of his childhood and to ask Julia and Isabella to do the same. And I would make one item for each of them that reminds me of dinners with them.

I can only presume how Matt must be in shock about the unforeseen invitation and the fact that I am suddenly living in some house in the hills. He doesn't like surprises, and I know he will think that I've lost my mind.

*Remember, while you are reading these words, I'll be in a peaceful place watching over all of you. I hope they will give you a sense of tranquility.*

**Word** [ wɔrd ]—noun: *a single distinct meaningful element of speech and writing*

*Matt, my boy: Embrace the unexpected and let life surprise you in ways you could have never imagined.*

*Isabella, darling: Never be afraid to live out your big dreams.*

*Julia, my Julia: You're the rock. You're the one who will keep this family together.*

*I see a big family: all three of you with loving partners and many kids. I see you celebrating Christmases, birthdays and weddings. I'll put in a special request to the Universe that life will turn out the way you want it to be.*

Now I can only hope that my Christmas plan will work out.

# DAY 25
## DECEMBER 21 | HOME

A loud banging noise shook me out of my sleep. It sounded like someone was running full steam ahead against my door. Alarmed, I jumped out of bed, knocking my knee on the nightstand, and in my search for the light switch, I stubbed my toe. Dammit! Through the curtain, I could see that it was still dark outside, which made me wonder what time it was. Another knock, if one can call such a loud banging *a knock*.

Without a second thought, I rushed downstairs, and, dressed in nothing more than a T-shirt, flung open the entrance door (it occurred to me later that this probably wasn't a smart thing to do in LA). And I found myself standing in front of the most gorgeous man I've ever seen. Maybe I'm exaggerating a bit. Maybe not. He was stunning.

His dark hair and skin reflected in the moonlight and left me not only speechless but also rather dumb looking. Let me elaborate: six foot four, deep brown eyes, beautiful smile, and muscles in all the right places. You know what I'm talking about. If only Freja could have seen me staring at him, she would have exploded with laughter.

"I'm so sorry to disturb you at such a late—actually, early—hour," he said in a deep and very sexy voice. Even his voice was perfect.

I just stood there and kept on staring at him.

"I'm looking for Baxter." There was a pause before he added, "My dog. He must have gotten out again, and I have a feeling he might be hiding in your backyard."

"How did he…?"

"I'm not sure. The last time I saw him, he was asleep in my bed."

And then I did another dumb thing: I invited the stranger into my house.

"What kind of dog is Baxter?" I asked, as I led him down the hallway, through the living room, out onto the terrace and into the garden. At that hour, just before sunrise, the backyard rested in a ghostly greenish grey.

"White, about seven pounds, a fluffy Maltese," he said.

*Don't coyotes roam around here at night?* I thought.

Suddenly self-conscious of my looks, I adjusted my hair as if it would make a difference and I rushed away from the light into the darkness, calling out, "Baxter, Baxter!" It took no more than five minutes before the cutest, very white fluffy thing shot out of nowhere and jumped straight into my arms. For a moment I pressed him against my chest, feeling his heart beating fast, and in return, he licked my hands and face.

Moments like these make me forget everything that's going on in my life. I call them *my happy moments.*

**Happy** ['hapē ] — adjective: *feeling or showing pleasure or contentment*

"I'm sorry, I didn't introduce myself," the stranger said, holding out his hand to me, "Sharquay Williams." I shook his hand and simultaneously handed him Baxter.

"Liz Taite." And I added quickly, "I'm glad Baxter is safe."

"Me too."

Pointing to Baxter he said, "We feel terrible for waking you up."

Now I recognized him—Sharquay Williams, the famous basketball player—but I pretended not to. I remembered that he retired maybe four or five years ago after a serious injury. Julia loves sports and had talked about him.

"There's nothing to feel bad about. I love early mornings," I said.

He turned around and waved. "See you around, neighbor."

"See you," I whispered before closing the door.

After Sharquay left, I went back to sleep for a couple of hours. These days, I take twelve pills—prescribed by Dr. Sternenberg and a colleague of his who practices Eastern Medicine—some medications I can't pronounce, and a mixture of nasty herbs that *may* or *may not* help me feel better.

When I was up and running again, I hopped in the car, and I was off to Malibu. Forty minutes later I strolled along a narrow pathway, past million-dollar properties, to a never-ending stretch of eggshell-colored beach.

Somebody once told me that the more complicated life becomes, the more crucial it is to set goals. Now more than ever is the time, so I set three for myself—one is to think as many positive thoughts as possible, the second is to live every moment to the fullest and my last goal is to take a walk every day for as long as I can. Some days I will walk three miles, other days maybe five or more. As long as I can walk, I know I'm alive.

This morning I walked at a steady pace, feeling the sand rubbing against my feet. I took in every breath— every second of my precious life. I felt so alive—*another happy moment.*

Earlier, as I was leaving the house, something stopped me. The basket! There it stood—still untouched—right next to the entrance. I have to admit that yesterday I glanced at it from time to time, wondering what was under the fancy Christmas wrapping.

And now as I'm writing this, I'm still hesitant to unwrap it, and perplexed by my self- imposed willpower considering that self-restraint has never been my kind of virtue. I could never wait for anything. I've always needed everything to be immediate and fast.

**Willpower** [ˈwilˌpou(ə)r ]—noun: *control exerted to do something or restrain impulses*

To my astonishment, I'm practicing patience and self-control. Maybe to prove something to myself. Still, I'm wondering who the basket might be from.

And then, out of the blue, I thought about Pete and wondered if I could have saved my marriage? *Enough, Liz.*

These are my final words for today before I'm off to bed.

# DAY 26
## DECEMBER 22 | HOME

I woke up anxious, immediately falling back into my old pattern of *if* thinking. What *if* my kids think that the invitation and me being in LA isn't important? What *if* Pete tells them things about me leaving our marriage that aren't true? What *if* the kids are angry with me for my silence and my unannounced reappearance? What if they don't show up? They aren't used to me behaving erratically. I have always been the predictable one.

**Predictable** [ prə'diktəb(ə)l ] — adjective: *behaving or occurring in a way that is expected*

My life used to be predictable, and now it's nothing but *un*predictable.

The scariest thought of all was: What *if* I'll be sitting in my new home alone on my last Christmas?

Despite the warm wind entering through the open bedroom window, these unjustified *ifs* made me shiver, and I pulled the duvet cover over my head and pleaded with the Universe to help me out here.

After a while, a bluebird flew past my window and snapped me out of my thoughts. One glance at my watch and I leapt out of bed. It was past 10 AM, and I wasted part of my morning on *ifs*. So silly! Nobody but me cares when I get up, or what I do, but every minute counts because time is passing rapidly. And I desperately want to stop it.

This morning, I decided not to go for my regular walk. (There goes my goal for today.) Instead, I meandered through the wide-open space of my living room and through the open door leading to my sacred garden. The scent was irresistible: flowery and sweet. I pushed my bare feet deep into the grass, wanting to feel a connection to this incredible earth—a link to take with me when the time comes. More than ever, I want to believe that in heaven I'll be able to feel the damp earth and the tickling grass on my feet, a thread leading me back to this house, and in a way, to my kids. Is that even possible? I don't know, but I want to believe that it is.

# DAY 27
## DECEMBER 23 | HOME

No two days are alike now. Today was as grim and as dark as it gets, not because of the pouring rain, but because of how I felt.

I still can't get out of bed. My whole body is aching. I hate being sick. I hate that I have no control over what will happen to me next.

All my good intentions of living in the moment have dissolved and I'm drowning in negative thinking, knowing full-well that it will lead to nothing. As hard as I try, I can't find the strength to be grateful. I'm sad and I feel like crying. I want to see my kids achieving their dreams. I want to see my grandchildren grow up, and I want to spoil them. I want to make a difference in other people's lives. But instead, I'm in pain. I'm in emotional distress, and for the first time since leaving New York I feel lonely.

In Southern California it rarely rains, but when it does, it's like the world is in tears; it pours endlessly for hours. The drumming of the falling droplets on my roof is monotone and there's something comforting in the rhythm of it.

Not only am I in agony, but I'm also angry. I want to scream.

I bellowed, "Why me? God, if you exist, then talk to me. Give me an answer! I need to know why, and I need to know it now!" There was no answer. Just silence.

Despite my failing marriage and some unfulfilled dreams, I can truthfully say that I've always loved life. That's why the inner torment I felt today was so unbearable. It was the type of pain I've never experienced before. All while my annoying inner voice whispered to me, *focus on the positive*. But how can I, feeling the way I do?

Hours later, on my way to the kitchen, the still-unopened basket caught my eye, and I thought it was the perfect moment to open it. Isn't there always an ideal moment for everything?

I ripped the paper off, and I was surprised how thoughtful the chosen items were as I plucked them out one by one: a pair of fluffy house slippers, an assortment of teas, several magazines, a gift card for a meditation app, lavender incense, a scented candle, a vanilla bubble bath, and body lotion. There wasn't a thing I didn't love.

Who was this person who knew me so well? I searched for a card and finally found one hidden in the book. It read:

*May your days be filled with joy in your charming new home. Call me if you need a friend. Susan*

I took my basket of goodies and went back to bed,

thinking that I must write a list of movies I love. Maybe funny movies can save me. I once heard that laughter can cure anything.

# DAY 28

DECEMBER 24 | CHRISTMAS EVE

Today was terrific, and I silently thanked the Universe for letting me have another day in which I felt like myself: pain-free and happy.

I took the presents I bought to the terrace and carefully began wrapping them—that's when tears started to flow; after all, this was the last time I would do this.

The morning passed too quickly, and suddenly it was noon. And it was warm, almost hot, not like the wintery Christmases I'm used to. It once again made me realize how much my life has changed in only a few weeks.

I began wondering why I didn't leave my marriage earlier. Why didn't I take that one step forward? Why had I been paralyzed, and to some degree hopeful that Pete…

"Stop it, Liz! Just stop it." I said out loud, then thinking, *Today is too beautiful to beat yourself up.*

I wrote a card for each gift. It took me a long time. I had trouble concentrating—lately, this happens a lot. For a long time, I watched a tiny ant crawling around the table and a bumblebee humming past me, back and forth.

Much later I placed the gifts underneath the tree. That's when I couldn't avoid it, the fear of being alone tomorrow hit me hard.

Tomorrow is crucial for me and now I'm contemplating if I should have handled it differently. Maybe I should have talked to the kids and explained why I didn't call earlier. The thought that I may have messed up makes me sad.

I want to see them so badly. I want to spend time with them. I need to hear their voices and feel their arms around me.

# DAY 29
## DECEMBER 25 | CHRISTMAS DAY

The early morning sun invited me to sit a little longer on the terrace, but I had less than eight hours left to make this my perfect Christmas. So instead of lingering in the garden, I tidied up every corner of my new home. And as I found more and more intriguing objects, a story about this house slowly unfolded.

Then I set the table with beautiful antique china, the outer rim of the plates golden with turquoise circles. I had found them in one of the dining room cupboards. Thinking, *Who wouldn't claim something so exquisite?* In the center of the table, I placed a wreath made of red roses. I chopped and cooked, chose music for later and cut yellow and purple flowers from my garden.

The garden, although enchanting, looks like a wild mess and I need to remember to ask Susan if she knows a gardener. Unconsciously, I'm trying to live my life in the most ordinary way, although nothing about my life is ordinary anymore. I want to be me for as long as I can.

So many years have passed and here I was, preparing

one last Christmas dinner for my kids. Images of their births floated through my head: their tiny, naked bodies lying on my belly, and Pete, his loving eyes on them and me. Pete loving us. For a short period, we were his world. And then we were not.

At five o'clock sharp I got dressed, and as so often before, the doorbell rang before I was ready.

The sound made my heart leap, and all my fears of my kids not showing up dissolved in an instant as I rushed down the stairs to open the door. There they stood, *my* most precious people in the world, right in front of me.

We hugged for a long time while I cried and wiped away tears, which made me wonder if they knew something was wrong. Then again, how could they? These were tears of joy.

All followed by a flood of questions.

"What are you doing here?" Julia asked.

"Why didn't you tell us earlier, Mom?" Isabella shouted. It was more an accusation than a question. She added, "I was worried, and I had to change all my plans."

I took her into my arms and whispered, "Thank you. Thank you."

It easily became one of the best days of my life. From the second my kids and their significant others entered the house, the sound of chattering and voices never ceased. Hours passed like seconds, which was the part I liked the least. We talked, laughed and unwrapped presents.

The house was alive, and I loved it. It was loud and busy and everybody seemed to get along. It was perfect.

Matt brought chicken nuggets as his favorite childhood food. Julia made French fries. She insisted that they need to go straight from the frying pan to the plate: hot and crispy. And Isabella brought vanilla pudding with raspberry syrup.

The questions kept coming.

"Mom, why didn't you tell us earlier?" Julia asked. Isabella added, "This all feels so weird. And why isn't dad here?"

Matt wanted to know how long I was staying and why I rented a house instead of an Airbnb. I tried to answer as truthfully as possible, and after a little while, the focus shifted from me to them. A moment I embraced with relief.

Once again, I've noticed that I space out. I wonder if my mind is preparing me for what will come, teaching me what to do when life becomes intolerable.

In one of these moments, I pictured Emma Whitaker, the previous owner, sitting around this same table with her husband and kids. Had she even been married? As quickly as I entered my imaginative world, I snapped out of it when Isabella snuck up on me and gave me a hug.

From the head of the table, I eyed Matt—6 foot 2, dark hair and deep-sea blue eyes—and his equally handsome boyfriend, Sebastian. They looked so happy and devoted to one another. I admire their courage to stand up for themselves at such a young age and not hide who they are.

I moved my attention over to Isabella's new

boyfriend, Nick—an artist. They both have still so much to learn, and I can't believe they'll stay together.

Isabella will suffer the most, not having me around, but I'm confident that Julia and Matt will take good care of her. They have the kind of sibling connection that runs deep. I've always wondered why they ended up living in the same city. Now I know the answer: to be there for each other.

Julia. Twenty-five-year-old Julia, genuine with a big heart. One day, her life will be much more settled than she could ever know right now. Next to her sat Jeffrey, his arm protectively around her shoulder.

"Jeffrey…" I began, but I was immediately interrupted, first by his smile followed by his words. "Liz, please call me Jeff."

"Jeff, how are your three kids?" I asked.

He hesitated, just for a second. "Four."

Not that I wanted to, but I repeated a little too loud, "Four!"

"Mom!" Julia exclaimed. I stopped asking. He never answered.

What possibly could attract her to him? After all, his height, looks and personality are just average. He adores Julia, but most likely because she's half his age. What am I talking about? He doesn't love her; he wants to possess her. But will he be able to keep her? I know he won't because I will interfere. I don't know exactly how, but I will. More than anything, I want my kids to experience "true" love and safety.

Looking from one of my kids to the other, I found peace tonight. In the end, everything will turn out just fine without me. It has to, considering I have a little more time left and absolutely nothing better to do than to shape their lives.

*Isabella, Matt, and Julia, I can see your surprised and slightly shocked faces when you read this. And I can hear your voices saying something like, "I can't believe Mom would do this! She never interfered in our lives like this before." And you're correct, under normal circumstances I never would have. What I want is for you to remember that I love you. My love for you will carry on. Remember this!*

And I love this journal. I love to write. I love that I can put into words exactly what I think and feel. (Now I've used the word love too much.)

# DAY 30

### DECEMBER 26 | SANTA MONICA
### AND HOME

A day like yesterday had no chance of being followed by an even better one. And in fact, it wasn't. Today I was forced to think about my fast–approaching physical limitations. After getting up, I felt a change in my body, like what Dr. Sternenberg had warned me about. A mixture of numbness and stabbing pain followed by nausea.

Feeling queasy didn't stop me from driving to the beach, which probably was a dumb thing to do. I had to stop three times, but I wasn't ready to give in to my sickness or maddening victim mentality. Not yet. Dammit!

The sky was cloudless and the most heavenly cerulean color—mystical. More than anything, I wanted to walk. That's not true. I wanted to run. But I was too weak to do either. So I sat in the sun. It warmed my skin, and my panic and anger gradually turned into stillness. Concentrating on my breathing, I reminded myself to enjoy the moment and not let it slip away. I was still alive.

I loved the feeling of sand running through my

fingers as I thought about yesterday, my kids, their partners, and what the future—the little future that is left—
has in store for me. Don't we all just make up a feasible
scenario and then hope for the best?

I thought about the inevitable outcome of my destiny.
Have I already given up? Am I without hope?

**Hope** [ hōp ] — noun: *a feeling of expectation and desire of a
certain thing to happen*

What hurts the most is the thought of leaving my
kids. It numbs me.

"I don't want to die! Do you hear me, whoever is
planning my future for me? I don't want to die!" I
screamed into the endless empty sky above the sea,
knowing (at least hoping) that nobody could hear me
over the roar of the ocean. Then I sank into the sand
and lay there until the sun began to burn my face.

For the first time I saw life as one journey, short or
long, with a beginning, middle and end. It's a voyage we
all must take—no exceptions—to gain wisdom, to
become compassionate, to love and ultimately, if we are
lucky, to learn the meaning of life. Life threw me an
unexpected twist. I didn't see this one coming, and now I
can't figure out how to deal with it.

While speeding along the freeway, then up Coldwater, I
asked myself over and over, *Why me?* And couldn't help it
but I cried until my home, bathed in the afternoon light,

came into view. After I stopped the car, I just sat there, staring at my house. My heart rejoiced. I was home.

The rest of the day I spent in my sanctuary sipping Earl Grey tea and reading some of my favorite pages of Pride and Prejudice. Until I was ready to explore more of my wild-looking garden. Every day I am in awe of how many flowers bloom during the winter in California. A narrow cobblestone pathway led me to a wooden shack. Strange that Susan hadn't mentioned this hidden treasure, almost completely shadowed by oak trees. Curious and eager to see what was inside, I tried to open the door, but it was securely locked.

After shaking the door multiple times, I walked around the cabin and peeked into the dust-covered windows. Not that I could see much, but the glimpse I got surprised me. There was a desk filled with papers, a chair, and hundreds of books. It looked like an abandoned writer's retreat. Who had used this, and when? I was intrigued, and I made a note to ask Susan about the key.

I couldn't have foreseen how much serenity this house would give me.

Still, there were moments when I feel like I'm trespassing. After all, I didn't choose any of the furniture, kitchen items, books, and objects placed throughout the house. I did not plant one flower. To some extent, it is odd to live in somebody else's home and call it my own.

Waving off that thought, I reminded myself that exploring is part of my journey. Giving in to my curiosity, I continued to stroll around the grounds, replaying the 'oohs' and 'ahs' of approval I heard when the kids walked through the house. Seeing their faces confirmed that I had made the right decision. They adored this place.

It seems like magic lurks in every corner here. For the first time, I spotted a gray stone angel on top of the fountain, expelling water from her wings. Before retreating to my hammock, I stopped and examined her every detail. Maybe the Universe placed an angel in my garden. Or is there a God after all? And did he place it there, just for me?

~

Yesterday my kids helped me to set up a turquoise hammock which now sways with the wind in between two palm trees. I can see myself using this hammock often, lying here and swinging from side to side while reading and contemplating, or doing nothing.

Now I think about things that only a few weeks ago I would have quickly dismissed, bizarre stuff like what the color turquoise means to me.

**Turquoise** [ ˈtər͜ˌk(w)oiz ] – noun: *a light greenish-blue color*

Turquoise, just like the Caribbean Sea. Like a summer dress I owned for years, eyes, curtains, tiles, gems, and the color of the dinner plates.

~

The sun was setting and as I swung in my hammock, I thought about how much I love to immerse myself in a book—a story, a new world populated with people I've never met, with the intricacies of their lives. Finally I drifted off, dreaming about heaven—*my* heaven—the one I'll travel to too soon. I pictured what it might look like. Maybe filled with puppies? But what do I know!

# DAY 31
## DECEMBER 27 | HOME

At the crack of dawn, my new home—which looks like a charming blend of East Coast country and Italian Villa—laid in total silence as I aimlessly wandered from room to room. The kitchen blends into the dining room; the dining room blends into the living room, which leads out to the terrace. Next to it is the cozy library. And the small upstairs office is sandwiched between two bedrooms and their respective bathrooms. This is my newfound piece of heaven. I LOVE IT SO MUCH!

Each room is filled with details from Emma's life, which, if I think about it, feels absurd. The only thing I know about her so far is that she lived in this house all by herself until she died at ninety-six years old. She left her story in this house and its many intriguing objects—sculptures, paintings, wooden boxes—all waiting to be uncovered.

As I explored, a myriad of questions and doubts filled my mind. Once again, I doubted my right to snoop around a stranger's life. What importance could her story possibly have for me? And why was I inclined to search for answers?

My time is precious, but despite all reasoning, a compulsion draws me to learn more about this house and the woman who spent a lifetime here. I need to understand why I ended up in this place, but like everything else now, I must do it on my terms.

# SUSAN

It's difficult to explain, but all my life I've had a keen intuition when it comes to people. And I shamelessly use it to succeed in my work. Of course, some people I read better than others. And I've become an expert on who to stay clear of: the two-faced, the deceitful, the liars, the narcissists and of course, the utterly delusional. There are many in Los Angeles.

From the beginning, I knew Liz was different. I was drawn to her quiet demeanor, her inquisitive eyes and her occasional unexpected (rather loud) laughter. I was intrigued, and I wondered what had brought her to LA. She told me she had left her husband, and that her three kids live here and that she misses them. It makes sense that she wants to spend time with them, but I bet there's another reason for her move.

Liz is a little younger than me, still I can see us becoming friends. We seem to have similar qualities, and the fact that she loved my favorite house made me like her even more. Her brown eyes lit up and sparkled with joy when she saw it. I could feel her excitement. It's an idyllic place that's been intriguing me for years, almost as much as Emma, the former owner.

I had only met her once at a party, and after her death, I tried for over two years to get the listing to sell the house. Then out of the blue, I received a call from one of Emma's sons—interestingly enough, just two days before Liz contacted me. Was this a coincidence or divine intervention? I can't recall anything like this ever happening to me before.

The few times I met Liz I felt a sadness in her. That's why I wanted to reach out to her and sent her something nice. I love putting together gift baskets. Something I started doing years ago for charity events and discovered that they bring such joy to people. Most people love surprises. I hope it will bring the same happiness to Liz.

# DAY 32
## DECEMBER 28 | HOME

The craziness of my illness is that things change so quickly from one day to another. Yesterday after Susan left I felt miserable, and today I feel magnificent.

I called Susan—not only to thank her for her thoughtful gift, but also to ask for the key to the shack, and if she would like to join me for one of my beach walks. In the past, I would have avoided inviting a semi-stranger to spend time with me. Instead, I would have written her a thank you note. I was never confident enough to make spontaneous phone calls. But this morning I did, and I made a new friend.

"I've been thinking of you. I was wondering how it feels to live in one of my all-time favorite LA houses?"

"I love it," I said.

Then she told me she would pick me up in less than an hour. Excited, I rushed to shower, get dressed and drink my healthy kale-yoghurt smoothie.

While I was getting dressed, it occurred to me that I might have missed many opportunities to make friends because I never dared to approach other people. I always felt like I was intruding. What a silly thing! By reaching out to another human being, I might not have always won, but could I ever have really lost?

I was still scrambling to get ready by the time Susan rang my bell. She, of course, looked stunning wearing an eggshell-colored leisure outfit with her straight blond hair in a bun. How can anyone look so elegant going to the beach at such an early hour?

During our walk, I understood that she always strives to look her best. I had such a great day. Susan is delightful. She's kind. And she's… fabulous!

# DAY 33

## DECEMBER 29 | ZUMA BEACH

It was early morning, and I was in the middle of choosing what to wear when my doorbell rang. To my surprise, Susan walked into my house geared up to join me for my daily beach walk, our second walk together. We had made no plans to see each other, and I guess I looked a bit stunned. Seeing my expression, she laughed.

"Ready?" she asked, and quickly added, "I thought you might want some company. I have no clients this morning, and I enjoyed yesterday immensely."

Truthfully, I was thrilled to see her.

While I finished getting dressed, I heard her shouting from the living room, "I brought you the key to the shack!" There was a brief pause before she continued, "And I love this house. Have you noticed how the sun travels from one room to the next all day long? It's magical."

*I love this house too,* I thought. For sure, Susan has come into my life when I needed her the most.

**Magical** [ ˈmajək(ə)l ] — adjective: *relating to, using, or resembling magic, something that has a delightfully unusual quality*

During our drive to Zuma beach and our walk, I welcomed moments of quietude. But mostly we chatted as if we'd known each other forever.

"I meant to ask you about that shack in my garden. Do you know what's inside?" I asked.

"No, I only got the key yesterday. I peeked through the window when I checked out the house after I got the listing. Not that I could see much through the dust, but to me it looked like a big mess."

"Doesn't anybody want whatever is in there?" I asked. "Or any of her things in the house? There's so much stuff, and some interesting art."

Susan shook her head. "Shocking, but no. It's all yours."

"That's just crazy."

"Oh darling, there's a lot of insane stuff going on in this town."

"I'm curious about her."

"Who?"

I laughed. "Emma."

Susan took a deep breath. "Don't you love the ocean air!" It wasn't exactly a question; she kept on talking. "All I know is that she lived a very secluded life after her husband died. And there were some rumors." She laughed. "It's LA, honey! Everybody has a secret. Maybe one day you'll write a book about her."

"Maybe." Of course, I wouldn't.

We continued to walk in silence, and for the first time, I felt a sense of peace.

"When did her husband die?" I asked.

"It must be at least twenty-five years ago."

I definitely need to spend an afternoon in the shack to find out more about Emma and her story.

~

The pouring rain had ceased only hours earlier, and the sun made the still-wet sand glitter like a million diamonds. Zuma beach was more than beautiful; it was hypnotizing.

We snooped around for unusual stones and that's when Susan told me that she never had children. For the past ten years, she's been living on her own in the hills above Sunset Boulevard.

I had to ask. "What are you doing with all the stones?"

"I paint funny faces on them and give them to the people I love. People who mean something to me," she said. "That way they can always remember me."

Susan is someone who lives every moment to the fullest. She makes decisions—good and bad ones—and never looks back.

Sometime during our walk, I looked up to heaven and, with one quick thought, I wiped out all my regrets (at least for now). I thought, *No more regrets, Liz. Just love. Just breathe.* The past was gone, and because there wasn't a real future for me, there was only the present. At that moment, I knew I was emerging from darkness into the light.

# DAY 34

## DECEMBER 30 | HOME

Only two days left until this year ends. That thought makes me dizzy. I'm hyperventilating. It's time to make my goodbye list.

IMPORTANT — MY GOODBYE LIST

1. Aunt Erica and Uncle Fred, both in their eighties, and my emotional support team over the years. Things changed when they moved to Montana. Our conversations became less frequent. They're probably wondering why I haven't called them in so long. They will be devastated to hear I'm sick.
2. Baley, my cousin. Baley and I grew up together, and although separated by distance, talked often. We have the same sense of

humor and our conversations, while never
that deep, have always been fun.

3. Victoria, my dear NYC neighbor and friend.
   Over the past twenty years we shared many
   beautiful moments, seeing our kids grow up
   together. I will miss you, dear friend.
4. Freja, my best and forever friend. My rock!
   We agreed before I left the city that I would
   call her and Erica when I was ready (Freja
   didn't keep her end of the bargain and
   already called me several times.).
5. Erica, my other best and forever friend. My
   voice of wisdom. I miss Freja and Erica. I
   miss them so much. I miss the gallery. I miss
   my old routine (at least sometimes). I miss
   living without being so aware of time passing.
   It makes me sad.
6. Dave, my dear friend. He doesn't always have
   the best advice on how to resolve problems,
   but he comes up with crazy solutions. He
   always makes me laugh and I love him.
7. Tamal, my oldest friend.

While writing this list, it dawned on me that there's some
truth to the saying that most people are lucky if they
have a handful of meaningful friends at the end of their
lives. Here are mine, in one brief list. I can't come up
with any other people who genuinely care about me. But
obviously, there is Pete. I might call him. I might. He
deserves to know. After all, he's the father of my kids and
we loved each other once. I, at least, had loved him.

After coming back from my walk, the initial stillness
of the morning rapidly turned into a welcomed frenzy.
First, I found yet another present—a set of hand soaps—

in front of my entrance door. Attached to it was a card that read: *Mom, we'll all be spending New Year's Eve at your place. Dinner at 9 PM. Dress up.* I felt a deep sense of joy. My kids taking charge like this put a smile on my face. It made me think that they are going to be alright.

However, I suddenly faced another problem. I hadn't brought any fancy dresses, not that I ever owned many.

Susan called, as she has been doing for the last few days. She's such a busy woman and I'm surprised that she wants to spend so much time with me. Not that I mind it, I actually enjoy her company immensely. And for a second time, she called me at just the right moment.

After I explained my wardrobe dilemma, she exploded in one of her sweet laughs.

"What a wonderful problem to have! I'll see you soon." I stared at my phone. She had just hung up on me.

One hour later, she rang my bell holding eight extravagant outfits. We have a similar slim build. Susan is just a couple of inches taller than me, standing tall at five foot eleven.

After playing fashion show for a little time, I decided on a black dress with a fine lace trimming at the top and bottom. It's simple and elegant.

"You look amazing. Much better than I ever looked in it. It's yours!" Susan insisted. One look at her face, I knew I wouldn't win this battle.

"I can't."

"Of course you can. And I have to run. I have three hopelessly annoying and demanding clients today." She sighed and made a face that made me laugh. Then she added, "And you look tired, darling. Lay down and get some rest."

With that, she hugged me, grabbed the other dresses

and was on her way. As the door closed behind her, I wondered how she could know me so well, and why she calls me "darling." I like it! I'm so grateful Susan came into my life. She just appeared like my own personal angel.

In the afternoon, after taking a midday nap, I drove to Beverly Hills and embarked on a shopping spree. Today, I determined, was all about me. I should have done this much earlier. Forgetting about money (just this time), I bought tons of unnecessary things. Practically speaking, they might be useless items, but they're not pointless for my soul. And who cares! My life has no more rules! Therefore jewelry, bikinis, shoes, towels, sweaters, sparkling candles, a hat and four singing ducks (though I admit, I'm not entirely sure why I bought *those*), among many other things ended up in a series of overly pretentious shopping bags with tacky logos.

But I wasn't done yet, so I did the same thing in a magnificent and overpriced grocery store, splurging on a gazillion items: Salmon, squid, hand-rolled pasta, truffles, chocolates, colorful candies, caviar, mini meatballs, crackers, sauces, a dozen cheeses and many other things that didn't fit any specific pattern or recipe. Nothing made sense, except that I had fun. I'm living. I'm living in the now.

# DAY 35

## DECEMBER 31 | BEVERLY HILLS

This morning Susan insisted we go to her favorite hairdresser where, miraculously, she could show up without an appointment even though it was New Year's Eve.

Georgio, middle-aged, with long salt-and-pepper hair and five earrings dangling from one earlobe, was skilled and talkative. In a matter of two hours, I looked and felt like a new person, and I suddenly had seven more guests on my growing dinner list: Susan, and a mystery friend of Susan's, Sharquay, my neighbor, and his five-year-old daughter, and now Georgio, his mother and his wife. Georgio told me he had been happily married for over twenty years. Once again, I was confronted with a lesson I still have to learn: one should never judge appearances.

The next stop was a nail spa called *Happy Place*. According to Susan a woman's hands and feet should always look manicured. Why I ended up with Christmas red, sparkling nails is a whole other story. But I can't stop looking at them. They look so glamorous! So not me. But

I wish I had lived this freely and spontaneously before my illness.

**Spontaneous** [ spän'tānēəs ] — adjective: *having an open, natural, and uninhibited manner*

Looking at the enormous amount of food I had bought yesterday, I realized it still wasn't going to be enough, and dinner was just hours away. Once again, Susan assured me it wouldn't be a problem. Getting to know Susan, I shouldn't have been surprised that a dinner buffet was no more than one phone call away. She told me to stop worrying. So I did.

If heaven exists, one day Susan will be on the express train over there. She's pure love, joy and generosity.

*Now, this is important, Julia, Isabella, and Matt. Not once today did I think about being sick. Happiness surrounded me all day long. And you three embody the purest form for me. There are moments in life when, no matter how hard you try, you will never be able to anticipate what happens next. You will never be able to predict the moments that will change your life forever.*

NEW YEAR'S EVE

Time flew by so fast that just a few hours later, as I write this, I have a hard time recalling what happened. The entire evening moved along in the most natural and effortless way.

It began with me standing on my doorstep—dressed in Susan's beautiful dinner dress—and then, in stepped Sam. He stepped into my life—into my soul—like nobody ever had before. He took my breath away. Literally. For a split second, I stopped breathing.

When Sam entered my home, it felt as if he had

been there a hundred times before. First, he leaned down to kiss my cheek, and all I could think was that he was so tall and *hot*. Yes, hot! And when he handed me a sweet bouquet of wildflowers, a box of Moonstruck chocolates, and a bottle of Dom Perignon, his blue eyes danced across my face. It made me feel something I've never experienced before, a mix of jitteriness and tranquility. I must have looked like a complete fool as I stood there and stared at him.

He took a step back and studied me. "Sam Hanley. Lovely to meet you. Susan was definitely right when she described you."

His voice was husky and comforting, and I wanted to ask, 'Right about what?' Instead, I blushed and barely managed to whisper my name, "Liz Taite."

What I'm about to say (write) might sound foolish. It seemed puzzling even to me, but I wanted to spend time with Sam. I wanted to be close to him. I felt that I'm meant to be with this man, this stranger.

I'm worried I'm going insane. Maybe the pills have side effects and make me imagine things. I don't know who this man is. And I'm dying. It's a terrible combination. This is undoubtedly not the right moment to fall in love.

Over the past few weeks, my world has changed dramatically and now, just like that, it's about to change again.

I wish I could remember all the details of this evening, but I can't. I lived it from inside a cloud. The "healthy" version of myself moved through the night completely unfettered by negative circumstances. I felt better than ever. I was free. Open to experiencing life. That's what I made myself believe.

And it was the perfect dinner party. Susan hadn't

exaggerated when she said the catering company was the best in town. The service was nothing short of fabulous, flawless. I barely noticed them as they prepared the delicious tapas-style food, served it and cleaned it all up.

But nothing mattered more to me than seeing how much love and joy sat at one table in my new home. I wish we could have many more dinners like the one we had tonight. I don't mean catered or expensive dinners, just us being together.

At first, I had been surprised to see Julia and Isabella without their boyfriends. But in many ways, I felt relieved. There was a lightness to them I hadn't seen at the Christmas dinner. And I witnessed Sharquay unable to take his eyes off Julia, especially when his adorable daughter, Natalie, fell asleep in her lap. And despite Julia pretending not to be interested in him, I could see a spark in her I hadn't seen for quite some time. No surprise: he is polite, intelligent, and seems to be a good listener. I could see them together, a lot more than I could see her with Jeffrey.

I need to remember to arrange for Sharquay and Julia to meet again. I will play matchmaker, just a little. They would make an adorable couple, and I want to see Julia happy.

Matt and Sebastian are considerate and respectful towards each other. I don't worry about them. They were lucky. They found each other.

Isabella couldn't stop laughing at Georgio's funny jokes and I was happy to see her at ease. She looked sad during the Christmas dinner and although I'm not exactly sure how I will do it; I have to interfere. Maybe she already sensed that her relationship with Nick was fleeting. If nothing else, I have at least to talk to her. I want to understand her deepest desires.

Love cures almost everything. And if Isabella falls in love before I die, then my death might be easier for her to take.

**Love** [ lǝv ] — noun: *an intense feeling of deep affection*

Lying in bed and writing this in the first hours of the new year, I'm trying to recapture as much as I can. As always, most of my memories come to me in pictures.

Sam was talking to Sebastian, but our eyes kept meeting. Eventually, he came over and handed me a glass of champagne.

"I thought you might need this." Then he sat down next to me. Our conversation flowed. I told him about leaving Pete and the gallery to be with my kids. In return, he informed me that he's a veterinarian, a huge dog lover, divorced (no kids). We opened up to each other, not exactly the way strangers do. He also told me a couple of funny stories about his four-legged friends. At some point, Georgio's wife, intriguing Georgina (yes, Georgio and Georgina) joined in our conversation. While she openly flirted with Sam — Georgina flirts with everybody—he glanced at me several times, smiling. It was kind of funny. There was an inexplicable familiarity between us.

Later that night, I couldn't stand it any longer and I had to ask Susan, "Are you and Sam..." I couldn't finish my sentence. Susan burst into laughter.

"Darling, are you kidding me! Sam is like my younger brother. We've known each other for a long time."

A wave of relief overcame me, and at the same time I wondered how anyone could just be friends with a man like Sam. But as Susan would put it later that evening in her straightforward way, "Sam is my best friend. Always was, and always will be."

It was such an extraordinary and fun evening. The air was filled with bliss and excitement. Susan sang halfway through the night, a lot of songs I've never heard before, joined by Matt and Sebastian. It became clear that they have what so few people can't even conjure. They have the love and the freedom to be who they truly are.

Now it's past 4 AM, and I feel some pain inching up my legs. I don't want to cry, but tears are running down my face. I'm crying because now I want to live even more. I want to see Sam again. I want to see where life will lead us. But it wouldn't be right to let him fall in love with me. I'm babbling. He most likely has no intention of falling in love. I'm talking so much nonsense. I have to stop writing. I'm tired. So tired.

# DAY 36

## JANUARY 1 | LOS FELIZ

The benefits of my frequent walks took effect this morning; despite staying up late, lack of sleep and the pain I experienced during the early morning hours, I felt good.

I have to admit, I hoped Susan would show up today. I love having a friend like her in my life. She is fun and easy-going, which are two exceptional qualities. As I strolled around my garden, I replayed the conversation we had during our first beach walk. After telling her about my marriage, I was eager to find out more about her.

"Have you ever been married?"

"No. It never felt quite right."

"Do you ever have regrets?"

She laughed, hooked arms with me and said in her direct manner, "Regrets. Darling, why would you ask such a thing? Life always turns out just the way it should: simply perfect."

That made me wonder about *my* life. Can I ever look back and say that my life turned out perfectly? I doubt it.

I romped through the house for a while, cleaning up here and there, when I heard the bell. Not sure who to expect (though I had an idea), I rushed to open the door. There stood Susan on my doorstep, dazzling as always. She looked prepared for some physical activity, but she was also holding an enormous bouquet of yellow peonies.

Before I could say anything: "They're not from me," she said, handing over the bouquet. "Read the card, put them in a vase, put on some comfy clothes and then we have to rush because we can't be late."

"Rush? Where are we going?" I asked.

"We're going to a private ninety-minute yoga and meditation session in Beverly Hills."

"On New Year's Day?"

"Darling, it's a private group in one of my client's mansion. She's been doing this for years. It's all about starting the new year on a pleasant note. And if you ask me, it's the only way to begin the new year: healthy, happy, and hopeful."

"And?" Susan asked.

"And what?"

"What does the card say?"

I quickly opened it.

"It's from Sharquay. He thanked me for a lovely evening."

"He's a gorgeous man. That body!"

"Susan!"

"Hey, a girl—even at my age—can dream."

"You're out of luck. I think he likes Julia."

"They would make a beautiful couple," Susan said, and she meant it.

There was something so liberating about Susan always having a plan. My job was nothing more than to follow her instructions. It was freeing not to have to make any decisions.

Obviously, there was no time left for our beach walk. Instead, we drove down Coldwater and cruised along Sunset Boulevard until we turned onto a small side street lined with hedges hiding multi-million-dollar homes and almost-blooming Jacaranda trees. After talking to a security guard, Susan entered the secured driveway and parked the car in front of a villa that was ten times or more the size of my new home.

We were ushered from the security guard to a butler, to a housekeeper, to a yoga instructor in a room filled with women in Lululemon all gathered for one reason: to relax. Not much later, we embarked on a ninety–minute journey of serenity, which included a sound bath, incense and aromatherapy. I bent and twisted in ways I never thought I could—quietly thanking the Universe for making sure I felt good—all to soothing sounds and scents, and the voice of the ultrathin instructor.

Morning yoga, like so many other things, had just entered my life.

Without me ever meeting "the lady of the mansion," I walked out in a trance. I can't remember much of what happened next, except that thirty minutes later I was lying naked on a massage table somewhere in Beverly Hills and a striking hunk with a lot of tattoos, a chanting voice and magical hands lulled me into a deep sleep. I dreamt of colorful butterflies guiding me up to heaven. Heaven: a place without pain. A place without fear. A place without regrets.

If the world could be just a tiny bit like heaven in my dreams, then we would all find peace.

This morning, amidst the trance-inducing New

Year's yoga and massage, the most significant internal change I've experienced so far took place.

At almost 55, I finally figured it all out: what matters the most was and still is carpe diem. The point is the moment—**the moment**—the very breath one is taking, the very step one is making right now. It's about our ability to live in the moment we're given. The choices we make. How we respond to our fears and pains. The now. It's the only thing we can be sure of.

After the most calming massage I've ever experienced, Susan and I drove to a tiny restaurant in Los Feliz where we could smell cinnamon, chili and the sweet dough of conchas from far away.

In this case, the word restaurant was a slight exaggeration. It was more like a pop-up.

"I thought after yoga and a massage we would go somewhere healthy," I said, and then added, "Shouldn't we be drinking shots of wheatgrass and eat carrot soup?"

Laughing, Susan linked arms with me. "Are you crazy? That would ruin the day. It's all about feeling joy."

"Mexican food?" I asked.

"Caliente, spicy and hot." She paused for a second. "Just like Sam." Her eyes resting on me a second too long for my comfort.

I didn't know what to say, so I opted to stay quiet, even though I understood what she was insinuating. Except, maybe, for the caliente thing. That sounded more like a Latin lover, not what I pictured Sam would be like.

The food, thanks to Susan knowing the owner, arrived instantly, and she reached for a mini enchilada stuffed with ground beef and red peppers, taking a full bite.

"This is incredible," she declared. "This, the tacos, and the margaritas. ¡Perfecto! Es tan delicioso."

In Susan's opinion, only Mexican food could turn all of this into a fantastic day. And once again, she was right.

On our drive home, I asked, "Do you always have such terrific ideas?"

Waving me off, she answered. "Of course I do! Always. After all, somebody needs to have them."

Everything about Susan is unique, but her kindness is what I need the most right now.

Later, as we sat on my terrace looking out into my garden with the wind caressing our faces and hair, I added one more perfect day to my growing list.

We sat in silence as the sun faded, and at one point I smiled at Susan and she smiled back, pretending not to see my tears.

# DAY 37
## JANUARY 2 | HOME

Yesterday and the day before were charged with emotion, but all this excitement exhausted me and I was afraid that if I didn't rest today, my cancer, in the cruelest way, would creep up on me sooner, attack my body and destroy the joy I've been feeling these last few days.

I can't allow myself to give in to these thoughts. They tend to spin out of control and make me feel awful. So I developed a new way to stop myself: when I catch a negative thought, I clench my fists and repeat over and over in my mind, *Stop, Liz.* And it actually works.

No morning walk for me today! Instead, I made a cup of pineapple-coconut green tea and went back to bed to read. Every couple of pages I stopped reading and let my thoughts drift off. The story disappeared, and Sam appeared. The way he held my hand when he said goodbye. The way he leaned down to kiss my cheek. Was I making things up, or had there been a spark between us? Even if there is a connection between us, that's as far as this story will go. I don't have the right to lead him on or fall in love with him. That wouldn't be fair. It would be selfish. And it screams hurt, loud and clear.

I tried to concentrate on my book. And concurrently, I asked myself if I should be doing something more meaningful with my precious time. Am I wasting it? I don't think so. Reading spellbinds me and diverts my thoughts. It helps me go from a dark place to a light one.

In the afternoon, I felt better and continued to explore my home.

**Explore** [ik'splôr ]—noun: *travel in or through an unfamiliar country or area to learn about or familiarize oneself with it*

As I wandered around the house, I stopped in front of the antique desk in my living room and I noticed a silver letter opener lying on top, engraved with the name *George*. Who is George? Maybe he was Emma's husband. The fact that she kept his letter opener tells me that George, whoever he was, meant something to her. Behind the letter opener stood a framed photo of Emma hugging a black lab. George, the lab? She must have been in her eighties when this picture was taken. Even then, she was a captivating woman with her green eyes, gray hair in a bun and delicate frame. Next to the picture stood a small Madonna carved out of wood. I picked the Madonna up, studying her in my hand I felt a sense of inner peace for the first time today.

Still holding the Madonna, I sat in Emma's desk chair, picturing her sitting in this very same place many years ago, looking out into her lovely garden. From there, I could hear the subtle splash of the fountain and the birds singing, and I felt a light breeze coming through the open window. It's magnificent.

Susan told me that Emma had four kids and none of them live close or care to get any of her belongings. It still doesn't make any sense to me. If my calculation is correct, her youngest son must be in his mid-seventies now. I pondered over why they don't care more about their late mother. It made me sad. Thinking of my kids, I never would want them to suffer when I die, but without a doubt, I want them to remember me.

"I'm thinking of you, Emma. We don't know each other, but in the end we shared the same home. And I have a feeling we'll meet soon." I said this out loud.

Later, while carrying a plant to the terrace, I caught sight of the desk drawer. I tried to open it. It was stuck. I pulled more and more until I finally succeeded, inch-by-inch, to open it. It was a narrow drawer and I slid my hand across the wood into the unknown space, not knowing what I might touch. To my surprise, there was only what felt like paper in the back corner. I pulled it out. A yellow envelope. A letter. Sealed. That's why, despite being curious, I left it unopened on top of the desk together with the letter opener.

# DAY 38

## JANUARY 3 | ANOTHER DAY AT HOME

This morning on my way to the kitchen, I saw Emma's letter, still untouched, lying on the desk. I glanced at it and instead of going into the kitchen to prepare a nasty concoction, I picked up the letter and went to sit in my favorite chair on the terrace.

**Letter** [ ˈledər ]—noun: *a written, typed, or printed communication, sent in an envelope by mail or messenger*

Feeling a little guilty, I was about to open the letter with Emma's silver letter opener when I realized it had been opened before. There was a subtle slit, almost invisible, at the top of the envelope. That changed things. It was no longer a letter somebody had left to be found; it was a letter somebody had read and kept hidden in the back of the drawer for a reason. My heartbeat sped up when I took it out of the envelope and unfolded it. The handwriting looked almost like calligraphy—a work of art—and it was dated June 7th, 1978. Emma must have been in her mid-fifties, around my age.

*Lovely Emma (love of my life),*
*There are no words that can make this easier. You must trust me now more than ever. And never forget that every day, every minute, every second with you was nothing but extraordinary. We had quite some life together. My heart was yours when we met thirty-seven years ago. With you by my side, I transformed from a somewhat irresponsible, adventurous boy (why would you choose me?) to a trustworthy man who loved his family more than anything.*
*I am writing this letter because I know I won't have the strength to put you through what the next months will hold for me. I don't want you to remember me as a broken man. Remember me the way I am now. Remember my love for you. Remember, it will never end. Remember, I will watch over you. My sweetheart, you have gigantic plans, and I know you can do anything you put your mind to. I will see your laughter, your published books and all the good you will do in the many years to come. I will see you at our home. I will see you decorating it for the holidays. Maybe not immediately, but later, I am sure you will find tranquility here. And I will always be by your side, loving you, cheering you on, protecting you and waiting for you. Forgive me. With so much love, forever, George*

I must have sat there for a long time. I felt shaken. I felt like I shouldn't have read it. Was this a love note? Or a suicide note? Did her kids never forgive her for not stopping it? Was Emma a published author? I had googled her name before and had found nothing. I couldn't wait to see Susan again and ask her if she might know someone who has more information.

When I feel better, I have to go to the wooden shack and look for clues. Just not today.

# DAY 39
## JANUARY 4 | THE BEACH

I couldn't sleep most of the night. My thoughts drifted between Emma, George, and Sam. As much as I try, I can't get Sam out of my mind. He promised he would call me, and I can't shake the anxiety (or is it excitement?) I feel when I think about seeing him again. I am behaving like a teenager, and it's so out of character? I'm confused! I want to get to know him, and I want him to get to know me. Maybe we can just be friends. Now, that's ludicrous.

Although I didn't sleep well, this morning I jumped out of bed—yes, jumped—and it was less than forty minutes before I dug my bare feet deep into the fine sand. During my two-hour walk, a million thoughts crossed my mind: maybe Sam was just being courteous and in reality has no desire to call me. But why do I feel so strongly about him? And if he calls me, will I do something incredibly stupid? Like fall in love. I hate this kind of disruptive self-talk! It's what has haunted me my whole life.

Despite having so little time left, I still must learn to

trust. I have to believe that somehow life will take care of me when I need it to. Regardless, I should know better. Life shows up when it wants, sometimes for good, other times… "Stop, Liz!" I almost screamed the words, but I stopped myself and mumbled them instead. "If Sam wants to call me, then he will call."

And then, I did something so unexpected (for me) — I dashed back to the car and drove to St. Mary's in Beverly Hills, a small Roman Catholic church built on top of a foothill, its red bricks washed out by time.

The church was empty. It was cold inside, and I was glad that I brought a sweater. I chose a pew in the middle and as I sat there in silence, a sense of peaceful-ness surrounded me.

I couldn't remember the last time I had set foot in a church; it had been too many years. In the past few weeks, it's taken extraordinary effort to warm up again to the thought that there might be some form of a God out there. However, today I didn't ask, "Why me?" I just prayed for guidance, and I asked for time. I want to live without pain for as long as possible. And after I left the church, I asked to see Sam again. I put it out into the Universe, knowing the second I did it, I was asking for trouble.

Before I stopped the car, I saw it glittering—velvety red with teensy sparkles—lying on my doorstep in the sun: a diary. A journal. A place for my thoughts.

This diary, the one I am writing in right now. Today, I cut and pasted the thirty-eight days from my other journal into this one, so it would all be in one place. The last volume of my life.

When I saw the diary, I felt dizzy and had to sit down. My heart was racing fast because I had a feeling that this might be a present from Sam. I slid my hand across the soft surface, back and forth until finally I opened it.

The inside of the cover read: *Dear Liz, or would you prefer I call you Lizzie? Meeting you was unexpected, and this is my first token of appreciation for having you in my life. Write your thoughts and feelings in here, and I will do the same in mine (which is neither velvety nor red). Maybe later, one day far down the road, we can look back, read entries out loud to each other, and laugh together.*

Oh, Sam, you don't know… later… later… My throat closed and I made a noise that resembled a sob. This was going to be complicated. And I couldn't help but think that the Universe had answered my prayer faster than I could handle.

*Let's get to know each other in the most unconventional way by taking the day off tomorrow. Unless I hear from you, I'll pick you up at 10 AM. Sam*

My heart pounded so fast I was afraid I would drop dead at any second. I need to be honest and let him in on my secret, but I also want Sam to know ME. Not some sick version of me. This is too complicated.

With the diary pressed against my chest, I entered the house, conscious that from now on Sam would play an important part in my life. I just didn't know how important, yet.

# DAY 40
## JANUARY 5 | ROAD TRIP

S am had it all planned out. Two minutes before ten, he stood in front of my house, holding yet another present. Susan warned me that he has more virtues than flaws. My guess is that among them are punctuality, thoughtfulness and generosity.

**Virtue** [ˈvərCHo͞o ] — noun: *behavior showing high moral standards*

He handed me a tastefully wrapped package—silky paper, ribbons and tiny roses. To my astonishment, I giggled, which in hindsight was a little awkward while unwrapping my gift. The box was as glamorous as the bathing suit that I pulled out from underneath the tissue paper. A bathing suit! There was a strange silence between us. I wasn't exactly sure what to think. My first thought was that it's unusual to give a woman you barely know such an intimate gift. I mean, it was stunning—the same white-silverish color as the wrapping paper—but it also appeared to be shockingly small, something a

Sport's Illustrated model might wear. Oh well, it ended up fitting me perfectly and made me look ten years younger.

"How did you know my size?"

"Liz, I know women," he answered with a grin.

"Oh." I didn't know what else to say. Then there was a long pause.

Sam could barely stay serious. "Lizzie, I asked Susan to buy it for me. Do you honestly think I give every woman I meet a bathing suit?"

I believe I blushed, but I wasn't sure if it were his words or the bathing suit.

Sam and the weather matched up to make this day one of the best in my life. Both so perfect!

Until now it never crossed my mind how quickly our relationship had developed. We skipped what is considered to be "normal" dating—going for coffee, drinks, lunch, or maybe a movie—and proceeded in the most unconventional way.

As we wound up Route 1, I caught a glimpse of Sam smiling at me in his quiet manner and it struck me: here I was cruising along PCH (short for Pacific Coast Highway) next to a captivating man, the wind blowing through my hair, beautiful jazz music playing—*I was alive.* I might die soon, but not today. Today, I was very much alive.

My thoughts raced and I wondered if it was possible to fall in love with Sam without knowing much about him. Months ago, my answer would have been no, but now I felt differently. The way one looks at life changes dramatically knowing that death is only weeks away. Sam is kind and quick-witted with gorgeous blue eyes to boot. Looking at him, I believe this journey led me, in some weird way, to find Sam.

When things get tough, I'll remember this day. I'll play it over and over in my mind.

Just before we arrived in Santa Barbara, Sam put his arm around my shoulder and caressed my neck. Goosebumps ran up and down my legs and arms. It felt so natural that despite being in such an early stage of "us," all of a sudden, I couldn't imagine a life without him. I'm in deep trouble.

*Julia, Isabella, Matt, as you read this journal, you'll think that I'm out of my mind. Truthfully, I would think the same. But in Sam's presence, I get this feeling of belonging that I've never felt before.*

Out of nowhere, this remarkable man appeared and for whatever crazy reason, all my insecurities vanished. Call me delusional, but I sense that he'll be with me until the end. The only unfair thing is that I already know the end and he doesn't. What am I doing?

Today, however, there was no fear, just outright happiness. Every second of this day felt supercalifragilisticexpialidocious (did I get that right?). Now I finally understand happiness. The type of happiness that comes in the quiet moments. In the moments of unexpected silence, in the eyes of someone you love.

We talked a lot about the past.

"I was married for ten years to a brilliant woman."

"Then why did you get a divorce?"

He smiled and looked at me for the longest time. For a moment, I thought we might drive off the road. "Liz, I had to leave her in order to meet you." I laughed, and unconvincingly I said, "Very clever, Mr. Charming. You didn't know about me until, what, five days ago."

"Would it sound crazy if I told you I've always dreamt about meeting somebody like you?" He reached for my hand, and I let him.

He continued. "She wanted a bigger life. One I couldn't give her."

"And did she get it?"

"Some version of it."

There were the many calm moments when we just enjoyed being together in that silence of unspoken joy. Strangely enough, we never talked about the future.

**Quiet** [ ˈkwīət ] — adjective: *a peaceful or settled state; absence of noise or bustle*

After driving through a mesmerizing canyon, we stopped in front of a cozy looking cabin. As soon as we stepped out of the car, a short and stout man wearing the whitest apron I've ever seen came running out of the door, throwing his arms around Sam.

"Qué sorpresa, mi amigo. ¿Qué te trae por aquí?" he asked.

"Roberto, this is Liz."

At first, I thought Roberto didn't like me. He scrutinized me for what seemed like a long time before he exploded in a wide grin and kissed me on both cheeks.

"Liz... Liz, you're so beautiful." Then he pointed at Sam. "And this is the best man in California, maybe America. Not Mexico, that's me."

Sam smiled and glanced at me. There it was again, that quiet smile of his. It goes straight to my heart. It didn't surprise me that Sam has such distinctive friends. I got a feeling that no matter where people come from or how wealthy or how poor they are, Sam treats everybody with the same kindness and respect. That's what makes him extraordinary.

Roberto continued, "And he's the best animal doctor."

"Vet," Sam said.

"Okay, vet. All the famous people go to him. You're girlfriend of a famous animal doctor."

I glanced at Sam, who leaned over and kissed my lips ever so slightly. Then he whispered in my ear, "He said girlfriend." Our first kiss. Tears flooded my eyes, and I had a hard time hiding them.

Later we took a long walk along the beach in Santa Barbara. Sam put his arm around my shoulder and squeezed me from time to time. Every so often, we stopped and kissed. I couldn't breathe, everything was happening so fast. I was taking one of my favorite walks with a man I was falling in love with faster than I ever thought possible. These past few weeks, so many things have happened that I can't try to explain. I'm making decisions that at any other time in my life I never would have dared to pursue. I'm so confused! And I don't like being confused—not one bit.

# DAY 41
## JANUARY 6 | HOME

We came back past midnight, and I was exhausted but happier than I've ever been. I fell in love with Sam so incredibly fast. It was love at first sight! And even though my heart perceives it as love, my head doesn't fully comprehend it.

Our first date wasn't what one would expect. Usually, I figure it's a lot of 'getting-to-know-you' conversations, but it felt as if we'd known each other forever. The simple touch of our hands and Sam's arm around my shoulder as we strolled along the beach in Santa Barbara felt new but also strangely familiar. That night, Sam pulled me towards him and kissed me in a way... well, I thought I would faint. I didn't, thankfully! But don't ask me what Sam and I talked about the rest of the evening because I can't remember.

This morning, I sat on the terrace trying to regain some of my strength. I sipped yet another awful mixture of ginger and an herb called panax ginseng, this time prescribed by an Asian doctor who practices Eastern medicine in Los Angeles. The green smoothie won't be my miracle cure, but it relieves nausea and reduces some of the on-and-off pain. In other words, it helps. To be honest, all the tinctures and special drinks haven't helped me regain my energy. Today, I feel ragged.

I miss my kids, but I also want to give them their space and not call them every day. Thus, I leaned back in my beloved chair and observed a tiny worm slide along a rock while the fan-shaped leaves of the palm trees swayed from left to right making a soothing swishing sound. The gardener Susan hired for me must have been here. Pink roses now adorn a stone wall that used to be covered with nothing but weeds. What would Emma have thought about all the changes I'm making to her home? Emma.

That was my cue. After I finished my drink, I went inside the house to get the key to the shack, a.k.a 'Emma's Retreat.' I had no plans for today, and I was curious to uncover more about the woman who lived here before me.

While strolling towards the shack, I pictured how Emma—in a long, beige linen dress, sandals and a dangling gold necklace, her gray hair in a bun—had walked this path before me.

At first, I struggled with the lock, and it must have taken me a good ten minutes before I heard a click and the door creaked open. An overwhelming cloud of dust, followed by the scent of sweet vanilla and old paper, greeted me. The room itself looked like a painting: A stream of sunshine filtered through the two windows and the open door, throwing light on an old Mignon typewriter, a fountain pen and masses of papers piled up on a wooden desk. There were hundreds of books crowding floor-to-ceiling bookshelves that covered an entire wall. Opposite that wall was a wood-burning fireplace, and on its mantel stood a dozen or more framed photographs.

My emotions were all over the place. I was in sensory overload. One second I felt like an intruder, the next I saw it in my mind that this could be an idyllic place to sit and write in my journal, while sipping tea and making my minutes count.

I was still debating when and how to begin the cleaning process when I heard a rustling sound coming from the door. Then, with one big swoop, something jumped at me and landed in my arms. I had no time to see what it could be, so I screamed until I heard a bark.

"Baxter!" I exclaimed, laughing while holding him tight. He was so soft and cute. A big surge of love poured through me. "Did you escape again, you little troublemaker?"

With Baxter in my arms, I looked around the (I'm guessing) 300 square foot room.

"What do you think, Baxter? Should we clean up this place and make it nice? We can buy a fluffy rug and sometimes you can sit with me. And maybe we can read some of Emma's papers. Do you think she left them here on purpose?"

"Can I come in?" I got startled, before I saw it was Sharquay. "I'm sorry for disturbing you. It's becoming such a nasty habit of mine."

Liz waves him off. "Not in the least."

"The garden door was unlocked, and I thought I might find my little escape artist here." He pointed at Baxter before looking around.

"Nice place. What are you going to do with it?"

"That's what Baxter and I were just talking about. I

think I'll clean it up and use it as my retreat—a place to read, meditate, write." Suddenly it struck me that Sharquay might have some information about Emma.

"Did you ever meet Emma?" I asked.

"Emma?"

"The woman who had lived here before me."

"Unfortunately she died before I moved here." He paused, once again looking around. "I heard she was a writer. A very prolific one."

"She was? I've never heard of her," I said. "And I read a lot."

"Me too," he said.

*Just like Julia,* I thought. She had said the same thing to me the other day.

"There might be a way to figure out a bit more," he said, as he stepped forward to pull a book off the shelf. Then he pulled down another, and another, and another.

"G. E. Cornell," he read.

"The famous crime writer?"

He smiled. "Unless Emma had some kind of obsession with this particular author, I would say she's the one. Because as far as I can tell, all these books here are by the same person."

I was speechless for a second. Then I replied, "I get it. G stands for George."

"George?" he asked.

"Emma's husband. She used his last name. I wonder why she didn't use her name?"

"We'll find out. George and Emma."

And for a moment, I saw Emma sitting in her chair in front of her typewriter, a shawl around her shoulders, looking out into her beautiful garden.

"Would you like a cup of tea?" I asked.

He nodded and gave me a perfect, ad-worthy smile. As we walked back to the house, all I could think about was how he's not only drop-dead gorgeous but also educated. That's when the chimes tinkled, and in the distance, I saw Julia walking through the entrance gate. Coincidence or divine intervention?

This time Baxter jumped in *her* arms.

The three of us sat in the afternoon sun, sipping tea. Our laughter filled the space, but more than our conversation, I was interested in the connection I saw developing between Julia and Sharquay since the New Year's Eve dinner. There was a sparkle in her I hadn't seen before and Sharquay didn't exactly hide his infatuation with her.

"The view from Soho House is incredible," he said midway.

"Oh, I've never been," Julia answered.

"Why don't we all meet there for lunch on Tuesday?"

"I would love to," said Julia. "Mom?"

They both looked at me. I knew that deep down they hoped I'd say no.

"I wish I could, but I already have plans," I said, smiling.

"What plans?" Julia asked.

"I might meet a new friend. But let's get together for dinner soon." I looked at Sharquay.

"Sounds great," he said.

"And please bring your daughter," I said. "And Julia, let your siblings know. I want to see all of you soon. I miss you." Julia looked at me inquisitively.

Time is passing far too quickly. More so in perfect moments like the ones I shared with Sharquay and Julia this afternoon, sitting in my lovely garden, surrounded by nothing but love.

# DAY 42
## JANUARY 7 | VENICE

S am called this morning, and I immediately felt that "special connection" with him. The kind that's impossible to put into words. There's a tingling sensation, a jolt I feel each time I'm in his presence.

This time he invited me to join him for lunch in Venice, and he asked me if I had time to spend the afternoon and evening with him. To say that I was excited is an understatement. I tried to play it cool for about two seconds, thinking *if it was normal to behave like a love-struck teenager.*

Dressed in my oldest gym outfit and without looking in the mirror, I rushed to Beverly Hills to buy a new dress. I wanted to look great and not think about anything else but Sam. Then again, I couldn't shake the thought that I shouldn't begin something new, something I most likely won't be able to handle. Deep down, I believe what I desired the most was to have one more day of being me. Healthy and happy.

It isn't easy to find the perfect dress in less than two hours. But I did it.

~

Dressed in my new maxi tie-dye dress, I drove to Venice. All the way visualizing how our day might unfold.

**Visualize** [ˈviZH(o͞o)əˌlīz ] — verb: *form a mental image of something; imagine*

And there I stood on the famous Abbot Kinney Boulevard with its eclectic shops and multitude of restaurants, my dress blowing in the slight breeze as Sam walked towards me. My heart jumped, twice. The image of Sam in his jeans and blue shirt matching the color of his eyes will stay with me forever. When times get tough, I will close my eyes and see Sam walking towards me, his eyes on me, his lips in a half-smile, his slightly crooked teeth and his arms open, ready to embrace me.

Which is precisely what he did. He wrapped his arms around me and held me for a long time. He smelled like a mix of musk, sandalwood and vanilla. I took a deep breath, keeping my eyes closed. Eventually, he stepped back and I had to steady myself.

"Lizzie, that dress looks fabulous on you. Beautiful."

"Thank you," I whispered. "You're looking pretty handsome yourself."

Then he put his arm around me as if he had been doing it for years.

"Have you been to Venice?" he asked. "Venice Beach, not Venice, Italy."

"Neither one," I answered.

"Then you are in for a treat." He looked at my sandals. "I hope those are comfortable."

"Very."

"Are you sure? Or should we buy you a pair of shoes first?"

I laughed. Another present. "I'm sure."

"Great! Because we're going to explore."

While strolling along Abbot Kinney, Sam explained to me that in 1891, Kinney and his partner Francis Ryan bought a tract of land along the Santa Monica beach, where he built a pier, golf course, horse-racing track and boardwalk. After the recreation area opened in 1905, Venice came to be known as the "Coney Island of the Pacific." Now it's one of the most famous, must-see, colorful streets in Los Angeles.

On the way to the restaurant, Sam insisted on buying me a present. After all, I hadn't let him buy me shoes.

"One tiny present," I agreed. *Was this man for real? He must have some flaws.*

He took my hand. "Let's do it."

The first store had a bunch of interesting miscellaneous items—scarves, hats, books, notebooks, pens, cards, jewelry, and countless other things. He asked me to choose whatever I liked.

"I can't. This is all so expensive."

"Lizzie, you can. I want to buy you something, it will make me happy. You make me happy." *Do I make him happy? Or does it make him happy to buy things for me? But why does it matter? Liz, stop the chattering.* It worked. I stopped.

We laughed and talked and the "one little present" turned out to be a pair of super-expensive sunglasses and

Sam insisted on buying T-shirts with surfer images for all of us.

Then we strolled to a homey restaurant known as "The Shack." Just like mine back home, only this one had the perfect outdoor space: six small tables amid an array of colorful plants. The Shack is one hundred percent vegan. We ordered two energy juices, leafy greens, cauliflower steak and three different hummuses.

"Why did you move to LA?"

I didn't want to lie to Sam. He deserves the truth, just not yet. "I missed my kids," I answered, which is partially the truth.

"I want to hear everything," he said.

I expelled some kind of nervous laugh. "Everything?"

"Yes, Lizzie, this is our second date and I want to learn more about what you love and hate. I want to know how you met your ex-husband. I want you to hear about your kids, your parents, your dreams, your goals, your past."

Suddenly I felt sick to my stomach, and I almost blurted out the truth. Instead, I took a deep breath and told Sam about Paris, and that I gave up my dream to move there and become a journalist. I told him about my New York home, how much I had loved raising the kids there, my friends, the gallery. I realized I wasn't ready to talk much about Pete. He was still my husband. He was the man I had loved for so long.

"What do you love now?" Sam asked.

"Right now?"

"Right now." He said, his eyes meeting mine.

"I love this moment." I could see that my answer surprised him and he quickly added, "And what else do you love?"

"I love animals, flowers, the beach, reading, cooking… and making love." Then he paused, raised my chin, and grazed my lips. Electricity shot through my body. Something I hadn't felt in a very, very long time. Maybe ever.

After lunch, Sam brought me to see the canals. An entirely different version of the real Venice canals. Venice, Italy—another place I haven't been. In my mind I added it to the list of places I will never see.

We strolled along the small pathways by the water, admiring the different styles of houses and the cutest ducklings. We talked and talked, and then Sam stopped and pulled me close, his lips touching mine—at first tender, then with urgency.

Somehow we made it home and into my bed. What happened next wasn't that kind of crazy first-time lovemaking everyone hears about. Instead, it was slow and thoughtful. It was, in a good way, as if we had known each other for a long time. Everything about it felt right, and I had no doubt that Sam was falling for me as much as I was falling for him. That makes all of this so much more complicated.

JANUARY 8 | HOME

T he house was so quiet as I was lying in bed watching the sun move towards the curtain edges. I was daydreaming and trying to remember every detail of last night. Sam brought me home. He took the key from my hands and unlocked the door, and I was so giddy that I stumbled over the hallway rug straight into his arms. We kissed and he carefully peeled one piece of clothing after another off me, slowly and deliberately. After that, the details are nothing more than an elating blur, but I recall that despite my exhaustion, our lovemaking didn't end until shortly before sunrise.

Today is a new day, and my body is aching. Big surprise! Still, I got up to follow my morning routine, wondering if I should drive to the beach. But as I entered the kitchen, it took me a second to take in what I saw. Sam had set the table for me with a bouquet of wildflowers, fresh bread, butter and jam. Even the coffee was still warm.

As I poured myself a cup, I saw a note peeking out from underneath my plate.

*Lizzie, I'm not sure if you looked more beautiful last night or this morning. It was the best day (and night) I had in a long time. I'll be back later—to cook. If you have other plans, call me, otherwise just relax.*
*Kiss, Sam*

Was I dreaming? Who was this man?

Despite being on cloud nine, my thoughts, like so often before, shifted into anxiety. In the past weeks, everything happened so fast: I found out that I'm sick, I left Pete, I moved to California, I found this amazing house, I saw the kids. And I met Sam. The thought of having to tell him (and especially my kids) about me being sick made me nauseous. It will change *everything*.

Not knowing when Sam would be back and wanting to distract myself, I decided to explore 'Emma's Retreat,' a.k.a. 'The Shack,' a little more.

It still was a mess of spiderwebs, half-burned wood, and dust. I must have been in there at least four hours when Sam appeared in the doorway, carrying two enormous shopping bags. He had found me sitting in between stacks of papers. We smiled at each other and without saying a word, he dropped the bags and leaned down to kiss me.

"I knew I would find you here." He sat down in Emma's old desk chair, looking more handsome than I remembered. It was almost surreal. Not something you could tell your girlfriends over coffee and expect them to understand.

"Did you find anything interesting?" he asked.

"On top of the fact that she was a famous author who wrote twenty-two mystery novels under a pseudonym because she didn't want to take any attention away from her husband or their marriage; she also volunteered for Hope for Paws and at a center for abused kids."

"She sounds fantastic."

"Everything points to her having had a loving marriage and a thriving career. That's why I'm having such a hard time comprehending her falling out with her kids." I piled up some papers. "It's strange that they don't want any of her belongings."

"There must be a reason, and I'm sure you'll figure it out," Sam said with a twinkle in his eyes. I think he was making fun of me (a little).

I ran out of time to think about it when he asked, "When are you going to see your kids again?" His question took me by surprise. He added, "I was wondering if you would like to invite them to join us for dinner tonight. I'm making the best carnitas tacos you can find in Southern California."

I beamed. That was exactly what I needed. I needed to be with my kids. And with Sam.

I need more time.

It became apparent that Sam was a master in the kitchen. And after Julia, Matt (and Sebastian) confirmed that they had time to join us for dinner, while Isabella promised to come by later, Sam went to work.

Frankly, I've never seen anybody so focused while cooking. He washed, peeled, and cut peppers, carrots, onions, and cilantro in no time. Then he marinated the pork in a sauce with a secret recipe from his great-grandmother, which he said that one day he would share with me. Three filet mignons effortlessly made their way on a hot skillet, and the aroma of fresh herbs, meat and smoke spread throughout the house.

It felt like home, and watching Sam made me sad and happy at the same time—an unfamiliar feeling for me.

With Sam, everything feels natural. The way he kisses and hugs me—which he does all the time. He walks past me, stops, turns around, smiles at me, and then he kisses me without saying a word.

Punctual as always, Matt and Sebastian were the first ones to arrive, bringing several bottles of wine and a decadent chocolate-vanilla cake. I noticed again how thoughtful and soft-spoken Sebastian was towards Matt. He always makes sure that Matt gets his time in the spotlight.

Silently I thanked him, knowing that I won't have to worry about Matt.

Despite urging the kids not to bring anything, Julia brought four different spreads—tomato-basil, olive, black truffle and mushroom—and three loaves of bread to go along.

Intuitive Julia caught me off guard when she whispered to me, "What's going on, Mom?" Me coming to LA, renting a house, and making Sam that quickly part of my life didn't sound quite right to her.

I never had to answer because Sam's voice interrupted us. "I'm in the kitchen," he announced, as if we had been a family forever.

〜

It's only as I write this that it occurs to me that my kids welcomed Sam's sudden presence in my life. There was no anger or resentment. They seemed to appreciate him for who he was. In the same way, despite everything, they accepted their dad.

Talking and laughing, we all gathered in the kitchen and Julia, who can be very practical exclaimed, "Is this going to be too much food?" I looked around the kitchen. Food was piled up everywhere. She was right, there was far too much. That's when I had an idea.

"I'll be right back," I said, and rushed out of the kitchen.

Ten minutes later, I came back with Sharquai and his adorable daughter, Natalie. Baxter was running around the house, sniffing every corner. I noted the changing expression on Julia's face, and the smile she had when Natalie hugged her. I knew I was on to something.

My next thought was Susan. I called her and caught her driving to a late appointment, but she promised to cut it short and join us for dinner. Everything about Susan makes me happy. She's so no-nonsense. She's quite extraordinary.

The table, thanks to Susan who rearranged and swapped items shortly after she arrived, was suddenly set, like something out of Architectural Digest. She had made it to my place in less than an hour, after crossing town in LA traffic, which is nothing short of a miracle.

**Miracle** [ ˈmirək(ə)l ] — noun: *a surprising and welcome event that is not explicable by natural or scientific laws and is therefore considered to be the work of a divine agency*

Looking at the meticulously set table and the loving people gathering there, I wondered for a moment if a miracle was coming into my life. I took a deep breath and shifted my attention towards Sam, who was in a deep conversation with Matt and Sebastian.

I closed my eyes and saw Matt as a little boy, his blue eyes—Pete's eyes—looking at me with so much love. My son. Then I took another deep breath and opened my eyes, only to catch Susan studying me. She gave me an almost imperceptible nod of encouragement. Can she sense what's going on with me? *Hey Liz, it's not all about you,* I silently reminded myself.

Everybody looked so happy, and I felt the most profound gratitude for the moment we shared.

**Gratitude**: [ ˈgradəˌt(y)o͞od ] — noun: *readiness to show appreciation for and return kindness*

Then the doorbell chimed, and I had an excuse to leave the table and compose myself. It was Isabella. She looked stunning in a red dress, and she threw her arms around me.

"My mama," she said. "I can't believe you're living in California now and I can see you whenever I like. I missed you."

My heart dropped, I felt horrible. Thankfully, she went immediately to say hi to everybody else and gave me time to pull it together.

It was much later when I found a moment alone with Isabella.

"Why didn't you bring Nick?"

She shrugged her shoulders. "It didn't work out. He's young."

"Oh," I said, thinking that he was her age.

"And I don't mind being single." She giggled. "Life is stupendous."

*And I'm going to be the one who will take this good life away from her,* I thought. I don't want Isabella to have to face my death by herself.

At some point, Natalie sat in my lap and leaned against my body, which made me think about what it might have been like to be a grandmother. I snapped out of the negative thinking when I saw Julia reaching for Natalie, who immediately went from my lap into her arms. Sharquay leaned in to adjust Natalie's dress and just like that, they looked like a family.

Susan saw it as well, and we exchanged a knowing glance.

Around eleven, Sharquay had to leave to put Natalie, who had fallen asleep on Julia's lap, to bed. This evening I overheard that Natalie's mother had left them several years ago and now lives in Australia. It's hard to fathom what drove this woman to leave behind her precious daughter. I guess in every life, somewhere, a sad story can be found.

It had been a couple of long and busy days with a feeling of all kinds, and exhaustion settled in. As if I had said it out loud, everybody got up and got ready to leave.

Except for Sam. He stayed. I wanted him to stay.

# DAY 44

## JANUARY 9 | MALIBU

This morning I walked along the beach with Sam. My feet dug deep into the warm sand.

Our playful conversation turned serious when he asked me, "So, why did you move to California?"

I was reluctant to lie again, but I wasn't ready to reveal the entire truth. "It was time for me to live my life without regrets, and I would have had too many had I stayed in New York."

"It's such a drastic move to give everything up: your home, your job…"

I interrupted him. "I'm sorry, but I can't talk about this right now! Not yet."

He looked at me with surprise, and I turned away, ashamed over my sudden outburst.

We continued to walk in silence. And then he reached for my hand. I let him. He squeezed it and I glanced at him and whispered, "I'm sorry." That's when he took me in his arms.

It wasn't hard to imagine that I could get used to this: the sun, the beach, and mostly Sam.

In all honesty, I am unsettled. Last night, after making love to Sam—our hands and mouths exploring every inch of each other—right then, I knew I would have to tell him that I'm dying. But before I can have that dreaded conversation with him, I have to talk to my kids. And I still have no clue how.

The waves crashed against our ankles, and I shrieked while trying to escape the cold water. Sam lifted me up and carried me to safety.

"You weigh nothing, Lizzie. I have to cook for you more often," he said with a smile and the most adorable wink of his left eye. I must have lost more weight.

Sam hasn't mentioned it, but even in this short amount of time we've known each other, I felt like he began to envision a future for us. A future I can't allow myself to see.

Trying to stay in the moment, I focused on the warmth of his hand in mine and I tightened my grip as I looked at the bright blue sky. Words directed at God floated through my mind, words I don't remember, but I don't think they were kind. All I wanted to do was bury my face in the sand until I ran out of air. Instead, I nestled my head somewhere on Sam's broad chest, hoping to hide my pain.

# DAY 45
## JANUARY 10 | HOME

Sam left early this morning after surprising me with a cup of green tea in bed and one flower that looked like a turquoise daisy.

I'm not feeling well, and instead of confronting reality, I do the next best thing: I panic. All of it is too much for me right now; I can't handle it. I am loved, and I am in love. But the problem is that I'm not just *in* love; rather, I love Sam. Love at first sight exists after all.

In the last few weeks, my life played out in such a heavenly but—considering my circumstances—delusive way.

**Delusive** [ dəˈlo͞osiv ] — adjective: *giving a false or misleading impression*

Susan and Sam have been nothing but generous and loving, and I am deceiving them. I've never misled anybody in my life. What am I doing? Susan already has a place in my life. And Sam is a part of me in a way I could never have imagined.

The doorbell rang. I had no idea who it could be, but I glanced in the mirror on my way downstairs, and only one word came to my mind: horror. I wasn't exactly presentable—my hair was frizzy, there were dark circles around my eyes, and my skin was blotchy—but there was no time to resolve the problem now. Semi-adjusting my hair in a loose bun, I opened the door to find both Sam and Susan. I was surprised, but I was also thrilled to see them and forgot all about my appearance—at least for a moment. Before I could welcome them into my home, Susan was already coming in, chatting away.

"I ran into Sam, and he made up some silly excuse about why we shouldn't march in here, something about you needing some alone time." She placed two bags in the hallway and then faced me. "I'm not sure why he would ever think that."

She was about to say something else but stopped. "Are you feeling okay?"

To be honest, seeing them made me feel better already.

"Just a bit under the weather," I lied with a smile. As much as I tried, I couldn't stop glancing at Sam, who walked around the living room examining one of the many things Emma left behind. Every day he finds something new that interests him. Today it's a wooden statue that looks like an Egyptian goddess.

"Lizzie, my art expert, how old do you think this is?"

I had studied the goddess the other day. "I would say 18th century."

"Wow!" Susan exclaimed. "Mucho expensive."

After one more glance at me, Susan was in charge. She forced me to sit out on the terrace in my favorite outdoor chair while she prepared some awful tasting ginger concoction, which would supposedly 'take care of everything.'

She made me sip the full cup, all while entertaining us with some of her intriguing stories.

"Just forget about LA for a second and picture lovely cottages, rough sea and innumerable white fluffy clouds. That's Martha's Vineyard." I don't think she has any idea that she's a fantastically entertaining raconteur.

**Raconteur** [ ˌrä kän'tər ] — noun: *a person who tells anecdotes in a skillful and amusing way*

"It wasn't a perfect morning. Quite the contrary, it was a complicated time in my life and I felt lonely and misunderstood by almost everybody. I wasn't exactly in a great place."

"I can't picture you feeling sad," Sam said with a twinkle in his eye. "You are the most loved and positive person I know."

"Don't forget, we're talking more than twenty years ago. And that morning I was miserable. Still, I got my act together and went for a walk." She searched for my eyes. "Just the way you do, Liz." I nodded, once again wondering if she knew more about me than she gave away.

"So here I was all alone walking and weeping along the wide Philbin beach towards the picturesque red cliffs of Gayhead, wishing for a change in my life.

"What kind of change?" I asked.

"I wanted more. I wanted a home. Love. Success. The list was long." She paused. "Anyhow, I came across a beautiful white cottage with green shutters and a terrace overlooking the ocean. All of a sudden, I had to use the ladies' room. Urgently. That's when I met Max and Krista. And it changed my life."

"You couldn't hold it or go behind a bush?"

"Hilarious, Sam!" Susan pulled out a pillow from behind her back and hit Sam on the head.

"He heard the story before," Susan said, "many times."

"Many times." Sam repeated, and Susan hit him with another pillow. Watching them, I began to feel better. My nerves calmed.

"Anyway, that day was the first of many dinners Krista, Max and I had on the Vineyard. They were like the parents I never had, and when they became too old to travel from Boston to the Vineyard, they gave the house to me. It's odd how the right people always appear at the right time." She looked at me, and this time I tried to avoid her gaze.

I added, "And the impact they can have on you."

"I want both of you to come to the Vineyard," she commanded. "The house is fantastic! Right, Sam?"

"It's a magnificent home." Sam said. He squeezed my hand and looked at me. "It will be amazing, Lizzie. We can eat lobster, explore the cliffs and lighthouses, ride horses."

I couldn't look at him or Susan. I barely managed to hold back my emerging tears, knowing that it would never happen. Even more than before, I felt like a liar. I hated myself. And I couldn't breathe.

# DAY 46
### JANUARY 11 | SANTA MONICA

Today was rough! Just the thought of doctors and hospitals transported me into an uncertain world—a place of discomfort, a place of the unknown.

Not that I wanted to listen, but there was an inner voice urging me that it was time to choose one of the doctors Dr. Sternenberg had suggested. One I can trust. The comforting thought of having everything in place for when I need it inspired me to make a half a dozen phone calls and to spend several hours on the internet after Sam left this morning.

Like everything else lately, it all fell into place quickly. Once I found a doctor who appeared to be the right fit for me, I found out that there had been a cancellation and I could get an appointment for today.

Surprisingly, I felt at ease as I strolled down Wilshire Boulevard, watching all the hubbub around me. It was very touristy, and everybody was so alive in a place where death didn't seem to be an option. Charged with positivity, I met Dr. Edward Katz, a first-class oncologist and an overall pleasant man in his late fifties.

He looked somewhere between shocked and puzzled after I told him my story—me coming to LA and making all these last-minute changes. His facial expression made me think that my story most likely didn't fit the profile of the average dying patient.

And he said it, "This is unusual. But I think it's also brilliant."

I liked him. He had warm and vivid eyes. I explained to him, "When the time comes, I want someone to be there for me to ease the pain. I don't want to prolong my life. But I want to make it bearable." He understood and never questioned my wishes. He respected my decision and I felt like I could trust him. At the end of our somewhat arduous conversation, I left him with all my information and earlier test results. He assured me that he could come to see me at home should I need him.

Leaving his office, I felt calmer and grateful.

On my way back to the car, I strolled around Ocean Avenue, relieved to have found a compassionate doctor. I wished I could live another thirty years.

# DAY 47
## JANUARY 12 | HOME

Reflecting on parts of my earlier life, I expect my brief time with Sam will differ greatly from what I experienced before. But as I'm writing this, it sounds ridiculous for me to draw any conclusions, considering how little I actually know about him.

What's happening between me and Sam feels so natural, yet still so unusual, scary and fast. And I admit, for the first time in my life, I'm being downright selfish. (I don't like it.) In the past, I would've never even considered doing any of the things I've done in the past seven weeks. It's as if my life has been split into two pieces: Liz before being sick and Liz after she learned she was sick. The old me would have thought about everybody else first. It always took me a long time before making any decision. But not anymore. From our very first interaction, Sam and I connected on some higher level. Although neither of us said it out loud, there was always "us" right from the start.

Occasionally, I still think I'm out of my mind. But

now, I'm on the fast track to experiencing life as much as possible before it all comes to a stop.

What hurts the most is thinking about the future. I want to throw myself into Sam's arms and tell him that later is now. I want to let him know that I'm not sure if there will be another spring or summer. Then again, how certain can one be? One thing I know for sure, there won't be another fall for me. I don't want to think about it. Fuck. I hate this part so much.

So far, I've refrained from asking Sam too many questions about his personal life. He's reserved, but I sense that he'll reveal himself to me when he feels it's the right time. Closing my eyes, I can see myself reaching for Sam's hand while we sit somewhere on the beach, or maybe on the terrace, and he'll let me in on his life.

That's why it came as no surprise when he just showed up. Precisely at 6:00 PM, Sam stood in front of my door. In one hand, he held a worn-out duffle bag filled with clothes for the nights when he'll stay over, and in the other hand, a tiny blue box with a large white ribbon.

"Do you mind if I leave some clothes here, Lizzie?" he winked at me, then gave me one of his seductive smiles and I couldn't help but throw my arms around him. He held me for a very long time. He always does.

In my mind, I had it all rehearsed to perfection. Tonight was when I would confess and reveal the truth. That was before I opened the blue box. Inside was a golden necklace with two hearts—it made me feel so excited and so in love. So much in love that I couldn't bring myself to reveal the truth, not just yet. Instead, I stepped aside and once again let him into my house, into my life, into my heart and soul. This time to stay.

P.S. Susan assured me that Sam isn't as perfect as he appears and, in her opinion, he has a fair number of significant flaws. I still have to figure out what they are.

# DAY 48
## JANUARY 13 | HOME

No two days are the same anymore. Some days I feel almost normal, but on days like today, I feel out of sorts. It's still dark outside and I can't help but think about my life in New York. I miss the city. I miss the noise. The people. And when I reach out for Sam, who is sleeping peacefully next to me, I find myself thinking about Pete. The young Pete, the one who loved me.

I dismissed that thought and gently touched Sam's tousled salt-and-pepper hair. It's odd lying in bed with a man who appears utterly familiar and like a stranger all at once. I know very little about this man. I know he's a divorced veterinarian who loves dogs, has no kids and was born in Laguna Beach.

He stirred. I didn't want to wake him, but I also wanted him to be awake. I wanted to look into his eyes. I wanted to talk to him. I wanted to be close to him. (What's wrong with me? Am I going insane?) I wanted to hear from him that everything will be fine, although I know it won't.

I kept replaying last night in my mind. We had cooked dinner together—spaghetti with tomato sauce, arugula salad and chocolate cake that Sam had bought earlier with vanilla ice cream. Afterwards, we talked deep into the night.

Sam shared with me that his ex-wife had been a caring and compassionate woman.

I had to ask, "Then why…?"

"We wanted different things," Sam said.

"Such as?"

"I wanted kids, and she wasn't interested. She claimed that having dogs was fulfilling enough. Not the same thing." He smiled. And our conversation made me think how much I love my kids. It's a special kind of love.

"What's her name?"

"Clara."

"I like that name. It's warm."

During our talk, Sam told me about all the places he would love to see with me, and then he looked at me like no other man ever had before. Once again, I felt like a liar pretending that all his dreams would come true one day, well knowing that they wouldn't.

His eyes locked with mine for what seemed like an eternity, and in that very moment, I understood that I had never wanted anyone as much as I wanted him. He must have sensed it because he got up and swept me into his arms to carry me around the house.

"And here, Ms. Taite, is a comfortable living room with a wood-burning fireplace. The living room leads out into a beguiling garden." He hummed some soft tune and whirled around with me in his arms until we got back to the bedroom. I was dizzy from all the spinning, and all my many thoughts dissolved. In bed, our hands moved along our bodies, while our eyes stayed on each other as we made love. It wasn't rough or eager; instead, it was thoughtful, slow, and fulfilling. I took my time taking in every stroke, every movement, and all my mixed feelings of joy and sadness. I'll never be able to travel with Sam to all the places we talked about today, but I've already gone with him to the most beautiful place of all: love.

# DAY 49
## JANUARY 14 | MATT'S HOME

I once read that truly loving another person means giving all of yourself without ever losing who you are. I like that. It resonates with me.

This morning, I watched Sam from the terrace as he strolled through my beguiling garden examining all the flowers. He reminded me of my kids when they were small, looking at every flower, leaf, tree and insect. The minute that thought crossed my mind, I saw him holding something up in the air. "Lizzie, look at this beautiful worm."

I nodded and couldn't stop laughing. Thinking, *A beautiful worm.* The thought of leaving Sam, even just for a short time, already hurt. But I want to see my kids as often as I can and spend time with each of them. I need to prepare them. Or is it that I need to *prepare* myself for what will come?

*Matt, Isabella, and Julia: I love you so much. Always remember, no matter where I am, my love for you will never end. You are everything to me, and this life has mattered because of you.*

After breakfast with Sam, I longed to see Matt, so I called him, and he was available.

On my way to his house, pictures of a young, sweet, and playful Matt floated through my mind. Blond, four-year-old Matt cruising through our apartment in his blue shorts—his favorite color—and a white t-shirt, always carrying his stuffed rabbit named Boo. Where did the time go?

In my mind, I played out how Matt would take the news of me dying. He probably would think of his sisters and what this would do to them, and what his new role would be. He will protect them. And at the same time, he will look for a solution.

When we're happy time races, and that's what happened this afternoon as I watched my son. He hadn't changed much. He was still the sweetheart he used to be. Sebastian made sure I could have some time alone with Matt. Later, he served us delicious snacks, and invited me to see the house, explaining every detail—and there were many.

He pointed to a beautiful, gigantic hand-carved elephant standing in the foyer. "Matt chose this one in Thailand after we stayed at an elephant reservation near Chiang Mai. He has such impeccable taste."

"What's your most cherished Thailand memory?"

He laughed. "Every moment with Matt is my favorite memory. In Thailand, riding the elephants at sunset is for sure the one." He faced me. "Matt is an incredible person. He's kind, smart, talented, and loving. You raised a wonderful son, and I'm a fortunate man." He paused before adding, "Thank you for accepting us… our rela-tionship."

I touched his arm. "Why wouldn't I?"

"My parents never did."

"I'm sorry. That must have been hard." And to fill the silence that followed, I asked an odd question, "When is your birthday?" I wanted to know.

"October 10th. A libra."

They were happy and in love, and I was delighted for them. Suddenly I couldn't speak anymore. My emotions overwhelmed me when I became conscious of the fact that I will be dead when Matt turns thirty. Sorrow must have crossed my face because Sebastian stepped forward and gave me a long hug.

This afternoon was essential for me, I understood who my son is *now*, the man he became while we were separated by three thousand miles.

*Matt and Sebastian: Today, you brought peace to my life, the peace of knowing that you'll be happy together. Matt, you are not only my son, but also one of the most thoughtful people I know. You and Sebastian are men of integrity.*

We had tea and talked about foreign places, design, kids, and dogs. Then Matt asked me why I moved to California and how long I planned on staying. I didn't want to lie, so I excused myself, pretending that I had something in my eye. And when I got back, I diverted the conversation.

Oddly enough, we never mentioned Pete until I was ready to leave and Matt said, "I spoke to Dad. He said he would have called you, but he thought you would prefer not to hear from him."

There was a sudden sharp pain in my chest.

"I always kind of knew. And I'm sorry, Mom."

I looked straight into Matt's eyes and touched his hand. "It was my choice. I wanted to set him free. Free to find happiness." I took a deep breath. "In some form, I will always love your dad." Matt embraced me, and I held him as tight as I could. It almost felt like a goodbye.

Back in the car I cried. My tears flowed freely as I was thinking that Pete would probably call a couple of hotshot attorneys and put them to work, so I won't get a penny. Money always ruled him, it still does. Little does he know that I'll be dead by then and that I'm living the last days of my life filled with love.

I mourned my marriage, my sickness, and the fact that I still hadn't told my kids that I'm dying. I want to, but I didn't today even though I had planned to tell Matt first. I didn't because I'm scared. How selfish of me.

# MATT

My life has never been better. I love my home, my job and Sebastian. And I love my mom. I would like to believe that life will go on like this forever, but after I talked to dad and then to mom, I got a bad feeling.

Mom looks skinny and appears to be more reflective than usual. I could tell she was withholding the truth about why she moved to Los Angeles. None of this vague behavior makes sense. Mom always thinks things through and she usually expresses her thoughts.

My parents' decision to separate didn't surprise me. I love my dad, but he hasn't exactly been what one would call a devoted husband, and mom deserves better. Despite all of it, it is so out of character for her to leave her familiar life behind. The gallery, her friends, her home, New York City. I would have understood if she had taken a month off to visit us. But moving here? She used to spend months planning a one-week vacation. Mom didn't plan this one. She escaped. Why did she leave in such a rush? And what's keeping her from talking to me? Then there's Sam. He appears to be a fantastic guy with a good sense of humor. But Mom wouldn't get carried away by a stranger and rush into a new relationship before finalizing the divorce. She's still married. She loved Dad! And I bet she still does. I don't understand any of it.

And if that weren't enough, Sebastian told me she almost cried while he was showing her the house. And when she hugged me, it was strange. More than a hug, it felt as if she was holding on to me. I'm worried.

# DAY 50
## JANUARY 15 | HOME

This morning I snuggled closer to Sam. He felt so warm and calm, but despite that, anxiety crept up my body.

I turned away from Sam and took three long, calming breaths.

It actually worked. A sense of peace engulfed me and I got out of bed, eager to start my day. I snuck out of the bedroom and sauntered to the kitchen where I prepared breakfast for Sam. I took my time watching the yellow of the yolk and its slight wobbly movement, the vibrant red of the jam and its tiny black seeds. This was it. I lived in the moment.

Not much later, we were sitting in the garden, with hummingbirds fluttering from flower to flower. My eyes rested on Sam while he was reading the LA Times until he looked up and gave me that smile. The smile that said it all. That smile that should have made everything so simple but made everything so much harder. That smile that said, "I love being with you." Then he took my hand in his and continued reading.

# DAY 51
## JANUARY 16 | HOME

Next to my comfortable bed adorned with soft yellowish blankets and downy earth-colored pillows, there are now two piles of books. Most of them I will never read. Not because I don't want to, but simply because I will run out of time.

**Book** [ bŏok ] — noun: *a written or printed work consisting of pages glued or sewn together*
*along one side and bound in covers*

These books aren't the ones I brought with me, I plucked them out Emma's collection. She must have left behind over two thousand volumes. Susan, once again, assured me that the books, furniture, and all other items came with the house. Still, from time to time, I feel like an intruder stepping across the boundaries of right and wrong.

I feel the presence of Emma every day. And I'm captivated by this obscure woman who had lived a long, seemingly peaceful life. As time goes on, her life gently unfolds in front of me, and I ask myself how her story might intersect with mine.

# DAY 52
## JANUARY 17 | HOME

S am left around 3 AM this morning to watch dolphins. Sam! He's been gone only a few hours, and I already miss him. I wish I could have said to him, *Forget about the dolphins because I will be dead in six weeks. Let's stay in bed together.* Instead, he believes we have forever. This is my dilemma! By not being completely honest about my situation, I'm depriving us of precious time together.

The day slipped away. I finished reading one of Emma's books, an intriguing psychological thriller about a female Hollywood executive and her quest to find out who killed her friend. Emma was the novelist I failed to become. Sometimes, I feel as though there are many things I didn't achieve, but in the end, I'm confident my life turned out the way it should be.

While resting in my hammock, random thoughts came to me. Was it a coincidence that I ended up in this house and that I met Susan and Sam? Funny! My two Ss— Sam and Susan. Just like my two Ps—Pete and Paris.

# DAY 53
## JANUARY 18 | HOME

I'm lounging in my favorite chair, perched on top of a plush yellow pillow, squeezed between two cozy midnight blue cushions. It's an odd-looking, crooked chair. Most of the morning, I sat on my terrace writing in my journal and reading passages out of yet another of Emma's books. I was also daydreaming and wondering what Sam was doing out on the ocean.

He had been a veterinarian for twenty-one years when he felt it was time to put his fascination for dolphins into words and write a book with a friend of his who happens to be an acclaimed nature photographer.

Two more days until he returns from his expedition, which feels like an eternity.

I want to use this time to be with my kids. Early this morning I called them to see if one, or all of them, would be available for lunch, but repeated voice mail messages greeted me.

With my kids being unavailable, I needed to distract myself and overcome the urge to count every minute and every second until I see Sam again and feel his arms around me.

Time can be such a bitch! In times of joy it flies by, but in tough times it can be agonizingly slow. And in my case, there will not be enough of it.

Not expecting any visitors today, on my way to The Shack—Emma's former hiding spot, and now mine—I startled when a young man stepped out of one of my flannel bushes (Susan told me what they're called).

"I'm sorry, didn't mean to scare you," he said, holding a pair of gardening scissors close to me. He caught me by surprise, and I wasn't sure if I should feel threatened by the scissors.

Seeing my expression, he lowered them to the ground and stretched out his hand.

"Ethan Walker. The gardener."

"Liz Taite. The renter."

He laughed, showing perfect teeth. "Nice to meet you."

"I don't remember hiring you?"

"Susan Marble did. She's friends with my mom and thought you might need some help around here. I'm also supposed to let you know that she already paid me for five hours."

Immediately I thought, *Of course she did. Susan, my generous realtor and part-time angel.*

"I study landscaping at UCLA and garden on the side to make some extra money." He looked around. "This is a fantastic space. With your permission, I'd love to transform it into more of a Zen space—you know, tiny waterfalls, stones, maybe a small maze."

"Butterflies?"

"They'll find this place on their own," he said.

Looking at this polite and lanky young man with

intriguing green eyes, all I could think of was Isabella. She goes to UCLA, and she loves green eyes.

"Of course, I would love that."

"Great! Would it be okay then if I come three afternoons a week?"

"Come whenever you like."

He smiled. "Thank you." And he picked up his shears, holding them up. "My weapon."

I laughed. He had a sense of humor!

I called Isabella again and left another message on her phone, asking her to meet me tomorrow at the old Farmer's Market for breakfast, hoping that afterward we might go on one of my walks together. A long walk with my youngest daughter would heal my soul a little and would give us some quality time.

# DAY 54

## JANUARY 19 | FARMER'S MARKET

I saw her striding towards me from a distance. Isabella is striking. Not only because of her distinct features—beautiful long legs, coffee-brown hair, deep brown eyes, full lips—it's more than that. She's refined with an impeccable style far beyond her years. But the way she moves, that is what makes people stop and look at her.

She saw me waving and ran towards me the way she used to when she was a little girl. I held her in my arms and my heart beat so fast. A wave of sadness got the better of me. I didn't want to cry, so I recalled a positive thought in my head. To my astonishment, it worked. I'm getting good at this.

The Farmer's Market has been around since 1934. Nowadays it features about a hundred stalls selling everything from baked goods, meat, fruits, and veggies to stickers, candles, and souvenirs. We wandered around, food in hand, before finding a seat at one of their dilapidated outdoor tables.

"Have you heard from Dad?" I had to ask. It's

important to me that Pete will be in their lives once I'm gone.

"You know Dad, he only calls between meetings." She patted my arm, something she never does, and assured me, "It's all going to be okay, Mom." I'm not sure what she meant by this, but I hope she's right.

"How's dance?" I asked.

"Great."

"Did you see Nick again after the breakup?"

"Definitely not! Out of the picture. Don't ask," she sighed dramatically. "Completely and forever."

After breakfast, we strolled around like two women without a plan, buying lots of knickknacks along the way.

I know Isabella will take my death the hardest and I'm worried. Pete will check in with them from time to time, but otherwise he will be too busy leading his own life, and she needs family. She needs to be loved. Don't we all.

Isabella is still so young, but I want her to find love before I die. Somebody nice who will comfort her and distract her. This could be my last big task as her mother—my ultimate interference. And with Nick out of the picture...

Later I will look on from heaven, and if things don't go my way, I will probably put in a special word with my kind of God. But for now, I'm still here, and I must do something. And that something comes in the form of Ethan, my new gardener.

# DAY 55
## JANUARY 20 | HOME

Thoughts about the kids, Sam, and sometimes even Pete, kept me occupied most of the day and well into the night. I wrote some on a piece of paper, mainly to clear my mind. Then around 5 AM, I heard a noise. A clicking! Followed by footsteps. Fear paralyzed me for a second, and not sure what to do, I crawled out of bed and headed for the entrance door, turning on as many lights as I could.

I'm uncertain what came first, Sam's voice calling my name or me seeing him as I turned the corner. Either way, I was scared and equally relieved, if that makes any sense.

Our eyes met, and I rushed into his arms. He held me so tight (I need this now more than ever), whispering the words I wanted to hear the most. "I've been thinking about this for the past few days…"

"Yes?"

"I don't take this lightly and don't ask me to explain it." He paused. "I love you, Lizzie. I love you a lot."

"I know. I know because I love you too."

He had come back one day early.

*For Sam: One day you will read this, and I never want you to doubt that I love you. I fell for you the minute I opened the door on New Year's Eve and let you into my new home and into my life. Everything happened so fast, some people might say too fast. There are so many unexpected people (like you and Susan) and things that appeared in my life, like magic.*

Note: I still need to call everybody on my list. Don't want to!

# DAY 56
## JANUARY 21 | STILL AT HOME

I have been up since sunrise listening to Sam's breathing. My thoughts traveled between a dozen different subjects until the word *death* came to my mind. I *despise* that word. Let's be real. Who wants to be sick and die?

The loud chirp of a bird in the distance caught my attention. Its song was sorrowful. I must have listened for some time because when I turned around, Sam's eyes were on me. He was observing me. Does he know more than I'm aware of? Without a word, he pulled me on top of him. And just like that, we ended up spending the day in bed, making love and talking. Sam made plans for the future and I listened.

# DAY 57
## JANUARY 22 | ON THE WAY

Looking back—something I rarely do these days—I noticed that I've received fewer presents in the last ten years than I have in these past few weeks with Sam. He spoils me, and I let it happen. These days, I feel so adored that it's painful to think about everything I've been missing all these years.

It had been one of those mesmerizing California days with a mild breeze sweeping through a cloudless sky. And I felt better than ever. Lately, feeling good worries me because I know it won't last. Any day could be the day when things turn around for me. That said, I felt perfect when I woke up and saw Sam packing. He was packing my clothes, and then his, in the same suitcase. One suitcase.

Once again, Sam had another surprise for me—this time it was a trip. *And I have a feeling this gift will mean so much to both of us later on.* Next time I see Susan I have to ask her if Sam always spoils everybody like this.

For a second, I thought about the dinner I had

promised to make for everyone, but it would have to wait.

And off we went, like college kids in love, on what Sam declared would be the best road trip of our lives.

(This part I added later!) Sam was right. This trip and Napa, I will never be able to forget. *Napa is now imprinted on my memory forever.*

We drove along Route 1 heading North, the stunning Malibu coastline to our left with its vast stretch of fine sand bordering the impressive Pacific Ocean. My hair was blowing in the wind, soft music was playing, and Sam was singing along. I couldn't view all of this as a beginning, the beginning of Sam and me. But then again, I wasn't ready to see it as the end.

I reached for Sam's hand and held it, his warm hand in mine.

# DAY 58
## JANUARY 23 | SANTA BARBARA

S am and I woke up before sunrise, jumped into shorts, and bought coffee and sugar cookies in a small bakery that opens at 4 AM. The soothing scent of baked goods was overwhelming. This place had been around for a long time, baking all kinds of breads, Danishes and croissants.

Sam told me, "My dad brought me here as a kid, and I'm so happy to see them doing well."

Sam always thinks about other people, and that is what I love the most about him.

After stocking up on goodies, we drove for about twenty minutes, maybe longer—I didn't look at my watch—until we reached an isolated beach cove where impressive grayish looking stones surrounded a small stretch of white sand overlooking the Pacific Ocean.

Somewhere far east, the sun, an orange-red looking ball, rose above the horizon while the seagulls, ready for their first breakfast, swooped over us. With the waves crashing against the rocks, this was a dream spot. We cuddled up under a warm fleece blanket. It was romantic and intimate as we took off each other's clothes. Slow, considerate, quiet. It was so much more than just making love; it was love.

Forever—I will remember the warmth of the blanket and Sam holding and kissing me. The look on his face when he caressed my body, his touch and the smell of his skin, now salty from the ocean.

# DAY 59
## JANUARY 24 | CARMEL

Carmel is mesmerizing. Red, yellow, lilac and blue wildflowers adorn gardens along its narrow streets, releasing a sweet scent. The entire town is wrapped in a cloud of perfume.

Yesterday we stayed at a quaint B&B, whose fascinating owner—a man in his sixties covered in tattoos, told us that he bought the inn over 30 years ago after spending four years in prison. He made a pact with himself to change his life after being released, and he did.

Our room was charming: flowery wallpaper, antique furniture, and a canopy bed with a plush duvet and an array of pillows, plus a wood-burning fireplace.

In the morning, after a luxurious pancake breakfast, I noticed that Sam was very quiet. He held my hand in his as we strolled along the picturesque side streets. Occasionally we glanced at each other and the only thing I could think about was that I want a lifetime with this man.

"Lizzie?"

"Sam?"

"I feel lucky. I have to pinch myself. It's like I've been waiting for you… *forever*." He said it in a way that brought me to a halt, and he pulled me in a little closer.

My heart dropped knowing I will hurt Sam the day I tell him my secret. Thinking, *There is no future for us. We are nothing more than moving clouds, fleeting images, paint strokes.*

We continued to stroll around, mostly in silence, until he grabbed my arm so hard it almost hurt. His eyes never leaving mine, he pulled me in his arms and kissed me, this time with a rush of urgency.

# DAY 60

## JANUARY 25 | ON THE ROAD

There's a small restaurant overlooking the ocean, nestled high up in the hills somewhere off Route 1 between Carmel and Napa. It resembles a ski lodge—scenic, dreamy, romantic.

Less than two months ago, I was a lost woman who had little self-esteem and lacked the courage to act upon my deepest desires. Somewhere along the way, I had given up both. I would avoid any confrontation and I rarely stood up for myself. Learning that I was going to die soon changed everything. At that moment, it was like someone pushed me over the edge and screamed, "Fly, Liz, fly!"

Sam studied me. "What is it, Lizzie?"

I shook my head. And instead of saying something, I placed my hand on his arm. That's how we spent our time sitting on this lovely terrace, tucked in between evergreens. There, with him, I finally understood who I was. With Sam, I feel free to express my thoughts and to be quiet when I need to be. I am myself. I AM MYSELF AGAIN! IT'S ME, LIZ!

At some point, he moved closer and I put my head on his shoulder. Without looking at me, he said, "Lizzie, I don't think you know how beautiful you are." Every time Sam says something loving to me, I feel appreciated, and every time he does, I feel like a liar.

That afternoon, the wind picked up and blew through my hair. I loved how the breeze caressed my skin. Sam kept on moving strands of hair off my face and putting them back behind my ears. Then he leaned over and kissed my cheek, a slight gesture that made me spiral out of control.

What I've observed in the past weeks is that life is never a straight line, it bends and twists. They float from hopeful to desperate, loved to lonely, courageous to fearful. There's no straight line!

# DAY 61
## JANUARY 26 | NAPA

It was one of those days that started in the perfect way: sunny and around 60 degrees. Sam and I spent the day driving—to be precise, being driven—from one magnificent winery to the next. Wineries have something dreamy, enchanting about them. I'm not sure what it is, maybe the fantasy of living an idyllic life.

I got a taste of it as we strolled among the grapevines and did a tour at Napa Cellar. We went into a cavern filled with barrels and bottles stacked along dimly lit and musty smelling walls. We sniffed, swirled and sipped our vintages, and when nobody was looking (I'm sure everybody still saw us and I didn't care), Sam lifted me up, placed me on one of the many barrels and kissed me. His kisses were soft and simultaneously intense.

We tasted a wide selection of red and white wines while nibbling on crackers and cheese. Not once did it cross my mind that I shouldn't drink alcohol, and frankly, I didn't want to think about it. What more could it do to me? I'm alive *now*. And I savored every second of this day.

Back in the car, Sam and I were cruising along some dirt roads. My hand was in his and our conversation was flowing as smoothly as the wine.

"Have you ever been to San Francisco?" Sam asked.

"No, I haven't."

"That's fantastic!"

I was a bit confused. "And why is that fantastic?"

"Now we have a reason to come back to Napa," he laughed. "Next time we'll fly to San Francisco, and we'll drive to Napa and Sonoma."

Tears welled up; it happened so fast that it surprised me. Sadness overcame me and I felt angry. There's *no* straight line.

Surprised, Sam glanced at me. "Talk to me."

I squeezed his hand, then let go of him and looked out the window.

There was a moment of silence before Sam put his arm around my shoulder. I sensed he was concerned as he kissed my forehead. I could tell he knew something was wrong.

Then everything around me began to spin, and I felt dizzy…

Note: This all happened a couple of days ago, but it's today that I'm writing this entry. You'll see why.

# DAY 62

## JANUARY 27 | ON THE ROAD

There was an unfamiliar buzzing sound. I was caught somewhere between a dream and reality, thinking that the sheets felt so different—rougher, not as smooth—and that I was having trouble opening my eyes. They felt heavy, as if someone had placed stones on them.

I must have slept for a long time because when I got out of the dream state and reentered into the actual world, I was lying in a hospital bed surrounded by three doctors and Sam staring down at me.

I knew it was daytime as my eyes followed the sun's rays dancing across my extra-starched white bed sheets. Except for the buzzing, there was a painful and deadly silence. The kind of silence I don't like.

My thoughts were going back and forth. *How much did Sam know? I didn't want him to find out this way. Why didn't I tell him sooner? I should have known better.*

*I want to stroke his hair and look into his eyes. I want to hold him, tell him the truth while we're intertwined in each other's arms.*

*I'm scared. And I can't blame him if he's upset and never wants to see me again. He could leave my life as fast as he appeared in it.*

*He has a right to know that I'm dying.*

Finally, the older looking doctor stepped closer.

"Ms. Taite, can you hear me?"

I nodded. My throat felt so dry.

"We are trying to figure out what happened. Why don't you rest. We'll run some more tests tomorrow."

I stayed quiet. I recognized what happened. After all, Dr. Sternenberg had warned me. It was time. It was time to make changes.

Last night, while in a drugged deep sleep, I had a dream. I can't remember all the details, but I do recall that Sam was there. I saw him standing on my favorite stretch of beach, his hand extended towards me. I tried to reach him. I ran towards him, but he moved away. As hard as I tried, I couldn't. I disappeared. The peculiar thing was that Sam was still standing in the same spot.

Is this a premonition? Will I just disappear? A poof. Gone.

# DAY 63
## JANUARY 28 | NAPA

This morning, after a couple of simple neurological tests, the doctors concluded—partly because they needed my spot back in their small hospital, and because they were not equipped for further testing—that I had been severely dehydrated, thanks to the almost fatal combination of a little too much sun and far too much wine. It all made sense to them, and Sam looked relieved.

They failed to do a simple blood test, which, of course, would have revealed the truth. Was their negligence a divine intervention? The Universe, once again, had looked out for me.

Of course it wasn't the sun! It was the combination of a lot of medications and alcohol and me declining faster than I want to admit. Dr. Katz, my doctor in LA, had warned me. And I had chosen not to listen and to enjoy life instead.

I am no longer living in denial, but that doesn't mean that I don't detest what's happening to my body. There's pain and a lot of fear. Even if I don't show it, I'm scared about what will happen to me.

Today, I was warned. Now it's time for me to step up and have the toughest conversations of my life with the people I love the most.

While I got dressed and waited for Sam to pick me up, I tried to figure out how many days I might have left. Eighty would be generous. Maybe forty. Or something in-between.

# DAY 64
## JANUARY 29 | ROAD TRIP

We drove back along the dazzling Pacific coastline, and I don't remember much that happened in those hours. It was ridiculous how much better I felt, less confused and far more relaxed. And exhausted! That's probably why I was in a sort of dreamlike state for most of the ride, forgetting about the future and enjoying the moment: the ocean, the beaches, the trees, the sun, the monuments. The world was flying by, just like my life. I closed my eyes and felt the warm wind on my face. My parents and my sister appeared in my mind, us playing hide and seek; me graduating from college; I saw Pete holding Julia; me holding Matt and Isabella; me running along a beach with my kids until we were all out of breath, all of us falling into the warm sand and making sand angels. Angels! There were so many angels surrounding me. I reemerged for a fleeting moment, only to drift off again, imagining myself riding a beautiful horse—brown with a long mane—my hair bouncing up and down. I must have been thirty years younger. The image made me laugh out loud.

"What's so funny?" Sam asked.

"Just a silly dream."

Then he grew serious. "You scared me yesterday."

"I know."

"What bothers me is that we both know that you didn't drink a lot. You barely tasted the wine." There was a long pause before he continued. "You need to go and see a doctor."

"I know, Sam. I do." And we left it at that. For now. Seriously, what should I have done? Scream against the wind, *By the way, I'm dying. Sorry.*

To my astonishment, we already drove through Santa Barbara towards the lush green hills.

Recovering from the weird conversation we had earlier, Sam glanced at me. "You have a beautiful soul, Lizzie."

I smiled. Once again, I wasn't sure what to say.

Minutes later, we abruptly came to a halt in front of a gigantic and antique-looking door. On its edges were Egyptian symbols carved into the wood.

"Where are we?" I asked.

Sam reached for my arm to lead me towards the door, and then he stopped and kissed me. My heart was beating so fast; I thought it would jump out of my chest. I had a premonition.

"It's a secret," he whispered. And I thought, I don't like secrets, but I'm good at keeping them.

The door sprung open and upon entering I was not only in for one more surprise, but also faced with my biggest dilemma.

We had entered the most adorable and romantic jewelry store, so small that it fit only three people. A distinguished, white-haired lady stood behind a counter and greeted Sam and me. Her eyes, full of life experience, were examining us in a somewhat uncomfortable silent way until, with a huge grin, she expelled one word: "Soulmates." My heart dropped.

From a small drawer, she pulled out a tarot deck and shuffled it.

"Just one card," she said, and pulled a card from the deck. She glanced at it and quickly put it back in the pile.

Looking at me, she said, "Never mind. Let's look at the jewelry."

"What did you see?" Sam asked the woman.

"Love. I saw love."

My breath turned shallow and afraid that I would faint again, I reached for Sam's hand, only to notice that it was firmly pressed on my back, guiding me from the necklaces, bracelets and earrings towards the rings. Under normal circumstances, this moment would have been exquisite, but these weren't normal circumstances. I'm dying. And I'm still married. By now, my heartbeat was so fast I felt like I was losing control.

Sam turned towards me, "We only met a few weeks ago…" He laughed. "Don't look so scared, Lizzie. This isn't a marriage proposal. It's nothing more than letting you know that no matter what happens, I will be committed to you." He searched for my eyes, and I could have died right there. I suddenly felt sick again.

The rings were stunning, beautifully displayed in an antique glass case. Diamonds of all sizes sparkled in the light, each of them telling a love story, each of them with a history.

What Sam and I have is nothing but the present. My feelings tore me apart. I wanted Sam to put a ring on my finger. I wanted his love and commitment. I wanted that one moment to take with me to another world, to wherever I was destined to go. But I also knew that all of this would make my last days so much more convoluted. And would Sam ever forgive me for not opening up sooner?

I couldn't accept a ring, not even as I stood in that marvelous gem of a jewelry store, not without telling him the truth.

That's why I did the only thing I could do. I ran out of the store and leaned against the house wall catching my breath. Tears flooded my eyes and I cried and cried.

It took a little while before I saw Sam leaving the store and walking towards me, more questions written all over his face. But he never asked. Instead, he lifted my chin and kissed me.

"It's all going to be okay, Lizzie."

I buried my face in his neck and whispered, "I'm sorry. I love you." But now, I'm not so sure if he heard it.

# SAM

Years ago, I would have said that Liz's inconsistent behavior and her propensity to cry were red flags. Bad news for any new relationship. Over the years, I have had my share of experiences with women, and I'm sure there's a part of Liz's story that I haven't heard yet. Nothing points to anything specific, and I have no idea what it could be. All I can hope for is that someday, she will trust me enough and unveil what is bothering her.

I have made several attempts to ask her, but she keeps avoiding my questions. It's odd and somewhat unsettling. Maybe it has something to do with her husband. I don't know. And not knowing bothers me.

It's been a long time since I've been in a serious relationship, and I wasn't looking for one. My life is filled with friends, my upcoming book and the animals I foster. It felt great—it felt like enough—until I met Liz.

Liz changed everything. She changed my life the minute she opened the door to her new home. Her smile, her slightly sad eyes, her somewhat deep, soothing voice and infectious roaring laughter—if I could dream up a woman, it would be her. We match.

But honestly, since I met Liz, I feel slightly insane. I do things I never would have thought of doing before, such as pursuing a woman, this quickly. Or moving partially into her home (after all, I have my own) and hiring a student to take care of my current foster animals—five cats and four dogs—all to be with Liz. There's an urgency I can't quite explain.

Susan cherishes her and her kids seem great. Still, I have to figure out what she's hiding. Whatever it is, I know we will have the strength to overcome all obstacles. I love Lizzie. She is my forever.

# DAY 65
## JANUARY 30 | MALIBU

Despite the sudden arrival of stormy weather, we decided to stop in Malibu at a small oceanfront hotel surrounded by cypress trees and oleander bushes.

Sam was quieter than usual. I had prepared myself to answer all his questions truthfully, but he didn't ask me about what happened yesterday at the jewelry store. And I want to find the right moment to tell him. I know it has to be soon. Very soon.

Instead, we talked about Max, his brother, who lives in Vermont with his wife and four kids. Sam visits him every year in the fall. It made me think of New York and how I loved to stroll around the city in the fall, the short period before the grueling winter months. Then we talked about my kids, and Sam asked about Pete. I told him about the good and the bad times of my marriage. Sam listened. Sam knows how to listen.

Eventually, we ducked into a rustic fish shack and perched on wooden benches, and we ate the most delicious popcorn shrimp and fish and chips. All at once, yesterday was forgotten (just for now), along with the many unanswered questions.

The sound of waves crashing against the shore led to an unforgettably entrancing night. Cuddled into Sam's arms, he read moving words to me written by Pablo Neruda from a book of poetry we found in our room. One of them, *Die Slowly*, made me shiver. Sam's voice, now so familiar, became a faint sound, "… who does not risk and change the color of his clothes, who does not speak and does not experience, dies slowly."

The words were so powerful that it was easy to imagine how they could change lives and make a significant impact on the world. They certainly affected me.

I tried not to think about how the words I have to say to Sam will change his world.

# DAY 66

## JANUARY 31 | MALIBU

We woke up early to sunshine reflecting on the water and a beach that looked like a bed of sparkling crystals. Seduced by this spellbinding place, we decided to stay another day. *We.* That tiny word that has changed my life. *We.* The word I dreaded for the past ten years; then again, it was the same word I longed for all my life.

Considering everything, shouldn't this be around the time when I dissolve into an emotional mess, hit cushions and walls, and scream? In reality, I feel nothing but gratitude sitting in this spellbinding spot with Sam by my side. Among billions of men, I have found the one.

We ordered breakfast—eggs, croissants, coffee, butter and jam—and sat on our small private balcony, watching the seagulls swoosh over the crashing waves. It was breathtaking!

It's difficult to explain why, during these incredible moments, my mind works overtime. I thought about Elisabeth Kübler-Ross's famous book, *On Dying*, and the five stages one is supposed to go through: denial, anger, bargaining, depression and acceptance. I went through these emotions, and not precisely in that order. I must have altered the process when I made substantial changes in the final days of my life. Who would, in a state like mine, leave their old life behind to begin a new one? I did it. I smiled thinking: *You're crazy, Liz.* Maybe I was a bit insane. Then again, it had been the best thing I've done in a long time.

When I snapped out of it and looked up, I stared straight into Sam's eyes, wondering how long he had been looking at me.

"You look sad, Lizzie." The roar of the ocean mingled with my racing thoughts. *Was this the right moment for the truth?*

"Why?" he asked.

"Can we talk about it in a little while?"

He got up and kissed my forehead. "Of course." And without another word, he returned to the room, leaving me and my thoughts alone for a little while longer. Leaving me loving him even more.

# DAY 67
## FEBRUARY 1 | ALMOST HOME

We packed. There was a sudden urge to get going—the need to move on knowing that our trip was over.

Despite the magnificent room—filled with antiques and whimsical items: fluffy cushions, books, and traditional stationery—we rushed out, driven by some invisible force.

We rode in silence towards Zuma—once again we were heading North, the opposite direction of my home—and I wanted to know what Sam was thinking. I was afraid that he would throw my question right back at me, so I didn't ask. After some time, Sam hit the gas pedal, and we bolted along the coast. My thoughts raced at the same speed as the car.

Later, as we slowed down, with Zuma on our left, Sam rolled through a private gate (which he explained was only possible because he had called a wealthy friend of his) past incredibly modern beach homes—the ones out of movies with enormous glass panels and sun decks overlooking the ocean.

We parked the car and I followed Sam past the house and tennis court until we found the wooden steps leading to the beach. I can't remember the last time I was so excited and giggly in anticipation of discovering something new. Sam carried our picnic basket prepared by the hotel: chocolate cake, strawberries, champagne (mainly for Sam), baguette, and cheese. Could it get any better? Today I feel better than I did in the past couple of days. So strange! And to my surprise, I still have an appetite. I do. For now.

All the tension I felt earlier was gone. We were just two people in love. So much in love that I couldn't take my eyes off him.

It was warm enough, so we gathered all our courage and briefly dipped our bodies into the freezing ocean. As the sun was setting, we were alone on the semi-private beach and I tasted the salt on Sam's lips as we danced to a melody he was humming. In that moment the world stood still, and the roar of the ocean turned into music. I looked at Sam and said it out loud, no more of the insecure whispering. A statement of conviction: "I love you."

He pulled me close and held me so tightly, I lost my breath.

# DAY 68
## FEBRUARY 2 | HOME

Until recently, I was never cognizant of how fast my emotional and my physical state could swing from one extreme to another. Above all, I was afraid I would run out of time too quickly. Was that the first sign that I was losing the battle?

It was absurd to think about dying on such a mesmerizing day instead of living. So, I forced myself to stay in the moment.

The sun felt warm and soothing as we rolled along Route 1 towards Santa Monica.

Wanting to learn more about Sam, I asked, "Did you ever feel you were missing out on something by not having kids?"

"Years ago, I did. But I guess the universe had a different plan for me. I became a good uncle and a dedicated veterinarian."

"Why did you give it up?"

"Being a vet?"

"Yes."

"Something bigger was waiting for me. And I'm still

a vet. Just an unpaid one who takes care of dogs and cats in shelters." Then he added, "And I love it."

And that's when I found out about Sam's conviction for drunk driving some fourteen years ago. We all have a story.

~

Back home. Sam left to meet his friend, the photographer who's working on the dolphin book with him. They have to take care of some photo printing issues. After that, he needs to meet with the students who currently take care of his foster animals and tend to all the other work that has piled up over the past few days.

In an attempt to keep busy, I had a closer look at the hundreds of books neatly lined up on an enormous mahogany bookshelf that spanned an entire wall in the house. That bookshelf gives the intimate library an additional touch of warmth.

I slid my fingers along one of the shelves and a swirl of dust greeted me. The books covered all subjects —art, gardening, animals, architecture, traveling—and there was also a wide range of novels, from romance to fantasy and crime.

I moved the library ladder and climbed up to reach the top shelf when a collection of Jane Austen books that looked like first editions caught my eye. I pulled out several of them to have a closer look, but when I reached for Sense & Sensibility, my wrist touched a small and barely visible button chiseled into the wood. I pressed it. Nothing happened. Then I turned it, and a panel, hidden behind the Jane Austen books, slid aside, revealing a box made of bamboo. Intrigued, I reached for it.

I reminded myself that for now this was my house. Even so I felt a little guilty, but I couldn't help being curious.

After all, the box might hold the ultimate clue to solving the mystery of this house, the secret I've been looking for: Emma and George's secret, if there is even one. Could it be their love story? Maybe it's Emma's story, from the time George died to her death.

My brain was filled with possibilities, and despite my reservations, I was about to open the box. I had turned the key halfway when the doorbell rang. Not sure what to do with the box, I shoved it under a sofa pillow and ran for the door, wondering who could be at the door.

It was Susan, ready to join me for coffee or a drink. She loves cocktails.

"Look who I brought with me," she said, as she pointed at Ethan, the gardener, who was carrying a heavy bag of soil to the other end of the property. Susan winked at me and said, "If only I were forty years younger." Her theatrical gesture made me laugh.

She continued, "Get ready. I want to hear every detail of your trip. The good and the bad." And before I could say anything, she added, "And Sam already told me that you fainted."

# DAY 69

## FEBRUARY 3 | HOME

As I'm writing this, I'm sitting in my "perfect" garden, watching Ethan transform the dead bushes and empty pots into a blooming Zen oasis, oozing with tranquility.

**Zen** [ zen ] — noun: *a Japanese school of Mahayana Buddhism emphasizing the value of meditation and intuition*

Most of the day I spent going through the books Emma wrote: thirty-two novels, mostly thrillers. I read some pages out loud. Her writing kept me on the edge of my seat and my fascination for her grew. It's kind of cool to think that I'm living in the same house she used to live in.

Although our lives are so different, it still feels as if mine is overlapping with hers. In the end, she became the author I always wanted to be and I feel privileged to get to know her, page by page.

My day was quiet without Sam. Too quiet. Between reading, thinking about Sam, and trying to figure out what I can do to bring Isabella and Ethan together, suddenly it was nighttime.

Isabella wouldn't want me to set her up with my gardener, although he's educated and intriguingly handsome with his short brown hair and endearing smile. The truth is, Isabella wouldn't want me to set her up with anybody. She would refuse and give me a thousand reasons why she didn't want to meet him. Then I remembered the dinner I had loosely promised to give. I would love to get everybody together. One (it could be my last one) lovely dinner in my home!

# DAY 70
## FEBRUARY 4 | HOME

It surprised me to hear one of my neighbor's voices greeting me while I strolled around my neighborhood. Few people here engage in conversations. So, I stopped.

"Good morning. It's a beautiful day, isn't it?" I said.

"Yep, another gorgeous day in fucking paradise." It was so LA! I was slowly falling in love with California and the many unexpected and often endearing situations and people I encountered here.

Today, indeed, was another stunning day. When I got home, I strolled through my garden and examined the extraordinarily exquisite work Ethan had done in such a short time. I was distracting myself from wanting to count the minutes until I would see Sam again. My time is precious, and I want to keep busy doing all the things I still want and need to do. If I like it or not, I have to prepare myself. That's when my thoughts were interrupted by the faint sound of my doorbell.

I rushed to the gate. A bit out of breath and flushed with anticipation, thinking that Sam might be a day early, I flung the door open only to find, to my surprise, my three kids standing in front of me flaunting gigantic grins. Immense joy overcame me and love filled up my whole body. I held each of them so tightly. I squeezed them, and it took me forever to let go.

We sat in the garden enjoying each other's company while drinking passion fruit iced tea and eating chocolate cake in the warm midday sun. Then suddenly, amid our animated conversation punctuated by lots of stories and laughter, I had an idea.

I went into the kitchen to call Ethan and ask him if he had time to stop by and finish planting flowers around the waterfall he had created between two jutting rocks.

Destiny once again revealed itself. Ethan happened to be in the neighborhood and Isabella happened to be at the gate because she was strolling around the garden when he entered. I also happened to be very close—not too close, but close enough (and fast enough) to dash up and introduce them to one another.

"Isabella, this is Ethan. Creator of this magnificent garden."

The look on Ethan's face was somewhere between "struck by lightning" and "just saw a ghost." He stared at Isabella wide-eyed. It was difficult to suppress my emerging laughter. In the end, Isabella saved him.

She stretched out her hand. "Nice to meet you, Ethan. I love your work."

Goodbye to whoever currently has his eyes on Isabella and welcome, Ethan!

Ethan joined us for cake and he fit right in. After his initial flash of infatuation for Isabella (she does that to men), he showed that he can hold his own. Later he went to plant Blue-Eyed Grass, Busy Lizzie and the Sierra Shooting Star (I'm learning my flowers). At one point, I eyed Isabella strolling over to the fountain where Ethan was gardening. My plan was working.

*For Isabella: I know you'll be angry with me when you read this. Remember, I didn't do much. I simply introduced you, and love was written all over your faces. I knew you would be attracted to each other. You're both still young, so I can't predict for how long, but I have a feeling that Ethan will be there when you need him. His eyes were glued on you, and I had never seen you look at any other man that way. Follow your dreams. Always follow your dreams.*

*For Matt: Today, as so often before, I saw how much love and respect you show your sisters. They will need you. It makes me so happy to know that you've found happiness with Sebastian. You're everything one can expect from a friend, partner and son. Never doubt the greatness in you.*

*For Julia: I will never be able to thank you enough for breaking your promise to Sam and telling me the truth. Him calling you and sending all of you to me this afternoon is one of the most thoughtful things someone has done for me in a long time. As always, you're wise beyond your years, and I'm certain you can handle whatever life throws at you. Sam is a wonderful man and after reading this journal (I know you'll read every single word, trying to make sense out of everything) you'll give him a chance. He will need to be with all of you because you three are part of me. Nobody has ever loved me the way he does. That's not true. Many years ago, Dad loved me just the same. I know he did because I loved him just as much.*

*Julia, you're my rock. You're a woman with character and dignity. I have no doubt you will watch over Isabella and Matt and keep this family together. And I will watch over all of you.*

God, if you exist, please don't let me die. Please don't let me die. I don't want to die.

# ISABELLA

Seeing mom today was kind of bittersweet. It's great that she lives in LA now, and I can see her whenever I like. Mom and I were always so close. Although I love to pretend I'm all grown up, I still need her. Just knowing that she's here comforts me.

But I've noticed that she's different. I can't explain it. Maybe it's because she constantly seems to be concerned about our future. She has always been worried about us, but now she wants to know every detail of our lives. She tried to hook me up with Ethan (she thought I wouldn't notice). Seriously! I mean, he's hot, so I don't mind. But then again, it was kind of out of character. Why would it matter to her?

On the way to the house, Matt mentioned that he was concerned about mom too. Mainly because she looks fragile and tears up a lot. I can see that. And usually she's so active, now it feels like she's slowing down. (Then again, she leaped over a bush to get to Ethan and me in time. That was funny!) Maybe it's just because she left Dad and her home and the art gallery—which doesn't make sense either. It's way-out, and now I'm freaking out. I love her so much.

# DAY 71

## FEBRUARY 5 | BEVERLY HILLS

In New York, I was always busy running around, either for work or to meet friends for lunch or dinner. And in earlier years, I was schlepping groceries and happily transporting kids to school, ballet classes, tennis tournaments, birthday parties, bar mitzvahs and playdates. For the first time, I concede that one can be happy doing nothing.

Just sitting and taking in the moment—that's what I was doing when my phone rang. It was Erica. Despite my request to them to wait for me to reach out, Freja and Erica have been calling me every few days. To be honest, I love hearing their voices, but it's also hard for me to hear about how well the gallery is doing and how they're moving on with their lives. I can sense how, especially Erica, holds back information just so I won't be sad. The way they are with me now foreshadows how everybody else will react once they know that I'm dying.

**Foreshadow** [ fôr'SHadō ] — verb: *be a warning or indication of (a future event)*

Both Erica and Freja mean so well, and I love them. I miss them.

And just as I hung up, Sam stood in the doorway earlier than expected, watching me. We made a fire—Sam did—and we had a glass of red wine. And not much later, drowsy from the wine and from not sleeping enough, we made our way to the bedroom, kissing.

More than ever, I feel horrible. Sam deserves to know the truth. I can't wait any longer.

The problem is that by talking about it, I'm getting closer to the end. And I want to live. I HATE THIS SO MUCH! I DON'T WANT TO DIE!

# DAY 72
## FEBRUARY 6 | HOME

Exhausted from the previous days, Sam and I slept in late. After breakfast we went for a walk deep into the hills, past impressive villas—some a bit too opulent for my taste.

This could have been the perfect moment to come clean, but as we talked about the meaning of love, he told me about his first serious girlfriend.

"She was unpredictable and fearless, and she loved all sports. Her favorite thing was mountain climbing, while I love surfing and swimming." What followed was a horrific story about her disappearance during a hiking trip in Colombia.

I believe I mumbled something about being sorry, thinking. *How can I possibly tell him now that I'm dying?*

"It was terrible," he added. "And honestly, I was angry at her for a long time for putting me second."

After walking in silence for a while, Sam stopped, faced me, and cupped my face in his hands. "First loves are very complicated." I looked straight into his eyes and put my hands on top of his. He continued, "This here, you and I, is different. We are like two separate beings who form this comparatively perfect unity." I'm not sure I knew what all that meant, but I began to cry, quietly. Then I sobbed.

And I'm still crying (I'm too emotional! Damn medications!) while I'm writing this, smearing ink all over the page. I want Sam. I want this life, right here, in my house with Sam. I want a million more walks, hugs and kisses. I want my kids to come and visit me. I want us—us having dinners. Beach walks. Conversations. Strolling around my garden. I want it for another thirty years.

I am postponing the inevitable talk, as if I could postpone dying. This is ridiculous! And I must make those dreaded phone calls to friends and relatives as well. My thoughts are making me dizzy.

*For Sam: I'm sure that by now you think I'm an emotional mess. Believe me, I've thought a thousand times about how to tell you the truth. I want to let you know that we, you and I, are nothing more than a fleeting moment. I wanted to… I really did. I'm sorry. I'm so sorry. Forgive me.*

# DAY 73
## FEBRUARY 7 | MALIBU

The waves crashed onto the shore, making me jump out of the water from time to time, and run inland to keep from getting my pants wet.

I didn't feel great yesterday, and this morning I felt worse. I was nauseous from the moment I got up, I felt like fainting.

Despite all of it, and after Susan called me, I decided it would be good for me to get out of the house and get some ocean air. Two hours later she picked me up and we drove to Malibu. There was very little traffic, which didn't happen too often in LA, and it took us no time to get to the beach. Once I felt the wet sand on my feet, the dizziness disappeared and I slowly felt better.

Susan, as always, was her vibrant self—laughing, twirling, and occasionally glancing over at me. I tried to focus on staying in the moment, concentrating on taking in the ocean air. I love the saltiness on my skin.

While we were walking side by side in silence, I looked at Susan and I realized I had been waiting for—

no, I had been wishing for someone special to talk to. I needed to talk about this. It was time.

"I love this place. It makes me feel good," I said.

"What's going on, Liz? You look pale."

She stopped walking.

"Please don't stop walking and don't look at me like that."

"I'm looking at you because I'm concerned."

We continued to walk, and I gathered up all my strength.

"I'll never own a house in Malibu," I said.

"Most people don't own houses in Malibu."

"Susan…" There's no easy way to talk about dying, especially to someone you're close to—even though I've only known her for a short time. I took her hands in mine, locked eyes with her, and breathed the words, "Susan, I'm dying." It was out in the open. There was no going back. I had said it.

Susan stared at me. She just stared at me for a long time. "Oh my God, Liz. Liz. Liz." She kept on repeating my name as she took me in her arms, and I cried and cried. There was no more denial, no more anger, no more bargaining. Just sadness, and maybe acceptance.

*For Susan: I wanted to tell my kids first. But today I needed to talk to somebody, and I'm glad it was you. Not only did I ruin this day, but I also ruined the days to come. We both know things will change.*

*Susan, you are an extraordinary friend and I will never be able to thank you enough for everything you've done for me. I only wish we could have met earlier.*

# DAY 74
## FEBRUARY 8 | HOME

There was a loud banging noise, and I dragged myself out of bed. Sick and dizzy, I barely made it to the bathroom. Dammit, this isn't fair! "It's me, God, Universe, Buddha, or whoever you are. It's Liz. It's the woman who loves her children. The woman who loved Pete. It's the woman who found love again." I pounded my fist against the wall until I heard an echo. I stopped banging, but the noise continued.

After I threw up multiple times, I managed to take a quick shower. The banging carried on, and I struggled to my bedroom window overlooking the garden. Sam was standing in the middle of the lawn, building another hammock for us. He loves building things. A double hammock in a coral color. It was so pretty.

I'm not sure what happened. I felt weak. Dizzy. My muscles were giving in all at once. I remember I wanted to help Sam, and I reached out for him and called his name. But he didn't hear me through the closed window. He was too far away. Or did he call my name?

"Lizzie." The next thing I saw was Sam crouching over me and pressing a cold towel on my forehead.

"Lizzie, you fainted." He looked terrified. I hated seeing him like this.

"I felt sick and I'm not…" I murmured.

"It's okay. Put your arms around my neck." He lifted me up and carried me to my favorite chair on the terrace while insisting that I call a doctor.

The fresh air helped me. Luckily it wasn't hot outside. I sat there for some time, resting and sipping some healthy, awful tasting juice.

After sitting with me for a while, Sam continued to work on the hammock and the fountain project Ethan had started the other day. And while watching him work, I fell asleep.

# DAY 75
## FEBRUARY 9 | HOME

Reluctantly, Sam left early this morning to take care of half a dozen dogs somebody found in a dumpster. Horrible! Who would do such a thing? He wanted to call Susan to take care of me, but I assured him that I felt better. But the way he studied me made me think he didn't believe me.

It wasn't exactly a lie. I did feel a little better. And bit by bit, I gathered the strength to get up and to fight my emerging anxiety by focusing on my breathing. Still, I couldn't help but wonder: What will happen to me? Is this the end phase? Is this what Dr. Sternenberg warned me about when I forwent all the treatments? I began to sweat and my heart was racing.

And then I screamed at the top of my lungs: "Liz, stop it!" And incredibly, I did. The anxiety stopped. My inner voice slid into calmness, and so did I.

After some time I got up and somehow found the strength to make some of my dreaded phone calls. It was like practice for the most challenging conversations, the ones with my kids. And later with Sam.

"Aunt Lucy, it's Liz."

"Liz, so good to hear from you. It's been a while. How are you?"

This was tougher than expected. I was trembling. How does one deliver bad news?

"I moved to California because I'm dying." Once again, I had said it. What followed was the dreaded silence. I waited. Nothing.

"I'm sorry, there's no easy way to say this," I continued. Why was I apologizing for having to die?

"I don't know what to say." I heard the quiver in her voice. "Do you want us to come out there?"

"No," I shouted. "I need to do this on my own. I just wanted to let you know I love you."

"We love you too. Please let us know how we can help." There was a pause. "And call again soon."

"I will," I said, knowing that I wouldn't. "Goodbye." And I hang up.

One by one, I called everybody on my list. The calls were brief and to the point. Their responses varied. In the end, most people simply don't know what to say when you tell them you're dying. With all of them, it was the same; there was an initial moment of silence, followed by the sadness in their voices, combined with some relief that I didn't want to turn it into a long and awkward conversation.

In the afternoon my nausea and dizziness, which came in waves, lifted and eventually disappeared. So, I drove to the beach where I could escape into my favorite moments: observing the seagulls, feeling the ocean breeze, and walking. Today my "walk" consisted mostly of sitting in the sand, watching the waves, and thinking about how fast my feelings for Sam developed, and I wondered if it's possible to love another person without building a solid foundation. How much has my sickness affected the decisions I've made?

And sometimes, I thought of Pete and my old life and New York.

Now as I write this, I'm back at home, and I feel like doing nothing. The house is too quiet, and that old unavailing sensation of loneliness and resignation has shown up, unannounced and unwanted. This time, I'm going to make it stop. I can't waste my precious time wallowing in self-pity. "Fuck being sick." I said that so loud, it startled me.

**Self-pity** [ ˈˌself ˈpidē ] — noun: *excessive, self-absorbed unhappiness over one's own troubles*

A little later a thought crossed my mind, and I remembered the bamboo box. The bamboo box I found days ago on the bookshelf. It must be still stuffed under the pillows.

With newfound energy, I made my way to the library

and searched in between the cushions. And there it was, exactly where I had left it. I laughed, mainly because I wasn't sure what I was doing. And once again, I felt a little guilty for wanting to open a box that doesn't belong to me.

# DAY 76
## FEBRUARY 10 | HOME

Two things happened. First, Susan called and declared that she'll visit as soon as she can and that I should prepare myself because from now on she will check in with me multiple times a day. And that she doesn't give a fuck if I like it or not. All of this made me smile and think about how lucky I was to have found a friend like her. That's why I waited for Susan to help me decide what to do with the bamboo box. (I knew she would love the challenge.)

And the second thing was that last night, once again, Sam surprised me. Once in a while I have to pinch myself to make sure that he's real, and not some figure born out of my imagination.

Our phone conversation began with him asking me about a hundred times if I felt better, and me assuring him that I did. This was followed by him telling me he would see me the next day, which wasn't true because he showed up around midnight and almost gave me a heart attack.

He blindfolded me and led me around the house

onto the terrace. It's incredibly unsettling not to see. With my bare feet, I felt the coldness of the stone floor followed by the unevenness of the wooden floor, and the slight breeze caressing my hair mixed with Sam's breath on my neck as he whispered, "Do you trust me?"

I didn't answer, but I was thinking, *What a silly question.* I don't think I've ever trusted anyone more than I trust Sam. I would jump off a cliff if he asked, knowing that somehow he would end up catching me.

His fingertips gliding along my back made me shiver as he piloted me to my favorite chair. Jazz music filled the garden, blending with the rhythm of my beating heart. Then I felt his lips on mine as he slowly removed the scarf from my eyes.

The first thing I saw was my garden lit up with candles outlining one big heart made of roses. The table in front of me was adorned with lightly scented rose petal candles and delicately displayed finger food. Everything was small and delicate, almost too exquisite to eat. Everything was so gorgeous, including Sam.

I couldn't help but ask, "Are you always this thoughtful?"

"Are you asking me if I'm romantic?"

"Yes. Romantic, attentive, charming."

He laughed, "Not always. Just with you, Lizzie. Just with you."

Despite being sick, I felt lucky. I'm experiencing love in a way that only a few people do. And now I will take this night with me wherever I go.

# DAY 77
### FEBRUARY 11 | HOME

Susan knocked at my door, unannounced as usual. On the phone, she repeatedly had told me she would come to visit the next days, but I had no idea when. And here she was! I noticed early on that Susan doesn't follow any conventional rules. She's a free spirit.

That's why quite often, to my delight, she just appears.

So, there she was, standing in my doorway.

"I had the most stubborn and annoying client this morning," she declared. "And if that wasn't enough, he also had the most atrocious taste."

She kissed me on the cheek and rushed towards the kitchen. I followed her, suppressing my laughter.

"I won't have a scotch, even though I feel like one. Badly! But it's before noon, I shouldn't."

"Water?" I asked.

"Oh, fuck it. Just give me the scotch."

I reached for a glass and the scotch bottle.

"And that moron asked me if I knew any young, pretty women. I mean, who am I?"

"And?"

"Of course not. The guy is stingy and tacky. A fatal combination."

I wasn't sure if she was pretending that we never had the conversation about me dying.

There was a pause, and I asked, "Do you ever have any regrets?"

Susan laughed, "Never! It's such a waste of time. I try to live my life to the fullest. Every day."

And just like that, I discovered: *That's part of the secret of life.*

**Regret** [ rəˈgret ] — noun: *a feeling of sadness, repentance, or disappointment over something that has happened or been done*

*For Susan: Thank you for all the incredible moments you've brought into my life, and for all the memories you're still providing me with as I'm writing this. As I already mentioned, one of my few regrets is that we met so late in my journey. Still, I'm immensely grateful that our paths crossed. How ironic: If I weren't dying, I would have never looked for a home in LA and, most likely, we would have never met. And I would have never met Sam. That's why meeting you, my dear friend, has been one of the best things in my life.*

Susan and I sat in the garden, enjoying delicious vanilla-caramel tea, one of my favorites, and chocolate cake with whipped cream (I just nibbled) that Susan had brought from a tiny bakery called *Sugar*, when I remembered to show Susan the bamboo box.

"I have to show you something," I shouted while already on my way to the library to get the box. Once back out in the garden, I placed the box on the table in front of Susan.

"Pretty!" she exclaimed. "What's inside?"

"I don't know. It's not mine."

"Whose is it?" Susan asked.

"I found it in the library. It might be Emma's or George's."

"Why didn't you open it?"

"I'm not sure… I mean…" I said.

"Don't be silly. They're both dead. And the kids don't give a damn."

And without hesitation, she tried to open it. But she couldn't.

Then she lifted the box and examined it from every angle. "It's a mystery box," she said.

"It's what?"

"We need to move pieces around to open it. Kind of a clue box."

For one hour, we moved small pieces of the box from left to right and from up to down. And just when I was about to give up, the lid sprang open.

"Finally!" Susan exclaimed. "And look at this."

The box was filled with postcards from all over the world. They all began with, "My darling E" and ended with "M."

"One thing is certain; M doesn't stand for George!" Susan exclaimed.

I was baffled. Now I really need to get back into "The Shack."

# DAY 78
## FEBRUARY 12 | HOME

In "The Shack," Sam was studying me as we looked through a mountain of papers left behind by Emma. I pretended to concentrate on the papers, but all I could think about was that I had to tell Sam about my cancer. I should (there it is again, that word *should*) have told him from the beginning. It tormented me.

"It's hard to think that Emma might have loved another man," Sam said.

"Not 'might.' After reading her letters, it's obvious she loved 'M.' It looks as if they went on vacations together and he also was with her at book events."

Sam held up a letter. "And what about this? Undoubtedly, it's a love letter she wrote for George." He read, "My darling George, Paris is not the same without you, and I restlessly stroll the streets trying to remember all the fun we had here."

"Maybe they had a love triangle like Sartre and de Beauvoir. Emma clearly loved two men."

"How many men can you love, Lizzie?" Sam asked.

I didn't answer his question. Instead, I took a big breath. This was the moment.

"Sam... I... I am not... I have to..." I heard something. A knock, followed by Susan's voice, and I saw her face trying to peek through the glass window.

"Hello, lovebirds. I don't want to walk into a situation that would embarrass all of us."

Not waiting for a reply, she entered and plopped into the only armchair. There was a sadness in her eyes when she looked at me. Still, she pretended to be happy. Susan told me earlier how busy she was, and I'm sure the only reason she came over today was to check on me. That's when I knew everything had already changed.

Before I was living, and now I'm dying.

"By the way, why did I see Julia walking towards Sharquay's door with a ton of shopping bags?" she asked, looking from me to Sam while winking with one eye.

I didn't know, but I would find out.

For a second, I had been so close to telling Sam. Damn! With every day that passes, it's getting more complicated. I loathe hurting him. And I'm terrified of losing him. How can he ever forgive me from keeping the truth from him? And now I hate myself for being so selfish, just because I can't imagine my last days without him. I want to cry. Any control I ever had over my life vanished with my sickness, and I hate that I'm dying. I HATE IT SO MUCH!

# DAY 79
### FEBRUARY 13 | THE BEACH

Last night, I finally calmed down while I was lying in Sam's arms in our new hammock, the one he had built for me. I pretended not to see how he was looking at me. I was prepared to answer all his questions. But he didn't ask me anything.

Maybe, deep down, he senses that this isn't a fairy tale with a happy ending.

This morning the Malibu ocean air was crisp, and I enjoyed every step, feeling the sand below my feet and between my toes. My new medication had kicked in, and even though I still felt tired, it had freed me from most of the pain (for now). It also relieved me of some of my anxieties.

I dreaded talking about death when life felt so good. I've only known Sam for six weeks, but in that moment it felt like a lifetime. Sam was walking next to me, his arm around my shoulder, and the warm sun was shining on us as we talked about everything and nothing: the ocean, beaches and dogs.

There would never be a right moment for this, so I stopped and faced him. My mind spun and I can't remember the details except that I exhaled the words, "I'm dying." I waited, but he didn't say anything. Nothing. For a second, I was sure if he had heard me. "I'm dying. I'm sick, and I'm dying." Seagulls shrieked.

There was no way to determine what he was thinking. He only gave the slightest nod, and then he held me in his arms so tight I couldn't breathe. It was as if he knew it all along.

I whispered, "I'm so sorry. I wanted to tell you earlier, but I was so afraid I would lose you."

I waited for him to step back and yell at me or run off and never want to see me again.

Instead, he kissed the top of my head, over and over. As he continued to hold me I melted into his body, and I felt like a fool. I should have known better.

# DAY 80

## FEBRUARY 14 | BEVERLY HILLS

L ike so often in my life, nothing I had anticipated actually occurred. Sam was neither furious with me, nor did he leave me. He made sure to stay close to me and when I woke up this morning, he was still by my side. One look at Sam and all my doubts vanished.

Thinking back, I used to doubt myself too much. I used to doubt my abilities and question if I was worthy of someone else's love. What a waste of time!

**Doubt** [ dout ] — noun: *a feeling of uncertainty or a lack of conviction*

This morning Sam had an appointment with an actor who had donated 1.5 million dollars to *Small Paws & Big Paws* animal shelter.

"I can go another time," he said, putting on his pants.

"Why would you?"

He looked at me, noticeably searching for words. There was a long pause before he said, "I don't want you to be alone."

"That's exactly what you can't do!"

"I can't do what?"

"I don't want any of that pity shit."

And then he broke my heart by looking at me with tears in his eyes and a forced smile. I despised that moment.

"Anyway, I don't have time. I need to see Julia and find out what she was doing at Sharquay's house. And I want her to help me plan a dinner."

If it were up to me, I'd be with my kids every second. But that's not how it works. They have responsibilities, friends, work, studies. I don't want to disrupt their lives. At least not yet. The very life they are living right now will be the one that will comfort them when I'm gone.

Since I arrived in LA, I always called at least one of my three, but I refuse to put pressure on them. Luckily for me, Julia had time to meet and knowing that I would spend my day with her exhilarated me. Since an early age, Julia has always appeared to be the most level-headed of the three, but I'm also mindful of her sensitive side.

Before making my way to the French Country Cafe in Beverly Hills, I finished reading one of Emma's books. She was a brilliant writer. A wordsmith! Her descriptions are so vivid, it's almost like watching a movie.

What narrative can I paint for myself? Can I transport myself into a world without pain, into a world where I will live forever?

I saw her standing in the sunlight, transformed from a sweet little girl into a powerful young woman. Julia isn't the stunning beauty Isabella is. With Julia, one has to look deeper. She has dazzling green eyes, wavy dark blonde hair, a deep voice, and a wise soul—there lies all her beauty.

She hugged me for a long time. It was strange. It was different. Usually, her hugs are brief. This one was long and meaningful.

We found an outdoor seat in the shade, ordered food, and talked non-stop. It's always easy to talk to Julia, she's such a good listener.

Eventually, I had to ask. It was important for me to understand her deeper feelings. "Susan came over yesterday," I said.

"I like her a lot." Her words meant a lot to me because I know Susan will be a wonderful role model for Julia when I can't be there for her.

"She told me she saw you going to Sharquay's house."

"Now I like Susan a little less," she laughed.

"And?"

"And what, Mom?"

"Do you like him?" I asked.

There was a long pause because the server interrupted us and we ordered dessert.

After he left, I repeated my question, "So, do you like him?"

"Yep. And I love his daughter." Her face changed, and I saw "love."

"What about…"

"Jeffrey? Let's just say, after we broke up he wasn't exactly heartbroken. He was too old for me anyway."

*And too many kids*, I thought.

We talked and talked, and then we went on a shopping spree. Julia never asks for anything, but I wanted to buy her something beautiful. Something meaningful.

As we contemplated where to go next, out of nowhere, we glimpsed a hidden store in a courtyard with a rusty sign dangling on the front door. The place didn't look too inviting to me, but it did to Julia. It was her afternoon; I wanted to make her happy.

One of my flaws materialized. I had judged too soon. I was wrong about the store. I have to stop that. I have to be more generous with my thoughts.

Indeed, the store was a tucked-away gem filled with colorful, frilly clothes that I'm too old to wear. But they were perfect for Julia. There was jewelry, fun books and all kinds of odd and somewhat useless—but intriguing— finds. I bought Julia a pair of earrings with three dangling emerald drops. When she wears them, she'll remember this afternoon and think of me. She tried on dresses and shoes. I wanted to see her smile forever.

*For Julia: Sweetheart, the way you looked when you talked about Sharquay and his daughter made me think that this is love. You're both so lucky to have found each other. All I see is a kind and generous man, and when (if) the day comes (I believe it will, I have that feeling), you both have my blessing. And you know I'll be there. I'll be there watching over my little girl dressed in white.*

The sun is setting and the sky is almost pink as I'm writing this. I can't stop thinking about life—my kids,

Sam, the gallery, Pete, my friends, and my upcoming dinner party. I want it to be one of those Italian dinners where the entire family sits around one big table eating, chatting and laughing. I need to speak to Susan. I'm sure she'll have some thought on how to make it fabulous.

# DAY 81
## FEBRUARY 15 | HOME

I had a premonition of what will come.

## MY DREAM

Weightless, I floated in a baby blue, brightly lit sky. At first I was alone, and it seemed as if I was there for a long time, until the sky turned darker and a wave, like an ocean wave, approached me. *That's silly!* I thought. *There are no waves in the air.* The wave transformed and became a circle formed out of all the people I've been close to who have died before me. My father was there in his favorite pjs, and my mother was there too. Funny, my mother was her usual emotional self. Then there was my grandmother, my stubborn grandfather smoking a pipe, my lovely sister and a childhood friend who had died in her twenties. They were dancing around me and reaching for me, but I was too far away. I wanted to talk to them and let them know that I love them. A force pulled me in different directions, maybe a wind—not like a hurricane, but more like a breeze—and kept me from moving forward until I woke up screaming.

Next, I felt Sam's arms.

Today it's pouring. Sam is sitting at the desk in the living room working on his book while I sit across the room in a snuggly window nook overlooking the garden. The nook itself was built for relaxing, with its soft pillows and warm blankets. Now and then, I stop writing in my journal and observe the raindrops forming fragile bubbles on the flowers and the leaves of the majestic palm trees—calm, still, unperturbed.

I look up and see Sam studying me.

"Let's fly somewhere exotic. Just for a few days!" he says.

I know he means well. He wants to create special last moments for me. For us.

"All I need is this, here. All I need are my kids and you."

He nods, and somehow I manage to smile. But it all hurts so much.

I continue to stare out the window into my garden, thinking about how spectacular this world is. This world filled with details we too often miss. Love we don't acknowledge out of fear. Love we fail to see at all. How lucky am I that I said "yes," twice. Pete. Sam. Pete. Pete. Pete. Sam. Sam.

# DAY 82
## FEBRUARY 16 | HOME

It was still pouring, so I planned my dinner party. It was important to me to get it right. Whom would I invite? What food would I serve? And what about small gifts? I wanted this to be an unforgettable dinner. I wanted it to be meaningful.

My oncologist increased my medication, and since then I've been forgetting things. All the things I used to remember I have to write down now, which is annoying.

The day passed uneventfully, and I continued to read one of Emma's books titled *Canyon Road*, a story of a wife's disappearance after a dinner party. Thrillers always mix well with love stories.

Soon enough, I will take my own voyage into the unknown. Alone and with no return.

**Unknown** [ˌənˈnōn ] — adjective: *not known or familiar*

With the growing pain ravishing my body, I've been practicing a lot of positive self-talk. It goes something like this, "Don't cry, Liz, not now. Don't let Sam see your tears. Enjoy this time. Live Liz." I can. And I will. I will be strong for my kids. I will be strong for Sam. I have to be.

# DAY 83
## FEBRUARY 17 | MALIBU

The torrential rains finally stalled. The sun poked out from behind the clouds, and Susan came back from San Francisco. She showed up this morning, straight from the airport, to see how I was doing.

"Did you come back early for me?" I asked.

"Of course I did. And like it or not, I'm going to be around a lot from now on."

"Thank you," I whispered as Sam walked into the room. He kissed Susan on the cheek, and they exchanged a glance. Things have definitely changed. And I hate it.

Sam had a meeting this morning, and I'm positive he had asked Susan to come back early to be with me.

All this worrying over me was exactly what I wanted to avoid for as long as possible. Before, I was just Liz. Now I'm Liz who has cancer. But I have to admit, I was grateful not to be alone.

After breakfast, Susan decided we should drive to Malibu to go for our usual walk.

Surprisingly I felt stronger than expected, and we strolled along an empty beach, seemingly into eternity. The vastness of the landscape reminded me of our friendship—never-ending.

It's so easy to be around Susan. We walked, we talked, and we laughed.

"You have no idea what kind of men have crossed my path!" Susan declared.

I could only imagine.

"I'm sure there must have been dozens of men who wanted to be with you," I said.

"I wouldn't say dozens. But there were enough who made me seriously think about it."

Now I was curious. "Was Sam ever one of them?"

"Never! I told you before, I love Sam; the way I love my brother." Thinking of Sam that was difficult to picture.

"Who did you turn down?"

"Well, there was 'Mr. Charming,' who turned out to be married with four kids under the age of ten. Thanks to his wife, I figured this one out after four months of dating him. Then there was 'Mr. Successful.' Eye candy, well-educated, well-dressed, generous."

"No way, he had a wife as well?"

"No! He was a gambler with a big fat zero in his bank account."

I laughed. Susan is the most interesting woman I've ever met.

She continued, "Let's not forget 'Mr. I-Want-You-So-Much,' whom I actually loved for a second. He showered me with attention and lies until he disappeared. Literally. Gone. And now it's Mr. Charles Wilson III." Susan grinned. "I met him at the airport."

"What?"

"Yes."

"Are you serious?"

"Yes. He was sitting next to me, waiting for his flight to Seattle and we got to talking about airport food."

I chuckled while kicking pebbles in the ocean. "Airport food?"

"Of course, not just airport food. He's 65, short, bold, three grown-up kids, one granddaughter, one ex-wife and is a partner of a hedge fund. He splits his time between San Francisco and Brentwood."

"How short?" I asked.

"Short. But I don't care."

"He sounds perfect," I said.

"We'll see. Remember…"

"I know, I know." Mimicking her. "I won't compromise my freedom, but I will adjust." Susan laughed and linked arms with me. "You're doing great, darling."

I can't remember the exact moment, but I'll never forget the way the sand sparkled like a million diamonds in the early afternoon sun when Susan turned to me. All the laughter was gone. We just looked at each other and cried.

After some time, she said, "I think it's time to talk to your kids."

Unable to speak I just nodded, and she squeezed my arm. I must tell them. I know Susan is right. And I have to talk to them <u>now</u> because I'm running out of time.

# DAY 84
### FEBRUARY 18 | SOMEWHERE

I was brushing my teeth when Sam announced, "I have a surprise." He handed me my morning concoction. A new tradition. Sam did a bit of research and now every morning he makes me a kale-spinach-banana-ginger-coconut-protein smoothie infused with flaxseed oil and a Chinese herb with an impossible name to remember. The drink won't save my life, but it gives me more energy and helps me battle the frequent attacks of nausea.

"Put on your favorite sweatpants and sneakers," Sam said.

"Where are we going?"

"Lizzie, if I tell you everything beforehand, then it won't be a surprise." He cuddled me in his arms and kissed me. "Get dressed and let's go."

Sam's old convertible sailed along the empty side roads and the hot, dusty wind on my face eased my panic. I'm not too fond of surprises. I usually only feel secure being in control, and lately I'm everything but.

We drove for about a hundred miles, mostly in

silence. After I told Sam that I'm dying, he became overly concerned. I can't blame him. I would do the same.

Our destination was a gigantic open field. And once I saw the hangar in the distance, it struck me that we were about to skydive. I grabbed Sam's hand out of fear and because I saw my three kids standing in front of a small plane dressed in jumpsuits. They ran towards me, screaming, "Surprise!"

Right then, in that instant, I loved Sam the most. He's making sure I get time with my kids and he's doing it because he loves me.

As we hugged and kissed, I saw Sam taking pictures of us.

"Let's fly like birds," he said as he leaned closer and whispered in my ear, "It's all about creating memories." More than for me, he meant for the kids. And hopefully for him too.

I was terrified at the thought of jumping out of a plane, even though the idea of dying has taken on a different meaning lately. My thoughts were racing and images of parachutes not opening got stuck in my mind. Followed by many other vivid images and I almost peed my pants.

Pressed against Sam thousands of feet in the air, I learned that he had parachuted dozens of times before. The sky was so blue and cloudless as I watched my kids with their instructors jump into the void.

Then it was our turn. By now I was numb with fear when I heard Sam's muffled voice. "Trust me, Lizzie. Let's fly." I spread my arms out like eagle wings as we jumped. We fell, we soared, we fell more, and floated through the sky. And as simply as that, I suddenly found myself a little closer to heaven than to earth.

# DAY 85
## FEBRUARY 19 | HOME

Yesterday I felt great. Today I don't. There's a pattern of good, bad, and awful days emerging. And I don't like it. Time is slipping away, and I often find myself either in utter joy or in a state of paralyzing agony.

Right now, as I'm writing this, I'm leaning towards the latter. I'm sitting in my favorite chair on the terrace while Ethan is digging tiny holes everywhere on my lawn. I watch him, and I wonder what I can do to bring him and Isabella together.

It's strange how life changes. Under normal circumstances, I wouldn't even think about any of this. It wouldn't be relevant. I wouldn't interfere. But now that I'm sick, I must make sure that my kids are happy.

I ruminated on how to get Isabella and Ethan together and concluded that the dinner party will be the best course of action. As if Ethan can hear my thoughts, he's looking in my direction, lifting one flowerpot for my approval. Naturally, I have no idea what flowers he's planting. Still, I give him a thumbs up.

Ethan is such a nice young man—hardworking and wise beyond his years—and I can see him with Isabella. Isabella, my dancer. My sensitive and often emotional girl.

Not much later, I drifted off and ended up sleeping most of the day.

# DAY 86
## FEBRUARY 20 | HOME

Planning my dinner party made me mull over a lot of things. For one, I find it almost funny how much time we lose planning things. We plan our lives and in the end it all turns out differently from what we initially had in mind.

The anticipation of the dinner party put me in a state of 'happy' agitation. I wanted it to be perfect. Who can blame me—after all, this would be the last party I would ever give.

**Party** [ ˈpärdē ] — noun: *a social gathering of invited guests, typically involving eating, drinking, and entertainment*

When I expressed all my concerns to Susan, she casually reminded me that a dinner party isn't such a big deal and that she will make sure everything is flawless.

She assured me, "It's going to be as perfect as it needs to be." I must have looked unsure because she continued, "Don't worry, it'll be easy. All you need is a guest list, delicate china, fresh flowers, scented candles, soft music and delicious food from a celebrity caterer. And you're in luck because I happen to know the right one." Susan always makes me laugh. For her, everything is so easy. How much better would my life have been if I had met Susan years earlier?

"Shouldn't we cook something?" I asked.

"Darling, are you insane? You will not cook. And I'm certainly not cooking. Nobody will care where the food comes from as long as it's delicious." That was that.

I was left with nothing more to do than to take care of the guest list. The plan was to get heaters and have dinner in the garden. The garden is my favorite place. There's always movement—butterflies, snails, humming-birds, crickets.

The garden is like a moving picture. At first glance it appears to look the same each day. But then, one by one, new details surface every time I have a closer look. I only wish I could have spent my life seeing the world the way I see it now—this magnificent, evolving world.

*Matt, Isabella and Julia: Susan taught me one of her many "life lessons" today.* **Nothing needs to be perfect because everything is already as perfect as it needs to be.**

# DAY 87
### FEBRUARY 21 | HOME

Today was a terrible day. Today was the worst day of my life.

Nothing much happened between yesterday and this morning, except that my mood shifted. All day today I was somewhere between panicky and dispirited.

From Emma's desk—now my desk—I saw Sam leaning against a rock. He was deep in conversation with Ethan. While I watched them, I was thinking about having to tell my kids that I'm dying. That's when I began to sob, those deep and grueling sobs that can't be controlled.

I pleaded with the Universe to help me. To heal me. To give me another chance. I needed a miracle. I didn't want to die. I didn't want to say goodbye to my kids. And I couldn't help but wonder where I'll go from here.

I locked myself in the bathroom to be alone until Sam found me and threatened to knock down the door.

"Open the door. Please, Lizzie, talk to me."

"My kids. I need to talk to my kids."

"You will. But first, please open the door."

After some time alone, I flung it open and buried myself in his arms. Sam held me for a long time. "Do you want me to call the kids and ask them to come to see you?"

All I could do was nod in between all the crying.

The second I saw my kids entering the house, their faces questioning why they were summoned on such short notice, I lost it. I did exactly what I had promised myself I wouldn't do. I cried in front of them. Sam put his arm around me, or at least I think he did; I felt too numb to be sure. But I know I saw him leave the room to give us space.

As I looked at my kids, my heart stopped.

"Mom, you're scaring us," Julia said.

It was time. Nothing could make this easier.

"I'm sick," I whispered.

Isabella's eyes watered instantly. "What do you mean, Mommy?" She hadn't called me 'Mommy' in years.

"I'm so sorry," I said.

Matt came over to hug me and I held him tight.

"Mom, what does this mean?" he asked.

"You are not dying!" Julia exclaimed. Or was it a question? Now she was crying as well.

I nodded. I couldn't speak. My throat closed. I gasped for air. I couldn't breathe. This was far worse than I had predicted. I tried to swallow and was grateful when Sam reentered the room and handed me a glass of water. We all stared at each other, unsure what to say next. There isn't much else to say when someone announces their upcoming death. There's no hope left.

Then I held my kids, one by one, the way I used to

for so many years and I answered all their questions about my cancer, my doctor, and my medication. Then I told them how much time I have left. I guessed.

At last, my so very down-to-earth Julia—*Julia, I hope you know how extraordinary you are*—asked, "What is it you want, Mom? What can we do?" And my answer was simple. I wanted normalcy. After all, I wasn't dead yet.

Once Sam and I were alone again, I understood how essential it had been to have him there today. Being with us today, Sam had bonded with the kids and in the most gracious, Sam-like way, he had let them know—without words—that if they want him to, he would be there for them. And with no resentment, jealousy or doubt, they accepted this man, this stranger, into their lives.

After everybody left, I took a valium and I fell asleep cocooned in blankets, sitting in what was once Emma's favorite chair.

This was my worst day.

# DAY 88

## FEBRUARY 22 | HOME

S am's voice sounded to me like it was coming from underwater. What was I doing underwater? Was this a dream?

"Lizzie, it's noon." Sam touched my arm.

I blinked and saw his face right in front of mine. He kissed me on my forehead, and everything that had happened yesterday rushed back to me. Granted, I didn't want to go there.

After taking a long bath, I joined Sam in the living room. He sat on the floor, surrounded by dozens of photos for his book.

"Which one do you like best?" he asked.

I sat down next to him and looked at the captivating snapshots of dolphins in open water and other undersea life. There was one photo in particular I loved: a dolphin captured in mid-air, the light reflected on the striking animal, before diving back into the deep of the ocean.

"This one." I pointed to it. And I remembered another small box I had found. Emma must have loved boxes. They surface everywhere in the house and "The Shack."

Sam needed to work, so I went to get the box and sat on the terrace. Surrounded by the twittering chatter of bluebirds and the humming of bees, I felt at home. The beauty of the palm trees, lilies and orchids was calming as I sipped my tea. Then—this time without hesitation—I opened the box and pulled out a yellowish paper, thinned by time. My heartbeat quickened in anticipation of what I might find as I laid the paper out in front of me. It was a list dated December 31$^{st}$, 1962, written almost sixty years ago. It read:

Travels with M.
1952 — Masala Dabba from India
1953 — Papyrus from Egypt
1954 — Silver Bracelet from Thailand
1955 — Small Painting from Italy
1956 — Origami Kimono Doll from Tokyo
1957 — Wooden Kiwi from New Zealand
1958 — Lacquer Jar from Vietnam
1959 — Ryijy Rug from Finland
1960 — Boomerang and Kangaroo with Baby from Australia
1961 — Chop Sticks from Hong Kong
1962 — And from San Diego, the most precious gift, M's typewriter

I couldn't believe that Emma would leave this list in a box that anyone could find, especially George. Or did she place the list in the box after George's death? Once more, Emma's story had added yet another layer and meaning to the house. It was indisputable that M had played a significant role in her life. Had Emma loved him more than George? Or maybe she had loved both men equally? And while I was studying the list thoroughly, I understood that I had become the last witness of Emma's love story. A woman who had lived to be ninety-six. A woman who had lived in this house and sat in this chair. Her life, in so many ways, interlaced with mine. With only one difference: both men she had loved died years before her.

# DAY 89
## FEBRUARY 23 | SANTA MONICA

Sam left early this morning. My news—although he pretends it isn't so—put his life in disarray. After a light breakfast—over the past weeks, I've gradually lost my appetite—I pulled out the list I had found yesterday. It was one way to keep my mind busy with something other than sad thoughts.

What on earth was a Masala Dabba? I had to look it up and determined that it was a spice box. I had a hunch that I would find these objects somewhere in the house or shack, which led me to call Susan.

She was in the middle of her weekly spa treatment: facial, mani-pedi, a 90-minute massage. Excited, I wanted to tell her in person about the list and about an idea I had, mainly because I wanted to see her reaction. So, I agreed to meet her in Santa Monica at Shutters.

Shutters is a fabulous getaway hotel—romantic and exclusive, with a spectacular view of the Santa Monica boardwalk, the beach and the Pacific Ocean—available only to those lucky enough to be able to pay the steep price.

I sat on the hotel's small outdoor dining terrace in the sun, tanning. And yes, I can tan as much as I want. Before skin cancer can get me, I'll be long dead. It's almost funny to think that now I'm permitted to do everything I want because nothing can hurt me anymore. What a paradox!

Susan stormed onto the terrace loaded with shopping bags, waving, smiling, and almost knocking over one of the waiters who looked like he just stepped out of a magazine.

"Stunning. Did you see him?" she said so loudly that everybody could hear her.

"I'm not blind," I laughed.

"Anyway, nobody can compete with Charlie." And she winked at me.

She threw all her bags on an empty chair before kissing me on both cheeks.

"I can't figure out what is so important that you can't tell me on the phone."

"Maybe I wanted an excuse to see you," I said.

"For a second, I thought maybe you got a quick divorce and you're going to marry Sam." I laughed. "I don't have to marry Sam to be happy." I took a deep breath, redirecting my thoughts to a far less important subject.

"I found a list," I said.

"What list?"

"One that exhilarated me and, I'm not exactly sure why, but it made me think I would be crazy if I didn't buy *the* house."

Susan stared at me, open-mouthed. She looked as if she would faint, but then I heard an unearthly shriek, followed by, "What house? Your house?" By then, everybody at Shutter's was following our conversation.

"Yes, my house, Emma's house." And I quickly added, "If I can afford it."

Years ago, I inherited a sum of money from my father and never touched it. There was some money from the gallery as well. Susan immediately assured me that the price would be right because she would find a way to make it happen.

I don't doubt that she will. This house will live on. One day, this house will be filled with joy, love and laughter. I know it. I can see it.

I closed my eyes, and as the sun caressed my face, I envisioned my kids and my grandkids playing in the garden. Sam was there too.

# DAY 90
## FEBRUARY 24 | HOME

A lot of good things happened today.

It all began with Susan coming over to watch the sunrise and enjoy an early breakfast with me. She was worried about me, and she wanted to make sure that I ate enough and that I wasn't alone when Sam wasn't here.

"You don't have to cancel all your appointments for me," I said.

"Darling, shut up! First of all, I didn't cancel 'all' my appointments. Secondly, I need some free time, and I don't need the money. So, here I am." And that was the end of the conversation.

Sam left to pick "something" up, and I had a feeling he wasn't telling me everything.

Anyway, while Susan and I were sitting on the terrace sipping coffee and nibbling on some lavender chocolate chip cookies, I showed her the list I mentioned yesterday.

"Fascinating. Have you found all the objects?" she asked.

"I haven't looked for them yet."

"Why haven't you?" She exploded into laughter. "You've waited for me. Oh Liz, this will be fun. We can have our own little scavenger hunt." And before I could say anything, she added, "Now we can be sure there is another love story in this house other than yours."

She took the list from me. "And what on earth is a Masala Dabba?"

"It's a spice box."

"You didn't know that, did you?"

"No. I looked it up," I laughed.

And we skimmed through the list.

"Let's start with the easier items," Susan said. "Like the Ryijy rug from Finland and the painting from Italy."

We walked around the house and found the rug in the hallway leading to the bedroom. It was woven in a specific way and Susan googled it to make sure we had found the right one.

The painting of a staircase leading up to a small bridge surrounded by an array of colorful flowers was hanging in the bedroom. In the right-hand corner it said, "Venice, 1955." The year Emma and M visited there. I had never heard of the artist, despite being quite familiar with European painters. On the way to the bedroom, Susan had spotted the wooden kiwi and I discovered that it's a bird, and not a fruit. It happens to be New Zealand's national bird.

The stuffed kangaroo with a baby in its pouch sat on the bedroom's bookshelf. I wondered if Emma had placed these objects around the house before or after George's death.

"Let's look for the silver bracelet," Susan said. "It's probably in her jewelry box."

"I still cannot comprehend why none of her kids

claimed any of her possessions," I said. "I mean we're talking about jewelry here."

"Anger… resentment. Who knows what goes on in people's heads? I don't think we'll ever get the answer, but your daughters will look dazzling when they wear Emma's jewelry," she chuckled. "Assuming she's hidden any around here."

The jewelry box was a small safe tucked in the wall in the back corner of the walk-in closet.

"We won't be able to open it," I said.

Susan pushed me aside. "Of course we can." She rolled the lock up and down. And just as I thought—*of course we can*—the safe magically opened in front of my eyes.

In Susan's world, there is nothing she cannot do. Except save me. She can't do that.

"Surprise!" she exclaimed. "All zeros."

Inside we found not only the silver bracelet, but also diamond rings, necklaces, more bracelets and a pair of stunning ruby-studded earrings. Magnificent antique items, some gold, some silver. Underneath all the pieces, Susan pulled out an envelope that read, "*Kids*." No names.

It was strange to think why she wouldn't put names on the envelope.

"What are we going to do?"

"I'll reach out to one of her kids and let them know about the letter and the jewelry box," Susan said.

"Great idea." And the box with all its contents went straight back into the safe.

"And if I don't hear anything…" There was a tiny pause. "Then I'll give it all to your kids."

Holding back tears, I blurted out. "Yes."

Susan touched my arm and whispered, "I'm so sorry, Liz."

"Me too." And while swallowing my tears I asked, "What's next?"

"Let's search along the bookshelves for the chopsticks, the jar, the boomerang and the Masala Dabba…" She paused. "I don't think she would have placed it in the kitchen and used it."

"Right," I said. "And there's also the origami doll."

We went from room to room and found everything but the boomerang, the typewriter, and the papyrus. Every time we saw an object from the list, we performed a small victory dance. I love Susan. She has a rare talent for making other people happy.

"It's going to be almost impossible to find the papyrus," I said. "And the boomerang might be together with the typewriter in 'The Shack.'"

We agreed to look for these objects another day. Susan had a late afternoon appointment, and I was getting tired.

Lying on the sofa, I heard whimpering coming from outside. I got up and ambled through the garden, searching for the source of the noise, and when I turned around, I saw Sam standing right behind me. He startled me and I shrieked.

He was holding the smallest yellow lab in his arms— a puppy wearing a red ribbon around his neck.

Everything about the picture was sweet: the puppy, Sam, and the grin all over his face as he struggled to hold the fidgety little barking thing. I cried again. Who can blame me! Sam pulled me into his arms, and we stood like that for quite some time with our adorable puppy squeezed between us. This could have been the perfect beginning, if only.

# DAY 91
## FEBRUARY 25 | HOME

This morning I woke up to Floppy licking my face, and I instantly forgot about all the nausea and pain I've been feeling.

We named him Floppy after his huge and floppy ears. He was so adorable as he circled on top of the bed to find the perfect spot to cuddle up next to me. Feeling his warm body next to mine, I drifted back into a half-sleep, thinking about Sam and the way he had reacted after hearing about me being sick. He hadn't blamed me for not telling him earlier, even though he had every right to do so. My whole life, I had tried to be honest and forthcoming, and when it had mattered the most, I had failed.

**Fail** [ fāl ] — verb: *to be unsuccessful in achieving one's goal*

As I'm writing this, Sam is in the kitchen preparing dinner. Not to sound dramatic, but I can feel the end approaching. These will be our last weeks together, if not days. These will be the days when everything happens for the last time. It's overwhelming. I want to stop time, but I can't. I want to be "me" again. All of me.

Sam is trying so hard to behave as normal as possible, but his face shows every emotion he's going through and it breaks my heart.

My kids take turns to spend time with me now. In a split second their world has changed, and I shudder at the thought of them facing all of this because of me. I hate that they have to see me like this. Why me? This isn't fair. It isn't fair at all.

*Sam: When you read this, please remember that you brought nothing but love and joy into my life. So unexpectedly.*

*On my last day, in my last hour, I hope we will think about how lucky we were to have this time together at all. Don't feel bad. Not long ago, I had so many regrets, but looking back I've been so lucky—so lucky to meet Pete (He'll need answers about the last few months of my life. Maybe you can give him some), to love my kids, and to love you.*

# DAY 92

FEBRUARY 26 | HOME AND MALIBU

## ANOTHER DREAM

I strolled along a narrow, serpentine path that led me through a garden filled with bright flowers. Each of them had an individual and intense scent: citrus, vanilla, musk, coconut. It was so potent; it became confusing. I rushed past the flowers until I reached a roaring waterfall that formed a pond at the bottom. I sauntered along its edge until I came to a steep stair-case—intimidating stairs made of jagged rocks—and it took me some time before I reached the top. The colors changed to a much darker shade and the world around me spun. I stood on a bluff overlooking a vertiginous descent. I began to shake and right then, the rocks, trees and flowers turned black. Somebody was screaming. Then I woke up.

Sam sat next to me on the edge of the bed, both his hands cupping my face. "Lizzie, you had a nightmare." He caressed my sweaty hair, looking worried.

"Did I scream?" He nodded. "I'm sorry."

He pulled me into his arms.

After getting ready, I went to find Sam. He was in the garden gathering wood for the fireplace.

"I'm feeling better," I told him, and it was the truth. I felt better than usual. Not as weak. "Can we do something fun?"

"Of course we can."

"And Sam…," he looked straight at me. "Let's pretend, just for one more day, that I'm not sick."

Swallowing hard he nodded, and I noticed how he forced a smile before turning away from me.

Today was just for Sam and me. Around lunchtime, we drove out to Malibu. The beach was empty except for a couple of surfers and flocks of seagulls that swooped in on us from time to time. I took it all in: the salty air, the stones, the sun, the sand, the birds, the roar of the ocean, the wind and Sam. Most of the time, we were lost in our thoughts. There was no need to say anything.

It was peaceful. My world now revolves entirely around the people I love. I have no more desire to achieve goals, plan vacations, please people, work harder or renovate my new home. Now, it's all about love. It's almost as if my world stands still while I—nothing more than a tiny grain, a molecule, a particle—prepare to dematerialize.

My world is changing, and I can't pretend any longer that it isn't happening. I need time to be with the people

I love. I need time to say goodbye. I need time, but time is slipping away.

At one point, Sam put his arm around my shoulder and I reached for his hand and held it so tight it must have hurt him. But he never said anything.

We came home after sunset and unloaded some groceries we had bought at a farm stand on our way home. Then we cooked dinner. Well, Sam cooked dinner—I sat in my favorite chair on the terrace. I was exhausted, but I didn't want to spoil our day. So, I pretended to read even though I was napping.

Later we ate the most delicious mixture of fresh farm vegetables, which Sam had roasted in olive oil, chicken, and for dessert we had fresh berries with whipped cream. To my surprise, I was hungry for the first time in weeks. After losing most of my taste buds and my appetite, eating had become more a chore than a pleasure.

After dinner Sam carried me up the stairs, whispering in my ear, "I love you."

# DAY 93
## FEBRUARY 27 | HOME

Sam's body was warm and I inched closer to him. His arms were cradling me, silently saying, I'm here. As hard as I fought it, this morning, melancholy took over my mind and I spiraled into an abyss. It felt as if weeks had turned into days, and I tried to figure out how many days I had left. It became painfully clear that I would never find a satisfying answer. All the crying, praying, and screaming would not help. I lost hope.

Susan, my angel, appeared on my doorstep, as always when I needed her the most. She helped me out onto the terrace where we sat quietly, and she held my hand. There was a slight breeze and the palm trees bent gently from left to right. A squirrel jumped from one tree to the next. At last Susan broke the stillness by asking about something I had been contemplating for the past week.

"Liz, do you want to leave letters or notes to Sam and the kids?"

"Yes."

She looked straight at me. I love this about her. Susan never hides, nor does she ever pretend. She simply said, "I think it's time." She was right. It was time.

After Sam left to take care of some abandoned puppies, Susan prepared a light dinner for us. She dislikes cooking. In her opinion, other people know how to cook much better, so why should she do it?

By that time, I was spent by everything that had happened. And for some bizarre reason, I wished to end all of it right then. It seemed there was no point in dragging it out any longer. After all, I'm doing nothing but hurting people I love. And it won't get any easier.

I poked around my plate pretending to eat, then I reached for Susan's hand. "There will never be enough words to thank you."

"Stop that. You would do the same for me."

"All the useless crying. I'm tired of it myself, but I can't stop it."

Susan looked straight at me. "Darling, I understand, thirty years of therapy." That was the first time today I laughed, thinking that the therapy was working well for Susan.

"Liz, darling, as excruciatingly difficult as this is for you, let me help you focus on the good moments."

I nodded.

"You once told me about your 'Happy Moment' list. I think it's time to work on it. I want to see at least a hundred moments on that list. It might help."

I wasn't sure. One hundred. That was a lot.

"Okay, Liz?"

"Okay," I said. "I'll try." If nothing else, I will do it for Susan.

People often enter our lives at the most unexpected moments when we need them the most. Susan undoubtedly came to me when I needed her the most.

# DAY 94
## FEBRUARY 28 | HOME

**Normalcy** [ˈnôrməlsē ] — noun: *the condition of being normal; the state of being usual, typical, or expected*

Normalcy is all I want, but this morning I seriously doubted that it could be an option.

I strolled through my home because I felt restless and weak, and I needed to distract myself from my increasingly negative thoughts.

The meaning of this house has shifted in my mind. When I first stepped in the door, I thought this was my house. But now I'm certain this will be my kids' house. Sam's house. A place with history—although most of it isn't mine—where they can gather and remember me.

Since I woke up, for no apparent reason, I've been feeling the need to connect with Emma on some higher level. And I have no clue how to do that. Maybe among the many artifacts around the house there's some link that will help us form a bond.

Over the past few months, while taking in all the details of life, I've certainly gained some knowledge on how to live. But I have the feeling I'll never understand how to die.

Earlier this morning, Susan had called.

"Liz, you won't believe it."

"What?"

"Are you sitting down? I just got off the phone with some attorney who represents Emma's kids." Susan more shrieked than talked. "The price for the house includes everything. I mean, everything! The artwork, the books, the jewelry—all yours. They don't want the letters."

"I can't believe it," I said.

"I told you," she laughed. "It's crazy."

"I'm repeating myself here, but how is it possible that not one of Emma's kids cares about her possessions?"

"Liz, there are just some things in life we can't explain. And this is one of them." Susan said. "And who cares?"

Do I care? I picture Emma, and nothing makes much sense. It's as if there's a missing puzzle piece.

Wherever I go, if I mention that I'm living in Emma's house, everybody has something nice to say about her.

*Hey Emma, up there, I care! I will see you soon and give you the full report.* Will she be one of the people waiting for me? Will there be anybody waiting for me? I hope so.

# DAY 95

## MARCH 1 | HOME AND DR. KATZ

I love the antique chaise lounge in the hallway, the one I'm sitting on right now while writing this. On the other side of the long corridor stands an impressive stone statue of a mother holding a child in her arms, and an alluring painting by some unknown artist portraying a hill overlooking the ocean. It looks like the one I dreamed about last night.

### YET ANOTHER DREAM

I was leaping down ancient steps carved into stone. One by one, step by step, I moved towards Sam, my eyes on him, smiling. At the bottom Sam stood still, looking up at me, his hair tousled by the wind. Dressed in navy pants and a white shirt, his broad shoulders and upper-arm muscles were clearly visible. Sam looked so young as he stretched out both his hands towards me. My eggshell white silk dress glittered in the fading sun like a million diamonds. I'm not sure if I ever reached him, but I'm sure he was there and that I was in my wedding dress.

I woke up feeling sick. I barely made it to the bathroom before vomiting all over the place. It was the ugly, violently ill kind of vomiting. The room reeled and my body trembled. Then I fainted.

I remember nothing between that and hearing Sam's voice. "It's okay, Lizzie. It's okay." We were on our way to Dr. Katz. I was half sitting, half lying on the front seat, and the pain was unbearable. It came in waves and I thought I would faint again.

Sam told me he had found me lying on the bathroom floor. While carrying me to the car, he had debated between driving me to the hospital or to my doctor, whom he had called while driving high speed down Coldwater.

In a hospital, I would have ended up in the ER, probably waiting for my turn, and then explaining my extremely long medical history. Driving me to Dr. Katz was the better choice. And seriously, what could have been the worst scenario? Exactly! I could have died a little earlier.

But I didn't. And now, here I was lying in Dr. Katz's office, asking him the question every doctor dreads the most.

"How long do I have?" I asked.

"I understand it is imperative for you to know," he said. He's not the type who avoids tough questions. I nodded. "But I can only make an educated guess based on my experience."

"Okay," I took a deep breath, "then guess."

His eyes never left mine. From the beginning I had liked his straightforwardness.

"Three weeks, maybe a little less," he said. And I think he's about right.

Three weeks. Twenty-one days.

My kids. I need time with them. I need to let Pete know that I forgive him. I need time with Sam. I squeezed Sam's hand and he took me in his arms. That's when I could feel his tears on my face.

# DAY 96

## MARCH 2 | HOME AND A DRIVE

This morning I woke up feeling depressed. Thanks to the new medication Dr. Katz prescribed me, I felt a little better physically, but a dark cloud had descended on me. To shake the ominous feeling, I strolled through my garden to find something to put on my 'Happy Moments' list. That's when I saw the small Zen garden Ethan had built for me. When did all of that happen? There was the Buddha Sharquay had given me as a present, standing next to a babbling stone fountain amidst a mini maze with a sign that read: *Liz's Tranquility Garden*.

Now I was sad. Actually, I was mad. One always hears about miracles happening to people. I want to be one of these people. I'm angry and scared. I'm not sure which one comes first.

Sam saw me agitatedly pacing around the garden when he suggested we go for a drive. But I didn't feel like it. Frankly, I wanted to go back to bed and cry or scream and punch something. That's when a thought, *Do you want to live life to the fullest or waste your time feeling sorry for yourself?* shifted my mood entirely.

An hour later, Sam and I drove along Sunset Boulevard towards the Pacific Palisades. The warm wind felt like summer, and I closed my eyes. I must have dozed off because I got startled when we came to a stop.

"Let me show you something beautiful," Sam said, and he took my hand as we walked down a narrow, dusty, winding path to a small, isolated beach cove. I immediately slipped out of my pants and sandals and dipped my feet in the cold water. And just like that, my depression vanished.

The warm sun felt so soothing on my half-naked body and I let the sand sift through my fingers, all while listening to the roar of the ocean. I felt his fingers sliding up and down my back. I felt his gentle kiss.

# DAY 97
## MARCH 3 | HOME

My dinner party is approaching fast and I'm glad. Having this dinner means a lot to me.

Isabella is worried. I saw it in her eyes when she stood in front of my door this morning unannounced holding an enormous fruit basket. That isn't her normal behavior.

For one, it was 7:00 AM, and Isabella never gets up before 10:00 AM unless she has an early class.

And now that I think about it, she's never given me presents other than the occasional birthday card.

She didn't say it, but she's right: I won't need most of those things any longer. Things. We want things so badly—a new dress, an extra pair of shoes (Okay, I admit I love shoes), another coat and useless other objects. In the end, what do these things really mean to us? Nothing. They mean absolutely nothing.

But Isabella, standing in front of my door, meant everything to me—her hugging me the way she did when she was a little girl.

"I love you, Mom. Please don't die," she whispered. That's when my heart broke.

I struggled not to cry. Instead, I touched her hair and said, "Do you have some time? I want to show you something."

"All day." And that was different too. Isabella never has time all day long.

We made some tea and sauntered to "The Shack." On our way, we ran into Ethan, who was pouring sand out of bulky bags.

"Good morning, Ethan. What are you doing?" I asked.

"Good morning," he said. And I saw sparks flying between Isabella and him. I guess I don't know everything after all.

"I'm still working on the maze."

"Thank you for the wonderful tranquility garden. I love it." I said, wondering if Isabella had told him about me being sick. Then I had an idea. "If you have some time, please join us for lunch."

"I would love to." Had it been my imagination, or did he wink at Isabella?

Isabella loved "The Shack" and the fact that Emma had been an author. We searched for the typewriter from the list. It wasn't difficult to find. The typewriter, with an M engraved on the bottom, stood, still covered in dust, between her novels on the top shelf. Who was M? A famous writer? Did George ever meet M? I doubt it. Then again, anything is possible. Can one love two men at the same time? I'm not sure I'll ever be able to answer all these questions. But as Susan said, does it matter?

We also searched for the papyrus but couldn't find it. Maybe it's hidden on one of the bookshelves, and one day one of my kids will find it by chance. I don't care enough anymore to spend my time searching for it. Emma's life is becoming less important to me, as my life feels increasingly more valuable.

When Isabella said, "Mom, Julia is coming over tomorrow and Matt will come on Friday," I knew right then that what I had anticipated had now occurred: my life had changed. My kids were worried, and I had become a patient.

I took Isabella in my arms and whispered, "I know you are going to be okay." I didn't want to let her go.

Thinking about it now, I'm not sure about the sequence of events. But somewhere during lunch, I excused myself and went to prepare coffee. I took my sweet time before reappearing on the terrace with a tray loaded with coffee and almond cookies.

By then, Isabella and Ethan were deep in conversation, strolling around the garden. And just like that, to my delight, I had been forgotten.

I wanted to give them time, so I pretended to read one of Emma's books. All my life I've loved to read, but now, considering that I only have a few weeks left, it seems so unimportant. Then again, words had made me happy my whole life. Maybe true happiness, after all, can be found in the little things.

I glanced at Sam, who had joined us, and he gave me that slight nod of approval. That's when I said, "Ethan, did Isabella tell you we're going to have a dinner party next Tuesday?" Hoping, as I said it, that I would make it until then.

Not waiting for his reply, I asked, "Would you like to join us?"

He smiled. "Absolutely. I would love to." His eyes met Isabella's and despite everything, she suddenly looked happy. She smiled at him. I hadn't seen her smile since before I revealed that I was sick.

# DAY 98

## MARCH 4 | BEVERLY HILLS

The doorbell rang, and I made my way through the living room and along the long hallway leading to the front door. It was Susan and Georgio, her hairdresser.

"I thought if you can't go, then I will bring Georgio to you." I couldn't say anything because she was already striding towards the kitchen.

"Oh, Liz…" Georgio said and hugged me. There's no formula or correct way to handle death. It's complicated, and everybody is doing their best.

While we were sitting on the terrace and Georgio was making my hair "fabulous" I invited Susan to join me tomorrow on what probably will be my last shopping spree. I hope I'll feel well enough to go.

I won't miss shopping, cooking or fancy restaurants, but I will miss my walks and books, my morning drives, laughter and art, my gallery, and the people I love the most—all things that can go on my Good Moments list.

Susan will be one of the people I'll miss and tomorrow will most likely be our last opportunity to spend alone time together. She's been doing so much for me and I would like to do something meaningful for her. Besides, Susan loves to shop.

Susan agreed that my plan to buy gifts for all my dinner guests was "a fantastic idea."

On my list are Julia and Sharquay. He's coming back early from a business trip to join us. He clearly adores Julia and I've never seen her so at peace with another person.

Then, of course, there's Matt and Sebastian. Isabella and Ethan.

"Is Ethan coming?" Susan asked.

"Yes, he is. Yesterday, I had the feeling he and Isabella were hiding something from me. And later, I heard her talking to him about her love for ballet and he looked at her with so much admiration."

"He doesn't strike me as a dancer, which obviously isn't the point," Susan laughed.

"How can you explain to a twenty-year-old what love means? It's such an abstract concept."

"What does it mean to you, Liz?"

"Love?"

"Not love. But Isabella and Julia finding love."

"It means… You know, before I…" I wasn't yet prepared to say the word in a leisurely conversation. Susan understood and waited until I was ready to continue. "It will be easier for them. You know, not being alone."

Susan reached for my arm and squeezed it hard. Our eyes locked.

"And they will have me. I am going to be here," she said, "for all three of them."

"For their weddings…" I whispered, not able to hold back the tears anymore.

"Don't worry, I'm going to be here to make sure that everybody is okay. And I will spank them if they don't behave." We hugged again, but this time, we also cried.

Susan dabbed her eyes and said, "If it's okay with you, I'm going to bring Charles to the dinner."

I was in the middle of blowing my nose, "Who's Charles?"

"Remember, the man I met at the airport—short, bold, rich." (Of course, I remembered.)

"I want you to meet him. As it turns out, he has a fantastic sense of humor and is very generous."

While sitting in my favorite chair on the terrace, looking through the small box of photos I had brought from New York, listening to the chirping of crickets, I reflected on the importance of love.

More than ever, I believe we live to love. The concept of love—why we love someone and why, when we do, our world suddenly seems to be a different place—is hard to explain. Everything surrounding us appears to be more beautiful: the sounds are sweeter, the colors are brighter, the food tastes better and we feel more attractive.

Somewhere in the distance, a nightingale sang a sweet song and Sam stepped out onto the terrace. He handed me a glass of wine before sitting down next to me. Then he reached for my hand, and we just sat there. Together.

# DAY 99
## MARCH 5 | BEVERLY HILLS

As planned, Susan picked me up and we went on our shopping spree. It was a sunny, perfect 70–degree Californian day. I pretended to feel good. The truth is, I'm rapidly declining. I walk slower; I have no more appetite; I have no strength and I keep forgetting things.

Susan proposed we go to a French bistro first.

"What can be better than French fries and champagne?" I must have looked at her in a funny way because she added, "Sex is better, but this comes very close." An hour later, we were both still giggling as we stepped out on the terrace of the restaurant in our high heels and colorful dresses. *I will miss this*, I thought.

My shopping list was long. Or at least I thought it was until Susan corrected me. "I have shopped for much more in far less time," she said, and I believed her.

*MY SHOPPING LIST*
*Matt — a watch*
*Sebastian — cuff links*
*Charles—just a little something, mainly for being there with Susan*
*(even she has no idea what to get him, this might be a problem)*
*Susan—a bracelet in white gold (I will pretend that it's for one of*
*the girls and let her help me choose)*
*Julia and Isabella—both necklaces with hearts attached to them*
*Sharquay—something golf related (Julia had mentioned that he's*
*picking up golf)*
*Ethan—books on architecture and landscaping, and a new bike (he*
*needs one badly)*
*Sam—a watch with my name and a heart engraved on the inside,*
*and his favorite cotton sweaters in as many colors as I can get them*

Ten, what a great number. We would be ten at the table. In numerology, ten is a divine number that shows the completion of a cycle. How appropriate! I'm about to complete mine.

"Did you bring the photos?" Susan asked.

I reached for my bag and pulled out three envelopes.

"The artist, she's fantastic. You won't be disappointed."

I leaned over and gave Susan a long hug. "Thank you… thank you for everything."

Of course, we ended up buying so much more than just the items on the list. There were dolls, puzzles, crayons and coloring books for Sharquay's daughter, for when she comes over to visit (which now is almost daily). Fun gadgets and bikinis for the girls, T-shirts for the guys, little fun objects that make unusual sounds. And many books I will never read, but the kids and Sam will.

After unloading everything in the car, arms linked and strolling along, Susan turned towards me. As the afternoon sun illuminated her face, she said, "I will miss you, Liz."

My last shopping spree with Susan. Straight away I reminded myself to live in the present, in this moment, and to be grateful for having found a friend like her. And, most definitely, for feeling after all quite well today.

# DAY 100

## MARCH 6 | HOME

I had expected Pete's call. I knew he would contact me eventually. Not knowing anything about me being sick—I had asked the kids not to tell him yet because I wasn't ready for his commiseration—he prattled on while I had the urge to scream and beg him to stop.

"It's not fair what you did, Elizabeth. You could have given me some warning." *He had never before called me Elizabeth.*

"Just the way you did when you went to see all your girlfriends and I was left wondering when you would come home to me?"

"All," he puffed, then quickly added, "Two."

"Believe it or not, you hurt me. You hurt me for so many years and I simply couldn't take it any longer." I whispered, barely moving my lips because I didn't want him to hear me, "I loved you too once. Be happy."

Then he continued to talk about how much money a divorce will cost him and how I could dare to do this to him. Obviously, I never mentioned a divorce. There won't be one. He will be free from me much sooner than he thinks. Physically free. Financially free. Mentally, I'm not so sure. In any case, I couldn't deal with Pete diminishing me for one more second and trying to steal my confidence. So, I hung up.

I felt horrible. I had spent a lifetime with this man, and this was our goodbye. Although the "monumental" love we once had, had long dissipated, there was still the knowledge of our past and the life we had built together.

Thinking back, I wondered if all those years ago I should have made a different choice. Now, I wonder if I had chosen Pete because he had been the one every girl wanted. In the end, I'm not so sure that I ever had him. Isn't it true that most people are just loaned to us for a brief time? Most enter our lives for a short period, while few stay forever.

All of this was such a long time ago. Too many regrets! It's time to let go. No more sorrow about the past. In spite of everything, I am grateful. I loved Pete for a long time. And in some way, I will always love him, because without him, I would not have had Julia, Matt and Isabella. I wouldn't have had the most fantastic time raising them.

I need to talk to the kids. Maybe there'll be a way for them to rebuild their fragile relationship with their father.

*For Pete: In case you ever read this. I hope you'll find happiness again. I do. Take good care of yourself. I forgive you and I love you.*

# DAY 101
## MARCH 7 | HOME

The day came sooner than expected that I was confined to my bed. I watched all kinds of uplifting movies and Sam checked in on me every fifteen minutes. Obviously, that wasn't how I had envisioned my day to go. But I had another fainting spell in the living room this morning. The thump itself was forceful when I missed the rug and hit the wood floor. Sam heard it while preparing breakfast in the kitchen. (Thump—lump, it rhymes. That's weird.) My thoughts are confused. Maybe I hit my head harder than I thought.

While I'm writing this, and still feeling slightly dizzy, I'm also about to watch my fourth movie. Sam insisted on turning this into a fun movie marathon day with ice cream and potato chips. The food was for Sam. If at all, these days I only eat tiny portions. Frankly, I'm amazed that my stomach doesn't rebel more. The new medication did partially restore my appetite, and I was instructed (as if it were that easy) not to lose any more weight. I'm trying. Smoking weed helps. I had forgotten how relaxing it can be to sit in bed, watch movies and smoke a joint.

Watching a great movie has the same positive effect on me as reading a brilliant book. I'm transported to worlds and places I would never go to otherwise. I meet people who make me laugh, intrigue me, annoy or scare me. Movies and books are the greatest escapes.

My reading list has now been long forgotten. Instead, once in a while, I leaf through one of Emma's thrillers.

With reading less comes the distinct feeling that my journey is ending. I've stopped bargaining with the Universe. That doesn't mean that I don't want to live. I want to live. I want to run in wet sand. I want to twirl in my garden. I want to watch many more movies with my kids. I want to see the world. I want to go back to Paris. I want to read more books. I want to curl up in Sam's arms.

"Hey, you up there, whoever you might be, do you have a widescreen and lots of popcorn?" I shouted. And then I cried. I'm scared. I'm afraid of dying.

# DAY 102
## MARCH 8 | HOME

It was past noon, and the clattering of dishes could be heard all the way to my bedroom, while Sam, Susan and Lucinda (Susan's occasional house-keeper, "pearl of the house" as she calls her) were busy arranging my kitchen for our dinner.

I heard Susan yelling, "What are you watching while we're working our asses off?" And she topped it with her warm signature laughter. Earlier, after talking to my doctor, Sam and Susan had forced me to stay in bed and rest. So there I was, scribbling and doodling flowers in my journal while watching Baby Boom.

Such a pointless thing to do, to watch movies, when I know I will die soon. But what else should I do? Lie in bed and think about my upcoming death? My funeral? Everything I did a few weeks ago that seemed so pivotal now seems rather insignificant. The only thing that matters now are the people I love.

I watched two Nancy Meyers movies. Now and then, I drifted off wondering who Nancy Meyers in the real world is. It was a bit of a strange thought. But lately, I've been doing that a lot, thinking about people I'll never meet. Weird!

Susan checked on me and said, "They delivered the special gifts just in time."

Then Matt came over. Then Julia. Then Isabella called.

Sam left to pick up decorations, assuring me that Susan would stay until he returned. Things have changed so much, and not for the better.

Later in the afternoon, I had to use the bathroom, and that's when I decided enough was enough. I made my way downstairs and through the living room, out to the terrace. I heard Susan instructing Lucinda how to pre-prep food for tomorrow. The fresh air and light breeze were precisely what I had been longing for and needing the most. Covered with a cashmere blanket— one more of my latest indulgences—I relaxed into deep breathing. I took it all in: trees, flowers, birds and insects who have had so much less time than me on earth. I wanted to make this moment count.

I just sat there, wrapped up in my blanket and dreams, listening to the birds chirping and waiting for Sam to come home. I wanted to ask him about how he's feeling. He needs to know that he matters and that I'm forever grateful. He had a carefree life before me. And now he has me to…worry about. It bothers me. How can I ever thank him enough for staying with me all the way? This must be love.

When I opened my eyes, Susan was sitting next to me, pouring me a cup of hibiscus tea. Her smile and warmth are two of my best medicines.

We sat for a while before she pulled her chair closer to mine, and with one hand on my arm she looked straight into my eyes and announced, "The attorney just called. The house is officially yours."

"It is?"

Just like that, thanks to Susan and the incredible price she negotiated, Emma's house became Liz's house. I nodded and Susan squeezed my arm as tears rolled down my cheeks. We just sat there watching the sunset—in my house, in my home.

# DAY 103
## MARCH 9 | HOME

Long before sunrise, I sat in my garden cocooned by silence, breathing in the crisp early morning air. I was excited. I couldn't wait, and it was only 4:30 AM. Sam was still asleep along with the rest of the world. Knowing that in just a little while the sun would warm my face, I couldn't stop wondering if I would die in this chair, in this garden, alone.

At precisely 10 AM, Susan stormed into the house loaded with bags containing items that, as she put it, "we absolutely need." In only a few minutes, she unwrapped scented candles, napkins and wind-up toys for the table, along with some obscure items like a small and naked statue of the "God of Love" and another of the "God of Success." There were others whose meaning is still very unclear to me.

The caterer, under Susan's supervision, had taken over the kitchen, and the smell of rosemary, garlic and onion mixed with the sweetness of freshly baked apple pie filled my home. My home. I can't stop repeating these two words. Knowing that I can leave this house to the people I love made me a little giddy, but more importantly, it gave me a sense of tranquility.

From the beginning, Susan had been my partner in crime. I had asked her not to mention the house—I wanted it to be a surprise—and now she was as excited as I was to unveil the news. She kept on rushing around the house, making these funny faces, like, "I know, but nobody else does." It made me giggle like a teenage girl.

Miraculously, all those pills did an excellent job today because I, Elizabeth Taite, felt marvelous. As great as one can feel in my situation. My fainting spells were forgotten (for now), and I moved around the house all morning—slower than I used to—decorating and rearranging. Susan and Sam were hanging up lanterns, and Ethan was creating adorable flower arrangements. Occasionally we would bump into each other, each time resulting in an outburst of laughter. Just once more I wanted to pretend to be healthy.

While we were decorating, for a moment I stopped in front of Emma's portrait, the one that hung in the library. And I stared at her until my eyes locked with hers.

"Emma don't be sad. Everybody I talked to loved you. I assume your kids still have to learn to forgive. You loved M and George. I understand. I do." I turned around to walk away, but instead, I turned and faced her one more time. "See you soon, Emma." Then I strode away for good, wondering if I'll be forgotten one day.

That's silly! Because I know I won't. I will be remembered. This house will be too. And this dinner will be. And Sam will remember all the love we shared here. Although brief, it has been more than other people experience in a lifetime. This ultimate journey easily could be the best of my life, if I… damn, I hate this.

For a second I felt like crying, but I didn't. Instead, I peeked out of the window onto the terrace and took in the beauty of the tablecloths swaying in the wind. The marvelous arrangement of white roses and purple wildflowers took my breath away. Everybody cared so much. Everybody understood how much this dinner meant to me.

Last week Susan bought me the most stunning dress. It's like a wave in the ocean and it flows when I walk. Midnight blue with silvery-white straps. I can't wait for Sam to see me wearing it. I can't wait to see my kids together around one table. I love this anticipation, and if I wasn't dying, this would be the perfect moment.

*Isabella, Matt, and Julia: By the way, you can find my 'Happy Moments' list on the last page of this diary. Hopefully this list will uplift you when you face challenging times.*

# DAY 104

## MARCH 10 | AFTER THE PARTY

I t's 3:00 AM and I can't sleep. So, I snuck out of the bedroom to write in my journal. In the hope of gaining some clarity, I want to put my feelings into words.

Last night was crucial for me. I needed to be surrounded for one last time by all the people I love. There was a mix of happiness, laughter and sadness.

Does perfection exist? Not that it matters anymore. After this dinner, however, I'm more tempted to say yes, it does exist.

**Perfection** [ pərˈfekSH(ə)n ] — noun: the condition, state, or quality of being free or as free as possible from all flaws or defects

It was a memorable night. Unusually warm for March—Susan assured me she had nothing to do with it—and the wind was mild, a soothing breeze.

Thanks to Susan, the table was immaculately set with

its white and silver-rimmed plates, and the delicious Italian food created a stunning setting. I had asked for as many candles as possible, and their sweet scent lingered in the air. As so often in the last months, I received exactly what I had asked for.

The food was heavenly and despite not having any appetite, I still tasted the truffle ravioli and panna cotta. But it wasn't about the food. This dinner was about the people I love.

Our conversation flowed, moving from Sam's upcoming book to his earlier life as a vet, to Sharquay's basketball career and his desire to establish a foundation for underprivileged kids. Ethan mentioned that he wants to become a landscaper for the Hollywood stars. And I was thankful for Charles being there. He took away some of the pressure and sadness.

Julia surprised me when she announced that her biggest dream is to have a family. I thought I knew everything about my kids. Not even close.

We talked. We ate. We drank. Time passed far too fast. In the end, we all gathered in front of the big screen and Sam leaned closer, "Susan arranged all of this with the help of your kids."

One photo after another came up, portraying my kids and myself over the years as I quietly cried. My life played out in front of my eyes. It was harrowing and beautiful at the same time.

Later in the evening, I saw Julia's eyes filling up, and Sharquay held her head against his chest and comforted her by whispering something in her ear. Then he glanced at me like he was saying, "Don't worry, I got this."

At some point, Susan embraced me and whispered, "Do you like Charles?"

I reached for her hand. "He's charming. A keeper." My emotions were all over the place, and I had a tough time holding myself together.

Seeing me die will affect my kids. There will be worries and sorrow. And I can't do anything to stop it.

My journey is ending soon (Actually, I'm surprised I made it this far).

Too often derailed by the tiniest setbacks in this life, I had failed to see the beauty right in front of me. But I will remember tonight until I take my last breath. Everybody will remember tonight. This evening wasn't just for me; it was for my kids, for Sam and for Susan. This was our first goodbye of what will be many more in the next days.

I tried to be strong, but before the end of the night, when Sam brought all the presents to the library where we had gathered, Isabella expelled a loud sob and that's when I almost lost it. I took her in my arms and at that moment, having to say goodbye seemed impossible. For a second, I wondered if there was still room for one more bargain with the Universe.

Sam, aware of how difficult all of this would be for me, didn't leave my side. I could feel his hand on mine, or on my back. He was there; I wasn't alone.

My plan to surprise everybody with the news of the house didn't happen. An inner voice urged me to hold back. I just knew there would be a better moment to tell the kids and Sam.

*Oh Susan, your face—your big eyes winking at me—once you realized I wouldn't say anything yet. It was priceless.*

When I had a moment alone with Susan, she asked, "What happened?"

"I couldn't. Not yet." She squeezed my arm.

Telling the kids and Sam about the house, in so many ways, was the end. And I wasn't ready yet. But will I ever be?

# DAY 105
## MARCH 11 | HOME

Dammit! Today I feel seriously sick—nausea, heart palpitations, vertigo and a pounding headache. If I had the strength, I would punch my walls. Instead, I'm too weak to get up. The past days of activity finally caught up with me.

I wish I could say that this horrific sickness is just one more task I have to complete, just one more thing I have to go through, and that if I'm brave enough, I'll emerge in victory. But that's not how this works. I will not win this battle. From the beginning I have been told that there is no chance to beat this form of leukemia. But in my quiet hours, I still did what I think everybody would do in my situation: I hoped. I bargained with some higher power. I tried to decipher: *Why me?* I fell into moments of depression, and I always knew that no matter what I did, the outcome would be the same: I would die.

And now, I'm dashing towards the end too fast, unable to slow down.

My fingers hurt. It's all blurry. My thoughts are fuzzy. I need to stop writing.

# DAY 106
## MARCH 12 | THE HILLS

Sometimes my thoughts drift to my sister and my parents, who all died far too young. The pain of losing them is still as vivid as it was when it first happened. I want to believe that I will see them again and that all my pain will be gone. I want to trust that it will magically disappear when I find security in their embrace. I try to visualize heaven (or some form of it), and I try to focus on how I will feel once I'm whole again.

Now and then, Pete crosses my mind, and I wonder how it would have all worked out if (only) we had made fewer mistakes during our marriage. If we would have stayed together and loved each other forever, the way we had promised.

At times, my parents will fade out and my granny-ma and granny-pa appear. After my parents died, I was heartbroken and fragile, but granny-ma (that's what I used to call her) tried to convince me that everything happens for a reason, and that if we search deep enough, we can understand why. Can we? Granny-ma was the strongest and kindest woman I've ever met. I can see her in my mind, stretching out her thin arms towards me. I can hear her saying, "*Lizzie, I've been waiting for you. It's all going to be okay.*"

Now, at the end of my life, I ask myself more than ever if I've finally have figured out *life*, and if it even matters.

My thoughts float along and blend like a winding river, from Isabella to Sam, to Julia and the Californian sun, to flowers I've never seen before and will never remember by name, to Matt and the Pacific Ocean. The exquisite moments I've been so lucky to experience in the last months of my life. Months filled with love and happiness. Months filled with so many blessings. And one by one, all my regrets disappear.

This afternoon when Sam checked on me, I declared, "I feel much better."

"Hungry?" he asked.

"A little." It wasn't true, but I knew it would make him happy. So I lied.

"What about a super-energetic-banana-peanut butter-almond milk smoothie and a short walk with this guy here?" He pointed at himself.

"Not sure about driving to the beach," I said.

"I was thinking more about a stroll around this charming neighborhood."

Not much time passed before we ambled along a dirt path, Sam's arm tight around my shoulders, surrounded by purple Californian bushes, passing imposing gates hiding more majestic mansions.

"Do you know the name of these bushes?" I asked.

He stopped and gazed at me. "Lizzie, among all the things in this world, you want to ask me about some purple bushes?" And then he pressed me against him, holding me so tight it almost hurt. For the briefest of seconds, I couldn't help but think if I should have asked about my funeral.

# DAY 107
## MARCH 13 | HOME

It was about 2 AM and I couldn't sleep, and despite my recent lack of interest in movies, I tiptoed to the living room and watched Pretty Woman and Notting Hill. The movies made me feel relaxed. Or was it the weed? Amazingly, my racing thoughts stopped.

Many years ago, when I was in my twenties, I used to stroll around Notting Hill, exploring its colorful market. Back then, I was happy and carefree, dreaming about an exciting future.

That was the last thought I remember having before I drifted off. I dreamt about people, horses and hunting in the English countryside. I've never been hunting in my life.

Sam found me curled up lying on the sofa.

"You talked in your sleep."

"What did I say?"

"I'm not sure it was gibberish." He leaned down to kiss me. "I have to leave for an hour, and Susan is on her way."

Things have changed once again. Nobody wants me

to be alone any longer. Not even for an hour. It's dreadful and I don't like to think about it. Sam kissed me again, and that's when he looked straight at me. "Have you lost more weight, Lizzie?" That's the second time I lied to Sam. "I don't think so," I said, knowing that I had lost four more pounds.

I was afraid of fainting again, so I remained on the sofa until Susan arrived. She now has a key to the house, just in case. One look at me and, without saying a word, she rushed into the kitchen to prepare her fabulous ginger—and who knows what else—tea. Honestly, I didn't like it at first, but now it tastes a thousand times better to me than any other tea.

Then in no time, like Mary Poppins, she transformed the terrace into what could have easily been an elegant English tea garden. It certainly looked better than the English countryside I had seen in my dream.

Susan, like no other person (even more than Sam), understands my erratic moments of sadness. She understands that I'm slipping away fast. Her eyes and words seldom show her sorrow. Instead, she guides me to live my life fully, staying in the present moment.

"All of this is so pretty," I said, adding, "thank you."

"Don't be silly, darling. I love doing this. You can drink the most awful tea as long as it is in a pretty cup." She added, "I used to prepare tea parties for a bunch of Hollywood actresses, my so-called friends."

"When was that?" I asked. There's so much I still don't know about Susan.

"Ten something years ago. I gave up on them. Far too much drama. And let's be honest, they never cared about me in the first place."

I listened to some of Susan's stories, and I closed my eyes for what only felt like a second. When I reopened them, I saw one of Susan's painted rocks placed right in front of me. She had painted it for me in different shades of blue. Blue like the ocean I love so much. Underneath, in black ink, she had inscribed *Forever Best Friends—Love, Susan.* I cried, and she held me as I felt her tears on my face.

# DAY 108
## MARCH 14 | HOME

The phone had been ringing all day long. First it was Julia, who wanted to pass by before seeing Sharquay. The second call came from Isabella to let me know she loves me, and to ask if she could talk to Ethan, who, despite the never-ceasing drizzle, had been working all morning to create "magic" around the pool. Then Susan called to let me know she had a super busy day planned with "a bunch of ungrateful, obnoxious clients."

Things, however, got strange when Matt called and after ten minutes of chitchat, he announced—as if it were nothing—his wedding day: March 20th.

March 20th, only six days from today.

"Wedding?" I asked.

"It's just an exchange of vows." There was a pause before he added. "We thought you would like that." Like? I was thrilled. "I love it," I said, thinking, *Please let me be strong enough.*

He had decided that a tiny stretch of Malibu beach would be the perfect setting. Before this, I had heard

Matt and Sebastian talk about getting married one day. One day! All of this was for me—the wedding, Malibu, us all being together once again. My next thought was Pete. Would Pete come to Matt's wedding?

The wedding news was the beginning of a whirlwind day, and I wanted to help. I wanted to arrange and organize things; after all, this was going to be my son's wedding. And it was my last wedding. Then again, it's not exactly anymore what I want. There is a much bigger plan for me.

It's quiet and I'm sitting all by myself, left with nothing more than my thoughts and a notebook filled with some words and many empty pages. I feel the excitement of the upcoming wedding, but I also feel scared knowing that I don't have many days left. I don't want to, but right now I'm having a hard time not feeling at least a tiny bit sorry for myself.

# DAY 109
## MARCH 15 | HOME

I t's strange but expected how my body goes through extreme ups and downs. Today it was a down day. I was too weak to write a lot. My muscles weren't behaving the way they should and I couldn't hold a pen for more than a minute. It was unsettling.

Sam was with me all day, sitting on the bed and working on his book. It made me sad to think that I will never see the finished copy. Sam looked so handsome, but I couldn't stop ruminating on how death will feel. How will my kids react when I'm gone? How will it feel to be without Sam? Will I be alone? Will I be scared? And how will it be for Sam to be without me? As if Sam could read my thoughts, he turned towards me and said, "I'm going to miss you, Lizzie. Every day."

Not much later Susan showed up.

"I have news," I said.

"Good or bad?"

"Good."

She took a seat next to mine and with her big smile, asked, "And?"

"Matt is getting married on Saturday."

"And you're just telling me now! Why didn't you call me?"

I smiled and reached for her hand.

"You were busy and I…"

She interrupted me. "Don't be silly. Of course, I'll help. What do you think that I would just show up as a guest?" And she added, "After all, it's your boy."

I noticed, despite our brief time together, she's slipping into a motherly role, and I was grateful.

"I have to make it until Saturday," I whispered and added. "And I have to stop crying. It's getting annoying."

"You have a right to cry, and you can be annoyed and annoying as much as you like. Let's make a plan," Susan said. Then she screamed at the top of her lungs. "A wedding! Liz, a wedding! I love it!"

Susan always makes me smile.

# DAY 110
## MARCH 16 | HOME

Fuck! Fuck! Fuck! I wasn't sure if this type of rare outburst would make me feel better.

Last night I woke up bathed in sweat and couldn't get back to sleep. I listened to Sam's regular breathing while thinking of Matt's wedding. As so often before, my thoughts about the present mingled with thoughts about places I had traveled—Mexico, Brazil, Paris, Italy, Sweden, England, the French countryside—I had been so lucky.

Hours later—I must have fallen asleep again—I woke up from the most disturbing nightmare.

THE DREAM

I traveled through space at supersonic speed, screaming for help because I couldn't stop. I cried out in pain. I was frantically searching for the people I love. I wanted to see them. I wanted to hug and kiss them. At first, I was in a midnight blue orbit. Then, I flew through the ice-blue sky until, with one bang, everything went black. That's when I froze. I was scared witless. This wasn't heaven.

I screamed. This time it was loud and real. Even I had heard it. I woke up with a jolt and Sam came running from the bathroom, taking me in his arms. That was heaven. Sam is my heaven.

All day, I tried to ignore feeling wretched. But it didn't work.

Finally, at sunset, I gathered all my strength and sauntered through my garden for about ten minutes before settling in the library. Sam had made a fire. I love the crackling sound and the musky, burned scent of the firewood. Not tired anymore, I reached for one of Emma's books and as I opened it, a photo fell out, a picture of Emma standing between two men. All three of them looked tanned and happy. I turned it over and it read, "Greece 1968—George, Mitch and I." Wow! M stands for Mitch. I knew it! Emma had lived her life on her terms. She had loved two men!

# DAY 111
## MARCH 17 | HOME

S am insisted I would stay on the terrace to relax, and he wanted to talk. He took a sip of his coffee as his eyes rested on me. "What do you need the most from me?" he asked.

I looked at him. "My kids, you know, I need to make sure that they will be okay."

"I'll be here, Lizzie, and I want you now to stop worrying." I nodded and reached for his hand. And then I let out one uncontrollable whimper. Thinking about never seeing my kids was too painful, and so was this conversation.

It was such a mesmerizing morning. The sunlight reflected on the narrow stone path embedded in sand that Ethan had built to "The Shack." The sand in the maze next to the path was shining like gold. The beauty of this day didn't match up with our agonizing conversation.

I took a couple of deep breaths and gathered all my courage to continue.

"It will be the hardest for Isabella. She's sensitive and

"

she's always needed my emotional support more than Matt and Julia. Isabella will probably pretend to be okay even when she's not."

"How can I help her?" he asked.

"Ask her questions. She will always give you an honest answer. And give her many hugs… from me." I paused. "She will want to talk about me."

"And what about Pete, will he be around?"

"I don't know, but I think he will try." I hope he will be. Isabella, deep down, loves her dad. She has more of a connection with him than Julia and Matt have.

"Julia is my rock. She's down-to-earth and practical, and she's always shown a lot of inner strength."

"Her relationship with Sharquay will be good for her. It looks serious," Sam said.

"Sharquay seems like a good man. It makes me happy to see them together. He will give her security, but also enough freedom to do all the things she loves."

"My feeling is that Sharquay will spoil her. Did you see the bracelet he gave her?"

"The diamond one?" I asked.

Instead of answering me, Sam pulled out of his pocket a small silver box.

"Remember the tiny jewelry store, the one you fled from. You silly girl!"

I expelled a weird laugh while crying, well-knowing what would come next. Sam slid the box over to me.

I stared at it before opening it slowly. In it was the most beautiful diamond ring—one square diamond circled by smaller diamonds. Sam took it from me, and it sparkled in the sunlight like a million stars when he put it on my finger.

"I love you, Lizzie. Forever."

The warm air made me shiver and tears rolled down

my face. "I love you. Sam. Oh, Sam. I love you so very much."

He lifted me out of my chair and carried me to the bedroom where I laid in his arms, snuggled up to him. I thought about how he had been listening to me from day one, how he had anticipated all my wishes.

After our conversation, I felt a sense of tranquility knowing that Sam would be there for the kids in a way that Pete never had been and never would—or for that matter, could—be. Sam would be there every step of the way. He would be present as much as they want him to be.

Yes, in the end, California has embraced all of us! We all, in our own way, journeyed here to meet Sam. I reached for his hand as my thoughts, one by one, dissipated; for the first time, I felt like it was okay to die.

As if my conversation with Sam had freed me, I began to feel much better. Following Dr. Katz's advice to keep moving whenever I felt up to the task, I strolled around my beautiful garden. The garden that for the past weeks had fed my soul.

Months ago, when I began this final journey, I promised myself that I wouldn't look back. But I still do it from time to time.

I often wonder how my life would have turned out if I had become a famous journalist like Diane Sawyer or Barbara Walters. A journalist who would make a difference, maybe even change the world. I had dreamt about traveling the world and interviewing stars and politicians and people with a story to tell. And now, there was no more time!

*For Matt, Julia, and Isabella: Here is a bit of your mom's wisdom: Live now. Follow your dreams and your heart. Travel the world, get married or don't, have babies or don't. Explore and live every moment to the fullest. Don't wait! Now is your moment.*

**Wisdom** [ ˈwizdəm ] — noun: *the quality of having experience, knowledge, and good judgment; the quality of being wise*

# DAY 112
## MARCH 18 | HOME

had avoided mirrors for the past few weeks, but today I couldn't help it and I got a glimpse of my deteriorating self. It was bad.

There's not much left of me, the "me" I've gotten used to seeing all these years. I've lost 26 pounds and my face is pale with deep wrinkles. My eyes are bulging, and my hair looks brittle and so much thinner. I used to have full hair. What could Sam possibly see in me? I'm nothing more than a walking corpse.

A mirror is a funny thing. Don't we only see what we truly want to see? Sam must see something that I don't. Knowing him, he looks much deeper than the surface. He most likely sees how much I love him. He sees my soul. He sees "me." I hope!

After calming myself down, I called Susan.

"I look like shit, and I need help."

As always, Susan showed up less than two hours later, armed with a variety of shopping bags.

Before I could say anything, she elaborated, "I didn't

do it all by myself." Then she emptied all the bags on the kitchen counter. "I asked my high-profile client if we could go shopping instead of looking at houses. È voilà!" Makeup: concealers, lipsticks, nail polishes, eye shadows, blush. And tons of clothes. "We can bring back everything we don't need."

I was speechless. And I already felt a little better.

～

Julia picked us up to drive with us to the caterer.

"Nice makeup, Mom," she said. And when I embraced her, she held me so tight, I didn't want to let her go.

She whispered, "I love you."

I went to get my sweater and overheard Julia saying to Susan, "She's so thin."

"But doesn't she look good today!" Susan said. And then, as I was stepping away from the living room, I saw them hug.

Susan is my angel.

～

On our way back home, I said, "I'm amazed Luigi, Italian caterer to the stars, has an opening on a Saturday. And on such short notice."

"It didn't hurt that I sold his first home for a stellar price and right after, I found him his dream place," Susan said with a wide smile.

"His food is divine," Julia added. "Matt and Sebastian, the food connoisseurs, will love it."

Then I stared out the window, mainly to hide my

sadness as we drove deeper into the hills. I caught sight of how the sun was moving with us and highlighting every detail of the mesmerizing landscape.

# DAY 113
## MARCH 19 | HOME

My bones hurt a lot and I move so slowly now. Things changed quickly. Only few weeks ago, I could walk miles.

This morning I talked to Dr. Katz, and he agreed to give me a higher dose of pain medication. He wants me to be as comfortable as possible, something we had determined early on.

"You call the shots, Liz." I like him. He's a fantastic doctor.

I keep forgetting a lot of things. I can't taste food as much anymore and I can only eat tiny amounts. I get cold easily. I don't like it.

But the worst part is seeing the pain in the eyes of the people I love. It hurts the most. This morning, I saw worry and sadness in Sam's eyes, and I knew (I can feel it) that it is time for me to die.

I shuffled to "The Shack." I wanted to be alone to write a letter.

. . .

*For you —Isabella, Julia, and Matt—the three people I love unconditionally. The three people who made my life.*

*I have loved—and still love—every minute with you. I have no regrets when I chose you over everything else that I wanted to accomplish. But as I have learned, we can't choose how much time we have. Time chooses us, if that makes any sense.*

*Never give up on your dreams. Have goals and pursue them with all your passion. Make your dreams come true. Life will put so many stones in your way, but you can always find a way around them, a way forward.*

*Remember, first and foremost to find happiness within yourself. You must do that before you can find it through other people. You will never be completed by another person. You are complete— perfect—the way you are.*

*And I know there will be times you'll miss me, but you won't need me to make the right decisions. I know you can make them on your own.*

*I questioned my life for so long—too long. I searched for answers for years and on my trip to Los Angeles, I sat across from a humble young woman on the train who told me her story. That was when I knew that love is the answer to everything. Without love, there is no happiness.*

*I had so many extraordinary moments in my life: The day I met your dad. When I married him. When you were born. When you spoke your first words and took your first steps. When I met Sam.*

*My love for you will never end. It's always within you.*
*Love, Mommy*


I sealed the envelope and placed it **here**, in my red, velvety journal.

# DAY 114

## MARCH 20 | HOME AND MALIBU

The increased pain medication must have kicked in this morning because I stepped out of bed, feeling more like my old self than I had in days. Everything that had been difficult in the past few weeks miraculously turned into some form of joy. There was a sense of calm within me I hadn't felt in some time. I took a bath and drank the healthy concoction Sam had prepared for me (it won't change anything, but I'm drinking it for him). Still in my bathrobe, I wandered around the garden.

Sam, right away, picked up on my sudden transformation because he kept on smiling at me. He looked less worried and more relaxed, although both of us knew that my current physical state wouldn't last long.

This morning, when I was about to walk past him to get dressed, he reached for me and pulled me onto his lap.

"You're the most beautiful person I've ever met, Lizzie," he said. I buried my face in his neck and whispered, "Thank you… for everything." We sat there for a long time, Sam cradling me in his arms. I didn't want to be strong anymore.

~

The dress Susan had brought me for Matt's big day was a stunning emerald-color dress—flowing and elegant. The dress, despite being too loose, added to my sense of well-being.

The sunshine, the mild temperature, the music, the smell of orchids and lilies and roses, the white tent, the sand, the ocean air, the exquisitely arranged food, Isabella, Julia, Matt, their friends, Susan and of course Sam—all of it made this day into a divine experience.

The guests arrived shortly before noon and while the band played a soft rendition of "Just in Time," everybody found their seats.

Matt and Sebastian walked down the aisle—a path of sand with tiny pebbles and some of Susan's stones for good luck on either side. I was at peace, maybe because of the enlightening words of the young pastor, or maybe there was love everywhere.

Matt and Sebastian looked so handsome in their matching navy-blue pants and white shirts. They are very much in love and content with their decision to get married earlier than initially planned.

The ceremony was brief—arranged for me. Matt and Sebastian declared their love to each other with words they had written and afterward they exchanged rings. Music played in the background and while holding Sam's hand, I drifted off for just a little into my newly found world of imagination. A world so extraordinary. A world without hate or pain. A world solely filled with love.

The lunch was picture perfect and tasted divine, so I was informed—truffles, caviar, pâtés. I didn't eat, but everybody else loved it so much. Matt, for as long as I can remember, has always appreciated the fine things in life.

A little later, Susan switched seats with Sam.

"The attorney made all changes and completed your will."

I reached for her hand. "Susan, I made it! I made it. What a beautiful day…" She understood.

She squeezed my hand. "Don't make me cry right now." And then she asked, "Do you want to tell Sam and the kids about the house?"

"Soon."

"Soon," she repeated.

"Just in case… I have it all in writing," I muttered.

The rest of this incredible day passed too quickly, and it bothered me that Sam and I never danced. I just didn't have the strength.

Life has passed me and only now, in my last days, I can see it. I can see life. And it's beautiful.

# DAY 115

## MARCH 21 | HOME AND MALIBU AGAIN

After a long day like yesterday, I expected to be exhausted this morning. But to my amazement, I felt a surge of energy. At least after taking more of the powerful and very effective painkillers.

I stepped outside to get some fresh air and to take in the morning's beauty, only to notice (once again) how spectacular the garden was that Ethan had created. He had turned the once-neglected piece of land into a tiny paradise. My absolute favorite part is one of the bubbling waterfalls (there are three) that makes its way down slippery rocks, sparkling in the sunlight, before landing in the pool. But there's so much more. There are the palm trees and the hammocks, the small bench at the gate and the variety of wildflowers I love so much. And of course, there's my favorite chair on the terrace.

Here, in my beguiling garden, is where Sam found me lost today, as I've been so often lately, in my thoughts and dreams. Dreams of this house and my family sitting amidst all the palm trees and flowers. Dreams of their children running through the grass, their conversations, their laughter. Dreams of Sam, much older, sitting in my favorite chair, remembering.

I startled and returned to reality when he approached me from behind and caressed my neck.

He had been on the phone a good part of the morning.

"Have you seen my wallet?" he asked.

"No. I hope you didn't lose it?'

"I've searched everywhere. Maybe it slipped out of my pocket yesterday at the beach."

So, we drove back out to Malibu, although I thought our chances of finding it were more than slim.

This is my favorite drive, and I was grateful.

I took it all in—the trees and flowers, the sun, the passing cars, the highway and Sam. Despite feeling okay, I wondered if this would be my final trip. Most likely, my last time sitting next to Sam in his car, my hair flying in the wind, driving along Route 1 towards my favorite beach.

I expected for us (for Sam) to meander along the now empty stretch of white sand, searching for his brown leather wallet, while I stayed behind to rest. Instead, I found a middle-aged man playing the piano next to a small open tent. In the tent stood a table, all in white, stunningly set for lunch. White roses and orchids were spread all over the table and onto the sand below.

The only word I managed to say was, "Sam."

"We never had our dance, Lizzie." He caressed my face and we kissed.

"It's so beautiful," I said while taking my place at the table. "That's why you were on the phone all morning."

"I used the magic word."

"Which is?"

"Susan," he laughed. "I called her and asked for help. And she made it happen."

The thought of Sam and Susan doing all of this for me made me well up again. I've been unusually emotional in the past month. Go figure!

Once delicious tapas-sized dishes appeared—by now Sam knows how little I can eat—I focused on the moment and gradually it all turned into a spellbinding blur. The warmth of the sun and the champagne—I only had a few sips—mixed with a substantial amount of medications transported me into a pleasantly cloudy state. Then I thought, *Now would be the perfect moment to tell Sam about the house.*

"I have something for you. It's a gift, and I want you to accept it." My ring, the one Sam had given me, gleamed in the sunlight. And images of Sam—Sam surprising me, Sam listening to me, Sam carrying me when I haven't been able to walk, Sam holding me when I've been in pain—floated through my mind.

"I've thought about it for a long time." I took a deep breath. "I bought the house. Emma's house."

"You did?"

"Yes. And I want to give it to you."

"Lizzie, I can't."

"It's my last wish."

"You have to give it to your kids," he said.

"They have their own places, and I can't give it to one and not to the other two. It's our place. And I'm certain the kids will come to you. I want you to invite them. They will remember it as the place where their mother was the happiest. And one day, you will leave it to them."

"Lizzie…" I put my hand on his.

"Please." Sam kissed me. I guess that meant "yes."

We talked, laughed a little, and cried while the piano player continued playing, his songs merging with the roar of the ocean. A couple of hours later, the sun began to set and just when I became tired, Sam pulled me out of the chair into his arms, and we had our dance.

Today was otherworldly, and I wish I could repeat it over and over. I want to live this life again, knowing, as I do now, to look for the details—the small moments. But I have to be grateful—in the end, I got it all—I had the time to love and raise my kids; I was loved by Sam and I believe by Pete, and I bought my dream home. Yes, I got it all.

One hundred and sixteen days ago (I've been counting) Dr. Sternenberg told me I had approximately one hundred and forty days left to live. That means if he's correct, I have roughly three and a half weeks left. I sense he isn't.

# DAY 116
## MARCH 22 | HOME

This morning I was curled up next to the toilet, vomiting. I had trouble getting up. A piercing pain was shooting through my entire body and the nausea wouldn't stop.

Dr. Katz passed by around 10 AM, pretending that he was in the neighborhood, which I knew wasn't true. Sam had called him.

He sat down on my bed and measured my pulse. I had not been wrong about him. He always took his time, as if I was his only patient.

"You know the doctor in New York who diagnosed me made a prediction," I said.

"What was that?"

"He gave me a hundred and forty days, give or take."

"That's precise."

"Do you want to make another prediction?"

He shifted into a better position and took both my hands in his.

"Sometimes, I don't like my job, and this is one of

these times." And then he added, looking straight into my eyes, "Soon, Liz, soon."

After Dr. Katz left, I stayed in bed and made a list of all the things I need to do. It's a short list: I need to say goodbye to the people I love. Then I asked Sam to call the kids. And to call Susan as well.

Sam, who now rarely leaves my side, did so when Susan showed up this afternoon.

It was still pouring, and he had to move my favorite chair under the deck so that I wouldn't get wet. While I was sitting there, my eyes closed, and thinking about what my last words would be, Susan materialized (like an angel) and quietly sat next to me. Despite sensing her presence, I kept my eyes closed, feeling the warmth of her hand on my arm. We both knew that this was the end.

Finally, I looked at my friend. "Thank you for introducing me to Sam. For being there for me without asking too many questions. For leaving everything, even your most precious clients, to rush to me whenever I needed you." She squeezed my arm, tears rolled down her cheeks.

"Sam will need you. My kids will need you." I knew this was a lot to ask of someone I didn't even know a few months ago.

A hummingbird flew around our heads and a yellow butterfly landed on my shoulder for a brief second. We smiled, just a little.

"My father used to love butterflies," I said, wondering if that was another sign.

Gradually the mournful atmosphere turned a little lighter.

"I brought you something," Susan said as she pulled a bunch of papers out of her oversized handbag.

"My house?"

"Your house."

"Sam's house," I said.

Sam came in and joined us. He sat down next to me, putting his arm around my shoulder. I slid the signed papers and a set of keys across the table. "Your house, Sam." I didn't care that Susan was there with us. I just had to say it. "I want you to find happiness here, the way you and I were happy. Despite everything, this is a happy place—a house for celebrating weddings, baby showers and christenings."

Eventually, I got tired and knew I had to lie down. But not before walking Susan to the gate. We walked slowly (very slowly). I had no strength left, but I also didn't want this moment to end.

I gave her the longest hug. And she tried to smile for me before she spun around and walked away. I watched her disappear in the distance, but she never turned back. I knew this was the last time I would see Susan.

# DAY 117
## MARCH 23 | HOME

Today was a bad day. I was too sick to do anything. Every movement jolted pain all over my body. This wasn't the way I wanted to say goodbye to my kids. And I was scared I wouldn't have enough time.

One by one, the kids passed by, promising that they would be back the next day. They looked at me with so much agony. *I can't stand it any longer.*

I slept most of the day. Pictures of my childhood materialized in my dream: my swing, my bike, my elementary school, the bakery around the corner, our driveway. As fast as they appeared, they also disappeared.

I heard Sam checking on me, but I couldn't open my eyes. My eyelids felt too heavy.

Later, I felt Sam next to me in bed, and I heard him, almost in a whisper, reading *Pride and Prejudice* to me.

Now it's 4AM, the *in-between* hour, and I am alone. More than ever, I'm convinced I have to do this alone. My way.

# DAY 118

## MARCH 24 | SANTA MONICA

As promised, the kids showed up early this morning, and although I felt a little better, I wasn't ready to say goodbye. I couldn't face it. I will never be prepared to say goodbye.

We planned to spend the day together again tomorrow. Sam assured them that he would call them immediately if there were any changes.

After they left, I wanted Sam to drive me to the beach. He argued that I was too weak, but I wanted to see the ocean one last time. It was imperative. So, covered in blankets, I sat in the passenger seat next to Sam and we drove to Santa Monica.

It was a cloudy day, and after parking the car, Sam carried me to the beach. I felt tired and shaky and I couldn't walk more than a few steps, so we sat in the sand. That's when I locked eyes with Sam and my heart broke. I whispered, "I love you, Sam. I've loved you from the moment I first saw you." He stroked my back, and choking on his own words, he said, "I know, Lizzie, I know." I leaned my head against his shoulder. I could feel his warm breath on my neck, the sand beneath my feet, and the ocean breeze. That's when I let go of this life.

As I am writing this, I'm thinking about how moments always pass. The good ones pass too quickly and the bad ones too slowly. But they all pass somehow.

I'm just tired…

# DAY 119
## MARCH 25 | HOME

I was sitting in the library when Isabella, Matt, and Julia arrived together shortly before noon.

They feared the worst; I could see it written on their faces. Although Isabella tried so hard, she cried non-stop. Julia and Matt looked like they might lose all sense of control at any minute as well.

Sam excused himself to give us space. I wanted to feel my kids close. I searched for comforting words, but I couldn't find any. Instead, I held them for a very long time, one by one, and caressed their faces and kissed their cheeks. I told them over and over how much I love them.

Then it was time to let go for the last time.

Before they left, I asked Sam to join us. Earlier, the kids had assured me it was okay to give the house to Sam, as long as he would pass it on to them one day. They also promised me they'd take care of Sam.

As we gathered on the terrace, I said, "We have to name the house."

"Something happy," Matt said, always the optimist.

"Definitely," Julia said.

"What about 'Sunshine or Happiness,'" Sam suggested.

"What about 'Villa Nirvana,' which means the ultimate state of happiness; an idyllic place," Isabella said. And for the first time today, she smiled. At that moment, I knew this house would bring all of them comfort, and that there would be so many more hours of happiness in 'Villa Nirvana.'

**Nirvana** [ nər'vänə ] — noun: (in Buddhism) *a transcendent state in which there is neither suffering, desire, nor sense of self, and the subject is released from the effects of karma and the cycle of death and rebirth*

# MATT
## MARCH 26 | VILLA NIRVANA

My Mom died this morning. Sam found her in her favorite chair. She just fell asleep.

When I opened her journal, the one she left for us, lying right next to her, I came across this empty page. My sisters, Sam and I will read it soon.

Right now, Susan is in the kitchen crying, and arranging everything for the funeral. Sam is in the garden with Sebastian, Sharquay, Julia and Isabella.

I called dad and as expected, he was in shock. This will be difficult for him. I know he loved mom, despite not always treating her the way she deserved to be treated. He's on his way to LA, which will be good, especially for Isabella.

Yesterday was our last day with Mom. She looked so tired. A few times, I closed my eyes and pictured her healthy, the way she used to be, with so much energy. She's always been the most beautiful, loving mom.

Eventually, it was time to say goodnight (or was it goodbye?), which was the most horrific moment of my life. I barely made it. I wanted to escape this moment, instead it will be on my mind forever. She held each of us until it was time to let go. I forced myself not to turn around for one last time. But I could hear her sobbing. She cried. My mom. She cried.

# JULIA
## MARCH 28 | VILLA NIRVANA

This diary was lying right next to my mom when she died, as if it were her steady and trustworthy companion. I haven't had the courage to read her words yet. I know I will soon. I only opened it to find an empty page to write this.

On top of the diary was a yellow sticky note. It read: *This journal is for you, Julia, Matt, Isabella, Sam. I love you.*

I think soon, all of us will sit down together and read every single word the way I know Mom wanted us to. We will when we are ready.

I love Sam for loving Mom. In all these years, I've never seen my mother happier and more fulfilled. ~~I loved~~… I love her so much. She was always there for us. She made us laugh, encouraged us, and wiped away our tears. I hope she knew that she never let us down. *I love you, Mom, and I miss you. Always.*

I know you wouldn't want us to cry, but that's a promise I can't make.

Everybody is sitting on the terrace waiting for the cars to arrive to bring us to the tiny Beverly Hills church you adored so much. Dad is here too. He's been crying. He feels horrible that he had no clue what was going on. All this time, we respected your wish and didn't tell him. As you asked, I told him that you forgave and loved him. I know how complicated life was for you and how much you tried to help dad and make him understand that we were his family. It's dad, you know! He did his best. Isn't that all we can do?

From where I sit, I can see Isabella standing in the sunlight. Despite her puffy eyes from all the crying, she's so beautiful. She's standing right next to Sam.

Matt is holding Susan's hand. She's been crying all morning, and she says she doesn't give a damn if her eyes are swollen for days or if she looks unpresentable. Even Charles flew in from San Francisco. Sebastian, Sharquay, and Ethan are here too.

It's a sunny California day, just the way you would like it. A slight breeze coming from the ocean you loved so much is blowing through the trees, the air is dry, and it's the perfect temperature.

I'll see you later, Mom. Later. I love you. Forever.

# DAY 1 - SAM
## MARCH 29 | VILLA NIRVANA AND MALIBU

We—Isabella, Matt, Julia, and I—didn't sleep last night. After everybody left, we cuddled up on the comfy green sofa in the library, the sofa Emma had sat on for a lifetime, a lifetime so much longer than Liz's. Now both have died, one young and one old. It was just as Lizzie would have liked it. We looked at old pictures Julia had brought from her home. Pictures from a time when I wasn't yet part of her life.

*Oh, Lizzie. My Lizzie. How will I ever be able to stop missing you? How will I ever be able to live this life without you?*

I didn't want to cry in front of the kids, although there was nothing I wanted to do more. I wanted to cry until there were no more tears left. But Liz would have been proud of me; I held it together for a long while.

I am not sure how, but we made it through the night and when I stepped outside, I saw the sun rising, its first rays illuminating the blooming garden. There I saw Lizzie sitting in her favorite chair for the last days of her life, smiling through the pain, applying a little makeup from time to time—just for me. Lizzie pretended to feel good. And she did it for me. Who am I that I deserved all her love, her touch, her smile? The way she would put her arms around my neck and kiss my lips.

She was the picture of perfection. A perfection only I saw because I loved her the most (at least that's what I want to believe).

*I so much want to be with you. I want to live this life with you. I want to be with you, Lizzie, until we are old.*

At some point, I must have drifted off to sleep because the next thing I knew Julia's hand was touching my arm and I was waking up.

Watching the kids she loved so much, I knew what I had to do. I had promised Liz to be present in their lives, so if they let me, I will love them. Susan will love them too. And their dad will love them.

So, I told the kids—her kids—my unexpected new family, "It's time. Let me show you Lizzie's beach."

We all got ready, jumped in my old convertible, and drove along Route 1 in silence, each of us remembering Liz in our own unique way. And as the wind blew on our faces, I finally cried.

On the beach in Malibu, we slipped out of our shoes and walked towards the sun, the expressions on our faces hidden by its rays. I walked towards heaven. But heaven seemed so far away.

Tears kept rolling down my face and I felt Isabella's hand—Lizzie's hand--reaching for mine. In my mind, I saw Lizzie just the way I had seen her for the first time, only months earlier: so full of life. She appeared in my life like an angel and she left me with the greatest gift ever: love. She loved me. And she taught me what love is all about. Yes, she left me. But she left me smiling, believing that there is such a thing as happiness.

Stunning, dark-haired, charming, tender, caring Liz had left me one tiny note.

~

*Dear Sam,*
*You will always know when true love comes along. Grab it and never let it go. I know because I did it.*
*I love you… until later…*
*Liz*

And then I let go as I watched the tiny piece of paper being carried away by a gust of wind. There wasn't a cloud in the sky and as we all walked hand in hand, I could see Liz's smile. I could feel her touch. I could feel her kiss. I could feel my tears.

MY HAPPY MOMENTS LIST

Seeing my kids smile and hearing them laugh
Breathing in the ocean air
Music
My bare feet feeling sand, wood, grass, stone
Sam holding my hand
Wet doggy kisses
Sun shining on my face
Paris and the Musée d'Orsay
Truffle ravioli
Art
Reading certain passages from books I love
Walking (especially along the beach)
Seeing Manhattan from the distance when driving
towards the city
Bubble baths
Twittering birds
Morning drives
Watching waves moving in and out and the sun rising
Coffee
Candles
Paper and pen
And my many memories coming back to me like the
waves of the ocean
(To be continued…)

# ACKNOWLEDGMENTS

There's no better place than to thank you, the reader, for taking the time to read my book. So, thank you. My wish for you is that you live your dream right now, and if you find happiness on the way, then I did my job.

And in no particular order, thank you Katherine Statton, Ella Pery, Gary Donzig, and Kristen Walstrom for reading an early draft and giving me your honest feedback. And to Susan Douglass for pointing out all the inconsistencies.

A huge thank you to the talented Hannah Lindner for the beautiful book cover.

Thank you to Mimi Kite for being my loyal and supportive friend. I love our conversations and many laughs.

Thank you, Tracy Charlton for always being in my life and your long friendship.

And what would I do without Tania Moore, true friend and superb writer, who always gives excellent advice on all subjects.

And Michael Kowalski, my confidant and friend for life. Thank you for loving me through the crazy.

And a huge thank you to my multi-talented brother, Engelbert Eichner, for creating my wonderful website and being part of my life.

And a special thank you to Camilla (see below) my skilled editor. Thank you! Thank you!

And Marieke Lexmond, who despite writing her own

fantastic novels always finds time to read my work and always is available for a lovely chat. Your friendship means the world to me.

And Heidi Mittermair, despite being separated by 6000 miles, our friendship not only survived but became everything a true friendship is all about. You mean the world to me.

And to Lorenzo, my before… and always an important part of our modern family. Thank you for still being part of my life.

And for Norm, I'll never be able to thank you enough for always loving me in the most unconditional way. Never once you fail to encourage me to go after my dreams.

And to my two C's—Camilla and Cosimo—words can never be enough to let you know how much I love you and how proud I am to be your mother. Everything I do is for you!

And finally, this book was written to remember all the people we loved and lost.

*In Memory of Carla Zanieri and Matt Ross*

# ABOUT THE AUTHOR

Olivia Barry, after writing screenplays for many years, turned to writing novels. Besides writing in coffee shops, she loves traveling, photography, reading, and going on long walks with her dog. Currently she lives in Williamsburg, Brooklyn.

You can find me at
www.olivia-barry.com

I would love to hear from you.

Your Book Club/Readers Guide is available to download on my website.

facebook.com/oliviabarrywriter

instagram.com/oliviabarrywriter